Skullduggery at Quanah

Dennis Boyd Call

To Justin
Thank you for
your friendship!
Dennis Call

ISBN: 9781702322652

DEDICATION

To the wonderful citizens of Quanah, Texas. There are many who have encouraged me in this endeavor. The community is filled with warm and caring people.

.

ACKNOWLEDGMENTS

This is a book of fiction, but fiction can have a relationship to fact; I have tried to accommodate both. The following folks have very freely given much of their time, and have shared their knowledge with me about the area around Quanah, Texas. I am grateful for their kindness and friendship. They are listed in the order by which we met.

Scarlett Daugherty, Hardeman County Historical Museum
Bertha Woods, Quanah Chamber of Commerce
Jannice Griffin, Quanah Tribune-Chief newspaper
Jeanene Stermer, Downtown Medicine Mound Museum
Nell Looper, Thompson-Sawyer Public Library
Steven Sparkman, Manager, Medicine Mound Ranch

Skullduggery:
underhanded or unscrupulous behavior;
also: a devise or trick
(Merriam-Webster Dictionary)

Author's Note

Over the course of time our culture undergoes changes, and we as individuals make adjustments to accommodate those changes. In some cases it seems that we actually attempt to re-write, or even erase history.

The material in this book, the story as it were, covers a broad span of time, and the terminology reflects the norm of the time. Thus, there are references to "Indian, American Indian, and Native American" depending on the setting and the thinking of the day.

It is my hope that no one is offended by the use of the above terms. My intent in writing this fictional novel is to bring entertainment into the lives of those who choose to read it.

-    Dennis Boyd Call   -

CONTENTS

PROLOGUE
Abt. 1855 – Near the base of the Texas panhandle

Chief Peta Nocona felt that his time on earth was nearing the end. It was a hot and clear day. A slight breeze helped lessen the impact of the heat, and he knew that it was time for a visit to the sacred place. The sacred place was a hallowed area where visions and instruction from the gods occurred.

There, four mounds arose from the flat plains, and miraculous healing events were common. On special occasions, such as Peta was now sensing, visions were seen and divine instruction was received.

Yes, he said to himself, *I must go to Medicine Mound, the tallest of the four mounds.*

It would be a three or four-day fast, and his son Pecos was to go with him as lookout. There were to be no interruptions.

The two of them loped leisurely astride their horses being careful to prepare themselves mentally for what was to come.

This will be good training for Pecos, Peta thought to himself. *I fear greatly for his future, and he will do well to wrap himself in sacred things. Otherwise he will become a scourge to our people.*

I oftentimes become concerned about him because of his unchecked criticisms of others in the camp, particularly his older brother, Quanah.

Peta Nocona loved his youngest son and knew him well. But he often became concerned about the path of behavior Pecos might take as he grew older.

Arriving at their destination they dismounted, and Peta gave some final instruction to Pecos. "My son, set up a camp for yourself right here, and do not leave until I return from the high place.

"You have provisions for four days. If someone comes, tell them that Chief Peta is on the mound and there is no space available."

With that, Peta went to the spring at the northern base of Medicine Mound; there he filled his water carrier which was fashioned from buffalo stomach. He began his trek to the top of the 350-foot-tall mound, the tallest of the four protrusions. It was to be a long and arduous climb.

The closer he came to the flat area of the uppermost part of the mound, the greater was his feeling of the presence a higher power. Peta felt the warmth and closeness of the spirits.

In fact, he had such a strong feeling of a hallowed personal touch that he began to know it was *his* personal spiritual guide descending upon him. He sensed an overpowering warmth on the inside, and he felt as though he could be outwardly glowing.

There was no question as to the importance of the chief's current vision quest … little did he know how important.

Peta Nocona arrived at his favorite, and pre-determined place on Medicine Mound. There he took pause and wondered: *Can I go straight into prayer or should I take time for cleansing first?*

Chief Peta knew that the spirits were close, and it was a temptation he had never before encountered.

He suddenly remembered the words of the old wise ones of the tribe from his youth: *Always remember this ... When you go for the good, the bad will try to intercede.* He proceeded with the cleansing.

Peta gathered some gypsum in his left hand, and poured in a small amount of water from his carrier. He swirled the mixture for several seconds then slurped the mixture from his left hand. The cleansing process had begun.

In prayerful reverence, the chief lay in a bed of the plentiful white gypsum powder, and then rolled while chanting words that only the spirits would understand.

As the sun went down in the clear western sky, Peta brought out the bag of peyote that he kept for these special ceremonies. The peyote was smoked sparingly by Peta; he knew the value of remaining conversant with the spirits. This ritual continued all day and into the night of the first day on the mound.

Apparently, the chief had satisfactorily prepared and cleansed himself because by early morning, well before the sun appeared in the eastern sky, Peta was surrounded by a quiet but piercing voice.

"Peta, you are to preserve the box, your secret box. It must be kept for the fifth son who will return honor to all generations of your children."

In his stupor, he rubbed his eyes and tried to make sense of what was happening.

"Peta, look and you will see," the voice continued.

Shaking his head a bit and trying with all his might to focus on what the voice was saying, Peta's mind began to clear.

"Over here, Peta, look over here and see your mission."

Peta turned to his left, and in his line of vision there appeared a panoramic view of himself fashioning a small stone burial container, just large enough to hold his secret box.

The length of the container was about two hand palms long and the width of two palms. The depth of the container was shallow, only about as deep as his pointing finger. It was rectangular, the top, bottom and sides all made of stone. The cover was a large stone, flat on the bottom with a rounded top. The entire stone case was tight, secure and unobtrusive.

"With a little dirt, leaves and gypsum scattered on top it will appear as just another small boulder protruding from the ground.

"Peta, you are to construct this protecting case for your secret box during this vision quest. Pecos is to go and get the secret box."

The vision had been seen and the revelation begun.

"You received the box and its contents from the tribal fathers many moons ago, and you have been faithful in preserving it all. Your prayers are now to be answered and you will know the purpose of the contents.

"But first, go and send Pecos on his errand; wait for the secret box, then return with it for more instruction."

Pecos was the only person alive, besides Chief Peta Nocona who knew of the secret box and how to retrieve it.

Later, after Pecos had delivered the secret box to Chief Peta; and when the sun was high in the sky, Peta returned to the sacred spot atop the mound. He was holding the secret box tight against his body. It was a treasure and was to be protected at all costs.

The voice began anew, "You have offered many prayers, seeking for understanding and knowledge. Now you will know. The crescent shaped object inside is inscribed with characters unknown to you; they will bring honor to your family."

Chief Peta was lost in his own understanding, and he thought he could see the form of a man from where the voice came.

"Some of your line will be cast aside; they will have no identity but will be preserved. Many will say part of your line is no longer pure. They say this for evil purpose. But the fifth son will come forth with proof that will restore honor to your whole family. He will know the inscription, and the tribal leaders will accept him."

The vision ended. Peta was struck with exhaustion and laid on the ground in a stupor. He stared at the sky, and then changed his focus to the brush surrounding him; his mind seemed lost. Then, just as he was gaining enough strength to stand, the vision was repeated.

Weak and unable to physically perform any tasks, Peta spent the remainder of the second night in thought and sleep. He pondered the meaning of what he had just been taught. He reasoned that the fifth son would come through his older son's line.

The fifth son would be the oldest son of each generation. *Quanah, my eldest will have much to be responsible for,* he reasoned. As Peta pondered and thought on the things he had seen and heard, he drifted off into deep slumber.

Spending the third day on the mound provided much satisfaction to Peta. He built the container by finding some appropriate stones, and fashioning them in a hole in the earth that he had dug.

He wanted the stone chest to be solid, secure and undetectable to the naked eye.

In the process he realized that he now knew the purpose and intent of the crescent shaped flat object inside his secret box. What he did not learn was the meaning of the inscriptions or the name of the object.

As his thoughts centered on the questions that arose, he received a quiet peace inside of him. His mind was filled with the words, *It is not important for you to know these things right now.*

Chief Peta Nocona'a heart and mind were satisfied.

Peta was too exhausted to return to the base of the mound that evening. He was so in-touch with the spirits and his experience, that he looked forward to another night on the mound.

But on the fourth day he came down from Medicine Mound; as he neared the base he saw confirmation of his vision. A bull buffalo was standing at the base near where Pecos would be waiting. In Peta's mind the sight was a symbol of success. "All will be well," he said to himself.

Suddenly, a shaft of lightning split the western sky; the shape of the lightning bolt eerily resembled the shape of the box's content. This further solidified the entire experience in Chief Peta Nocona's mind.

The present is inextricably
Shaped by the past

Chapter 1 – Jonathan

His name is Jonathan, and he has now reached full manhood. Jonathan will be celebrating his eighteenth birthday in three days and that is about all he knows for certain about himself. The word *celebrates* as applied to his birthday is a gross misnomer but that's how everyone he has ever known refers to their birthday; so Jonathan applies it to himself every year.

In a sense, he knows birthdays are important because every year, his father has said to him, "Today is your birthday. You are now … (whatever his age happened to be that year)." No other recognition of the eventful day has ever occurred … except for his twelfth.

Now, his eighteenth birthday is on the horizon, the thirteenth day of September. He wonders what is in store for him. Jonathan is not a worrisome fellow, but he considers his actions with very careful thought.

In truth, as he reflects on the past years, he has learned quite a lot, but he hasn't been certain how much of it applies to him. What he really is certain about is that he must be at a certain spot near the Texas panhandle early on his eighteenth birthday. He feels that he is prepared for whatever will occur.

Sitting there by himself just outside of Krum, Texas in his private spot, his mind wanders. He begins to think and contemplate all that he can recall about his life, his parents, and the mysteries that have seemed to surround everything he has ever known. His has been a thoughtful, introspective and reflective life.

****

Jonathan's musings this day begin early. It is Sunday morning, and he is at the Super 8 Hotel in Denton, having spent the night there. It is located only a few minutes east of Krum, and it is quite adequate for him.

He is trying to hurry to the free breakfast buffet before it is all picked over, but the reflections just keep rolling through his mind. This slows him down a bit. Actually, today's thoughts really began as he drifted off to sleep last evening and it seems that the thought process continued without changing throughout the night.

> *Even in my very early years, I probably knew more about life in general than about myself. One of my very earliest memories is of the regular relocations of our small family of three.*
>
> *I think I was about four years old at the time of my first recollection. My father, whom I have always called "Sir" walked into the kitchen of our home and simply said, "It is time to move." My mother, Ma, gave a cursory nod of her head and said, "Ok, I will have my things ready by noon." We packed up our belongings, and were on the road within hours.*

Jonathan's dreams last night covered a lot of territory, timewise speaking. He had retraced the early years of the his life, confirming the family's somewhat odd lifestyle.

The young man's reminiscing continues as he moves through his morning transformations. He goes from his sleepy state of mind to being fully alert, and ready for the day while trying to be the first in the hotel breakfast line.

We had moved with some degree of regularity, from Texas to Colorado, to Missouri and back to Texas. It was always in that circular or triangular rotation.

Whenever Sir announced, "It is time to move," we were soon loading the van and driving away from our home. We seldom stayed in one location more than six months or so. But each new place that we called "home" was in the same general area where we had lived sometime before; and it frequently presented a bit of a new challenge for me.

Reaching the hotel elevator, he anxiously pushes the button and the doors open immediately. *Wow, a really good sign!* He smiles inwardly at the thought.

Actually, the challenge was two-pronged. First was my apparently inborn desire for my own personal space. I really wanted to find a physical spot where I could be by myself and just think. Ma called it my place to dream; Sir called it a fantasy world and disapproved of any time being spent in such idleness.

I sure did not know how to define it, but I knew that I felt something very special while in this secret place. Second, I was a relatively small kid in the beginning but as I grew older, I also grew taller ... and heavier; I am now six feet-two inches tall and weigh about one-hundred-eighty pounds. Seclusion seemed more difficult with each relocation.

Oops, I forgot to push the down button and now the elevator is going up instead of down. Dangit! Jonathan is getting irritated at his own lack of attention, but the reminiscing does not stop.

No one really knew what was going on in this private place, and I wasn't so sure either ... at the beginning. I just knew how good I felt inside myself whenever I spent time there.

3

I even had a special name for this place, but I just kept it to myself; I don't know why, but I guess maybe it is part of my desire for privacy.

My first experience in one of these places occurred when I was about age five, and I found it in an area of tall trees with a lot of underbrush. There I fabricated a "room" where I could see out, but no one could see in.

Ma works a lot with reeds to make baskets and the such. She calls it weavin' and I picked up the knack from her. So, when I discovered my place in the trees, it was easy for me to weave the tiny and small branches into a sort of see-through blind.

I named the spot The Big Trees; from then on, every secret place regardless of its makeup became The Big Trees to me.

In this really neat and private place, I have had a lot of happenings that are both exciting and mysterious; they are each spiritual and emotional in intensity. These experiences are actually why I am here today.

Jonathan finally makes it to the eating room in the hotel. Loading his plate with his favorite breakfast food, sausage gravy and biscuits, he checks the scrambled egg warmer. His intent is to see if he might want to include some to his already filled plate; he adds a couple of large scoops of eggs to the top.

But, he thinks, *I sure wish they would add some small dill pickle pieces to the eggs.*

Bowing his head as Sir has always insisted, Jonathan offers a silent *thanks* and begins to eat. However, not even the hearty breakfast can take his mind off of the impressive happenings of his younger years; those years that have brought him here, to Krum, Texas on Sunday September 10, 2017, three days before his eighteenth birthday.

The first time it happened, I was really left in a stupor. I was only a kid ... nearing my sixth birthday ... but a very inquisitive kid. It was comforting and scary at the same time.

During my fifth or sixth time in The Big Trees, I was thinking about Ma and Sir; their kindness and how I liked being with them. My mind was roaming and I drifted into sleep.

I didn't see anyone ... or did I? I have often wondered about that. I was certain that I heard a soft female voice coming from some sort of form inside of my secret room.

The voice whispered tenderly, "You are smart. You have a good memory." The message was whispered to me several times, and when I awoke, I felt really good. There was a neat, warm feeling throughout my body. I liked the feeling, but I also felt as though I had been transported to another sphere. It was such a time of wonderment and joy; I guess a sort of awakening had begun.

I remember as a youngster, time at the special place became very important to me. I returned to The Big Trees often, as often as Ma and Sir would allow, sometimes three or four times in a week; The voice was something I always hoped would attend. Frequently it did, and the message was the same ... at first.

He recalls their next family relocation.

It was important that I find a new Big Trees place. Beginning with this move, the voice and form visited me less frequently, and the communication changed a bit; the messages became more tutorial as the years passed.

But I still always felt that comforting warmth inside. It was a feeling that I had become familiar with, and I knew that there would be a day sometime in the future when I would fully understand the purpose of these special visits.

Finishing his breakfast, he glances around at the other occupants in the room. They are mostly older folks who had helped themselves to food portions just a fraction of the size of his.

How do they seem so healthy and well-fed when they eat so little? he wonders.

Chuckling, he heads for the elevator which will take him to his second-floor room. Simultaneously, his thought process moves to another aspect of his life.

> *I have always wished for a little brother or sister; in fact, I brought it up to Sir once; the answer was a resolute, "One is enough!"*
>
> *One day, I had told Ma that I wanted more kids in the family. She told me to ask Sir about it; that was the end of any conversation about adding to the family.*
>
> *At times, when I was small, Ma would hold me on her lap and sing songs to me as we rocked in her old wooden rocking chair; the chair had once belonged to her father, "Gramps." She spoke of Gramps to me often, always with a sort of wistful tone of voice.*
>
> *It was clear that she loved the old man; he had died about twenty years previous at the age of eighty-seven. Gramps was forty-five years old when Ma was born; his wife had died when Ma was age four.*

Unaware to Jonathan, Sir had seen to it that his son would have this day alone in the area of Krum because of the symbolic relevance of the place.

Sitting for a moment in his hotel room, he is trying to give his head a rest from the memories. Jonathan decides that this is a good day to visit the local Big Trees area; the area where he has spent time during three or four previous family relocations. In fact, Jonathan begins to feel the familiar pull to escape humanity and be totally alone. *In order to do that, I must go to The Big Trees.*

Jonathan makes a quick stop at the nearby Valero station to pick up some snacks. He decides on some licorice, chips, Dr Pepper and a couple bottles of water, pays the bill and is on his way. His anticipation of returning to The Big Trees continues to be heightened.

****

Being alone today in The Big Trees, Jonathan suddenly recalls that this is the very same place near Krum where he first fashioned his secret place so many years ago. The same little weaved hideout no longer exists, but he is able to find solitude among the many trees.

It is also where he first experienced the quiet serene voice. *I wonder if Sir arranged it this way for me?* His curiosity is piqued, and thus, Jonathan also begins to gain a greater appreciation for his parents. His reverie then turns to them.

Ma seems to always find the good in our nomadic existence. Her agreeable attitude is very encouraging to me. Really, we have a rather enviable life together, the three of us; there are moments of laughter and pleasantries when on the road, and getting settled in a new home is an adventure that Ma and Sir seem to enjoy.

During those nice, enjoyable times, Sir often uses a pet nickname that he gave me; the nickname is Quanah. There has never been an explanation, just Quanah; then Sir simply smiles broadly, and often dances a sort of jig as he speaks the name. He us such a good man

Despite our many moves, I have never felt totally alone. It is as though we fit nicely into our new surroundings; although every place we have lived is in a remote area.

I find it interesting that we have never lived in a "normal" neighborhood; I really like it that way. Solitude is a word Ma uses to describe my desire to be at The Big Trees. Plus, I really like my private friend, the voice. Because of the fact that everyplace we have lived has included a secluded area, I never consider it strange. It is just a part of our itinerant life.

I have often wondered about Sir and his employment. It seems that all of the other kids that I have gotten to know have a dad who holds a job. What about Sir?

He always has money for us, and we never have to go without. in fact, he is funding this trip for me; the hotel bills, gasoline and anything else I may need. Sir gave me plenty of money.

Sir never speaks of his work and that is part of the mystery. The older I get, the more curious I become: Just who is Sir? He has never offered any information about himself, and somehow I know better than to ask questions about his heredity. Is he being secretive or just thinks it is not important?

Hmm, maybe that is where I get my desire for privacy, he thinks.

One thing that I have slowly become aware of however, is that every new place to which we locate seems to require Sir to be away from home for two days shortly following the move. When he returns, Sir always seems much more relaxed than he had been the previous two or three weeks.

"Ahhh, this is really what I like," Jonathan sighs as he stretches out, leaning his head against a small fallen log cushioned by the small pillow they always carry in the family van.

More questions come into Jonathan's mind, and in his fanciful world he imagines the possibilities.

Is there a connection with Sir's income and our frequent moves? Is Sir a bank robber? Maybe he has a secret investment to collect from. Could it be that Sir owns a business near every new home from which he earns money?

Why is he so secretive if he is an honorable man? If he weren't honorable, why would Ma continue to be happy with him? She seems to be supportive of all that he does. Also, she laughs a lot during our time together. But there is something I am not allowed to know!

As Jonathan has grown older, he decides that he must learn more about Sir. Perhaps he might gain some information about his father during a future episode in The Big Trees; surely the voice will know everything.

But then, will we still have time together in The Big Trees; my mentor and me, after this upcoming week? Oh my gosh, I have never considered that she might leave me!

A sort of panic is felt within, but it is replaced by sleep which is pleasantly accompanied by a slight rustle of the leaves above; a sound that has for years signaled peace to the young mind. The thought process that Jonathan has been experiencing seems to have replaced the voice that he pines for, a sort of narrator for the memories that continue in his light sleep.

I think perhaps she has come to be with me. I feel the warmth right now ....

It is Ma that I feel drawn to, more so than Sir. She tries to fill in the vacancies that I began to sense as I became older and went into childhood, then into my teenage years.

In some of the places where we have lived, there have been other kids. But, whenever I've seen them at play and tried to join in, I have been made to feel like an outsider, kinda' like a trespasser. I am just more comfortable being by myself.

Ma is not just my parent and teacher, but most of all, she is my only permanent friend. We have never settled in one place long enough to register and attend public school, at least this is what I have been told; and I wonder if that is true. Ma became my teacher and she is determined that I learn to read and write because, "It is important."

Equally, she said that I must learn to be independent, and learn to drive the family van when I turned sixteen; Sir saw to it that I did! Oh, how I love to drive!

With renewed energy Jonathan tries to focus on the upcoming week; but his mind continues to be attracted to the past. It seems that for some reason he must secure his past life and memories in his mind.

Doing so, he considers the passage of time, and his becoming a teenager. That was the time when he had sensed an increased intensity in schooling.

There has never been a "normal" school year, but we have had an every day session of reading practice, writing tutoring and "culture class" recitation.

The culture class' main focus has been centered on "America's First" as Ma calls it. America's First class consists of learning the oral history of the indigenous people in the areas where the three of us have always lived. It is a sort of triangular enclosure where we move every few months.

Jonathan continues the pause as he contemplates his own musings. He chuckles at his use of the word "indigenous."

I remember when Ma first used that word in class, I struggled all year trying to pronounce it! She has always been a really neat teacher. Funny how I remember certain silly things.

The presence of the feminine voice is verified when she speaks, "Jonathan, Jonathan, I am leaving you now. There are other duties that I must prepare for. Never forget that I will always be near. Just remember: Pay attention to the quiet voice of the mind. Be wise in all you do."

Momentarily, the sound of rustling leaves increases in intensity, and a sense of loss is felt by Jonathan, but a deeper feeling of security encompasses him as he awakes from his light slumber.

She was here with me ... and ... and it is interesting that she used the quiet voice phrase. He instinctively lowers his head and offers up a sincere thank you.

Jonathan's mind returns to Ma and his relationship with her.

Except for occasional new history lessons, new reading words and penmanship practice in school, all else is just routine. I know that there must be more than this to my existence. I have had twelve years of schooling now, and I think that I may have begun to come of age educationally.

Ma sometimes, in a vague sort of way, speaks about her younger life, but she speaks most frequently about Gramps. She tells of the stories that he told her, rather than of their relationship with one another.

However, she rarely speaks of her mother. Of course, she had never really known her mother, but Ma does know that Gramps loved his wife very much and missed her greatly. Ma and her father had a good life.

Gramps had inherited some oil something-or-other that provided income for as long as he was to live. But, when he died, the income stopped.

For some reason, Ma has not wanted to talk about other parts of her younger life; only about Gramps and his endearing stories, which she cherishes. I just know that there has to be more to Ma's life, and I would really like to know what there is. But right now is not the time to pursue the topic. I can't help but think how much I love and appreciate her for all she has meant to me. However ...

****

Adjusting his reclining posture in The Big Trees retreat, Jonathan reaches for his open bag of red licorice sticks.

Good, there are a lot of pieces left so I should be satisfied for quite a while, he comfortably tells himself.

Recalling his twelfth birthday, Jonathan remembers where they were living at the time, it was in the Texas panhandle. He thinks of their drive through a lot of flat land and seeing a sign that said, "Welcome to Quanah." He spoke to Sir about it.

"Is that where my nickname came from?" I asked.

"Sure is," was the reply and that was it. Sir immediately changed the subject.

Ma seemed relieved when the town of Quanah was behind us; this really added to the questions in my mind. Someday I will know and understand the truth; Quanah is either a good place or bad place. One day I will know how it all fits.

However, Quanah seems both an attraction and a disconcerting place to Sir and Ma. A long time ago I decided that this small town near the southeast corner of the Texas panhandle contains some secrets; perhaps some secrets very close to my parents. There has to be some reason for Ma to become troubled whenever we go through the area.

It will be better to wait and learn, rather than ask questions of Ma or Sir.

Jonathan stands, stretches and considers leaving The Big Trees, but is impressed to remain; he feels it must be important to continue in his contemplations. Taking a lengthy drink of water he settles back into his comfy position, and continues to ponder about his twelfth birthday.

Someplace outside of Quanah, I remember stopping in a remote place near the Texas panhandle. We had turned from Highway 287 onto a lonely road; I think we turned south. As we were driving slowly along the gravel road, Sir said, "You are twelve today. It is a special day and you must do something to prove your manhood." I had no idea what he was talking about. We then continued driving in silence for several miles.

In my first six years of schooling, I had been taught in America's First class about traditions and practices of the Native Americans. It seems that I wondered constantly: Is there a family connection?

Ma has never indicated any Native American heritage. Her complexion is rather light but she claims her mother's skin was somewhat darker.

Sir is just "Sir." He is a rather large, dark-skinned man who never, ever speaks of his family. Hmmm, I wonder if Sir could be a Native American. If so, then I am too, but I know better than to ask.

Another sip of water and his mind snaps back to the significance of his twelfth birthday. Sir had given to Jonathan some instructions that were to prove his manhood.

After we stopped in some isolated place in the Texas panhandle, Ma stepped outside of our large family van and tried to make herself comfortable in the shade of the vehicle; apparently this was to be a man-to-man discussion between us guys. It seemed almost ceremonial in nature to me as Sir began to speak.

"Quanah, my son, there is something that you must never reveal to anyone, not even to Ma. You are to memorize this location. You now have one hour to yourself; find special landmarks that you can remember. There will be a day in your future when this spot will mean everything to you. Remember this saying, 'Quanah bananah is the key.' Never forget it. I will never say it to you again."

I remember his words well, "Now, take the next hour to search the area. Find those things that are permanent, and things that will help you identify this spot in the future. Now go!"

I recollect very clearly how I felt as I began my one-hour exploration. I was scared, excited and very much alone. I knew that I was not abandoned, but I did feel totally lost and without a guide. Oh, how I wanted my friend from The Big Trees!

I am sure that Sir expected this to be a mysterious odyssey of education, wonderment and anticipation for me. But as I quietly exited the van and walked away from Sir's presence, my mind was wrapped around the question, What is the meaning of "Quanah banana is the key," and when will I need it? I still have feelings of surrealism just thinking about the experience.

****

The late afternoon sun begins to peek through the branches and leaves of the trees; Jonathan realizes that this Sunday has been a good day. As it comes to a close, this day seems like the departure of a good friend because it has been so comfortable and enjoyable.

Coming out of his musings into reality, Jonathan knows that he has something more relevant to consider ... the here and now of his life.

I must now focus on my quest for additional knowledge and personal direction. The encounters with my mentor at The Big Trees have taught me a lot about my purpose in life; things that I have been instructed to not share with anyone. This is both an honor and a burden. I realize that very few, if any young people have had the opportunity to grow intellectually the way I have. But I am also sure that there is much more to come.

It is interesting that I have been instructed to have my cell phone with me, but to keep it turned off except in the case of an extreme emergency. The only reason for the off position that I can think of, is that I cannot be tracked. I dunno, but there must be some explanation.

I think that the meeting this week, at someplace near Quanah, will not be the end of my mission. It will probably be a new beginning, the start of an adventure that I have no idea what it is. I can only hope I will complete it with exactness.

Gosh, I'm not sure exactly where to go; only to the "place that will mean everything to me someday," and that is still three days away.

Sir made sure that I have a room at the Best Western hotel in Quanah, and that is where I will go first. I can only trust that I will be led by the voice.

Knowing that the time to leave The Big Trees is approaching, Jonathan begins to gather his things. He finishes his Dr Pepper and drops the empty bottle into the Valero imprinted plastic shopping bag. He thinks again about Sir, and some of the advice he had offered.

At Sir's suggestion, I spent several hours yesterday studying the stuff on display at the Krum Museum. Sir proposed that my route to Quanah include some time in Krum.

He had said, "Visit the museum. You will find a lot of information about the Finley side of your ancestry, your mother's side; they are wonderful people. Perhaps someday you will have opportunity to meet them."

Those were Sir's closing words earlier Saturday as he and Ma stood outside of the van telling me good-bye. It was a love-filled good-bye. I am sure they feel as much anticipation and concern as me.

I am really grateful that Sir has allowed me to use our new family van for my drive to the Texas panhandle. It will be a relatively short trip since we are now living a few miles south of Krum, somewhere between Ponder and Justin.

Taking time to clean up his area, and making certain that he leaves no trash behind, Jonathan looks around at the place that holds so many memories for him. He eyes the spot of his first room, and the hand-crafted blind he weaved with the small branches.

Remembering those beginning times with the voice, tears form in his eyes. He has always been a sentimental type of kid, and today is no different. He wipes away the tears with the back of his right hand.

Gosh, I'm sure that I will have many more things to think about during my drive to Quanah tomorrow.

I would like to write all of this stuff down, but I have been specifically forbidden to write notes or make records of any kind regarding what is expected of me, except where expressly instructed to do so. All directives are to be held within my memory.

Taking his first few steps toward the van, and with a humorous twist he says aloud to himself, "Sure hope I don't get anything backwards!"

DENNIS BOYD CALL

How beautiful upon the mountains are
the feet of him that bringeth good tidings ...
(Isaiah 52:7)

CHAPTER 2 – PRAIRIE FLOWER

On the drive back to the Super 8 this evening, Jonathan is compelled to reconstruct more deeply in his mind, all that has happened in his lifetime.   Birthday twelve was undoubtedly the most significant birthday in Jonathan's life ... up to that point; and, he muses, possibly the most significant day *ever* in his life. That was the day Sir had sent him on his coming of age odyssey.

Sir gave me one hour to detect, memorize and mentally photograph those landmarks which would help me recognize that special place in the future.. This piece of north Texas terrain is supposed to "mean everything" to me someday is what he told me. I had to question my capacity to deal with all of this; I was only twelve years old, for goodness sake!

There were so many things to internalize; I was much too young to understand and deal with some realities: The voice in The Big Trees, the frequent family relocations, the source of Sir's income and all the questions that surround my heritage!

Wow! He acknowledges to himself, *All of this comes together as an insurmountable mystery.*

Over the next six years I tried with all my might to bring things into focus. Were it not for the cool tutoring that I received in my frequent Big Trees meetings, I would have felt completely overwhelmed. The voice has been a source of comfort,

19

knowledge and prophesy since the beginning of our meetings. I became very curious about who the voice belonged to.

It is only a short drive to the hotel and Jonathan relaxes a bit as he begins to near the intersection just prior to the railroad tracks. He has his eye on the black Volvo SUV on his right as he begins to enter the juncture, but he pays it no attention; he continues in deep thought.

One day in a brave and unplanned surge of courage I asked the voice, "Who are you?"

The response did not fully answer my question, but it gave me a lot of peace and confidence.

"A Prairie Flower is your friend and confidant," she said.

From that, I did learn that I am permitted to have two-way dialogue with my invisible mentor. That fact alone has fed my feelings of trust and confidence, both in her and in myself.

Sooo, it has just seemed a natural reaction for me to refer ever since, to the female voice as Prairie Flower.

Suddenly, the Volvo lurches forward with a squeal of the tires. It starts a left turn in front of Jonathan who hits the brakes heavily, and swerves to his right to avoid the collision.

Stopping in mid-intersection, Jonathan begins to perspire profusely, his body shaking uncontrollably. His mind's eye sees vividly the grin on the face of the other driver.

Oh my gosh! What is going on!? Jonathan is totally overcome by fearful emotion.

Pulling the van to the side of the street, Jonathan lays his head against the steering wheel and tries to regain his composure.

But, he thinks, *why such a ridiculous grin on his face? It has to be just an incompetent driver ... I hope, anyway ... Surely he would not do such a dumb thing on purpose!*

He pulls back onto the street and continues his drive to the hotel where he parks the van in an available parking space. He sits in silence for several minutes, giving thanks to whatever force or higher power had been his protector.

As he reaches for the door handle to exit the van, he sees a black Volvo SUV backing into the spot two vacancies over. His heart sinks as his head begins to swirl, and in a dazed state he witnesses the driver exit the Volvo and walk toward him. *Oh, no! Now what?*

He begins to tremble again. Sir and Ma had taught Jonathan to avoid conflict, and he isn't certain how to handle what might be coming.

The driver is a young dark-skinned man with hair to his shoulders, his demeanor seems pleasant but determined.

He speaks, "Jonathan, I am sorry, but I had to get your attention in a dramatic way. I have been given instructions to deliver a message and an envelope to you.

"The message is this: 'You must be careful in all you do.' And here is the envelope. Further, you must not open the envelope until you have been instructed to do so by Prairie Flower."

The fellow returns to his vehicle and drives away, leaving Jonathan speechless, relieved and confused, all at the same time.

Weak-kneed and quivering, he arrives in his hotel room and sits limply on the side of his bed. He tries with little to no success to make sense of what has just happened.

A shower might bring some calmness to me, he decides as he removes his shirt.

Refreshed and ready to call it a day, Jonathan feels he can soothe his mind by returning to his mental recollections of the past. He lays back on his bed, fluffs up the pillow and turns on his right side, his "comfy side." Closing his eyes his contemplation continues.

> *Since the beginning of my thirteenth year, following my twelfth birthday experience, I have been really eager to learn from the voice. It was about this same time that I learned of her name, although I have no idea if there is any significance to it. Heck, I don't even know if Prairie Flower is her name; it just seems to fit.*
>
> *What I do know is that my tutoring has been progressive: The first sessions taught me self-confidence, then trust, then honor.*

Shivers run up and down Jonathan's spine as he recognizes the extremely broad impact Prairie Flower has had on his life over the past eleven or twelve years. *She has been my guide, friend and comforter.*

Thinking of his added maturity, his thoughts continue.

It seems that the training has been a sub-conscious construction of my thought process. In the progression of the tutoring and as I have matured, the intensity and urgency of the messages have increased.

I also know that the messages and lessons delivered by Prairie Flower are for me and me alone. This entire situation, as exciting and comforting as it may be, is causing me some anxiety; especially given the episode this afternoon! But, the existence of Prairie Flower has been confirmed to me.

Not only am I forbidden to share the strange but all-important phrase "Quanah Bananah is the key," there are other matters. I think that I adequately explored, took mental notes, and visually photographed all landmarks and distinctions of that all-important

*spot way back on my twelfth birthday. I remember the hour spent ...
But, what if ...?*

*I know it was off of Highway 287 outside of the town of Quanah,
however I may not recognize the correct country road to take. I was
so focused on the exact place that I failed to notice if the road had a
number or a name.*

*Oh my gosh, I remember the smallest detail of the location, but
forget how to get there! I sure hope Prairie Flower will be with me
to guide me.*

*Then there are the additional things that Sir shared with me. How
can I possibly recall everything?!? Sir had confided additional
information at the completion of my hour-long adventure. He said
some things that I did not comprehend. I remember the words, but at
the time had little understanding of their importance.*

*He spoke of the loss of integrity, the loss of privilege and the devious
nature of many people.*

*"But," said he, "eaglets learn to soar so beautifully high in the sky
because they overcome terrifying odds. You my son, are an eaglet."*

An interesting visual Jonathan concludes, as he considers what his
options may be when his birthday actually arrives in three more
days.

Fingering the six-by-nine inch envelope handed him earlier this
afternoon, the nervous young man feels weight upon weight on his
shoulders.

*I am not even sure what this entire adventure is supposed to
accomplish; yet I know I am doing the right thing.*

He tries to visualize what Prairie Flower might look like, and in a
sense he tries to place responsibility on her for everything.

Additionally, Jonathan is carrying the instructions and lessons brought by his mentor. It feels to the youth that it is more than he can possibly comprehend; except he knows the great empowerment brought to him by Prairie Flower.

He is not specifically sworn to secrecy, but he knows that his mentoring is meant for him alone; it is not to be spoken of to anyone. The teachings and learnings are between Jonathan and Prairie Flower only.

Then he wonders aloud to himself, "Who is Prairie Flower? Why is she the one to be with me?"

It is only a fleeting thought, not even a real question, but something tells him that the time will come for him to know all of the answers. He continues in deep thought, a trait he developed in his many hours at The Big Trees.

Communication between Prairie Flower and me has always flowed seamlessly. She has developed my mind into a confident personality, even advancing me to a sense of self-assurance. Not only have I developed a great trust in my unseen friend, but Prairie Flower has put a mighty responsibility on me. The training has moved from intellectual development to instructive training.

Oh, my gosh! He suddenly grasps a new observation: Not only have I grown to physical adulthood, but I have closely approached full maturity of thought, reason and plan. Similarly, Prairie Flower has transitioned from being the unknown stranger, to the kind understanding character that I need.

In the beginning, the messages from Prairie Flower had seemed vague in substance, yet direct in meaning. They caused me to puzzle over what was happening, but I never failed to feel warmth and security following one of our sessions.

Many years have passed, and I have not only accepted my unseen friend but have learned to totally rely on her messages. A word that I have heard, but never paid much attention to is pounding hard in my mind: "Faith." Faith truly has a genuine meaning .

Contemplating the word faith, Jonathan re-aligns his thoughts.

We are not a religious family, at least not formally. Occasionally we do attend a church service ... But Sir seems uncomfortable there, and Ma is content just attending a couple times a year ... And an Easter service most years. But there seems to be a contradiction ... That is Sir's reliance on some divine power.

He insists on saying grace over meals; "We give thanks to our Maker for all that we have" ... Often, Sir speaks of the importance of living to a standard higher than is commonly accepted.

Sir has always taught me truth, honesty and integrity. Many times he has said, "Pay attention to the quiet voice of your mind." That is a form of faith, isn't it?

Prairie Flower used the quiet voice phrase just recently! Jonathan gulps in amazement at the similarity of Sir's and his mentor's teachings.

Maybe these are the reasons that it has not been difficult for me to accept first the voice, then the tutor's encouragement, followed by her instructions.

The Big Trees have become a sort of sanctuary to me. It is a place where conversing with Prairie Flower is not only hoped for, but I know that it will happen ... But only if I am prepared with an open mind, and am eager to learn.

Ma and Sir have been very focused for my entire life on helping me become a good person. I think that Sir may not realize the full impact of his compulsion for my good behavior. Maybe he has unwittingly been helping me prepare myself to receive Prairie Flower's messages.

Jonathan has come to understand that he has a special position in life; a purpose which he could not know without years of tutoring, training and coaching. It is this realization that brings him to understand the application of faith in his life.

Sir taught me to listen to the quiet voice; Ma taught me patience and respect; Prairie Flower is teaching me value, confidence and assurance for the future, a future that is both exciting and causes me fear.

But wait! Fear of the unknown is a contradiction because as I have been tutored, my knowledge of my role in the future is actually opening up to me. Having faith in Prairie Flower's guidance will most certainly help me overcome fear.

Gosh! The six years between ages twelve and eighteen have really been vital in my enlightenment. They are vital in that my knowledge and acceptance have kinda' merged. They seem to have morphed into a singular mission to which only I can respond. I guess that I have taken ownership of whatever is to come.

The hour upon hour of dialogue with Prairie Flower during our remarkable times at The Big Trees, have drawn me into a sort of partnership with her. But over the years, what was regular dialogue has become an almost constant companionship with her mind.

It is hard to describe, but it seems we have begun to communicate without dialogue. Is this what Sir means when he says to listen to the quiet voice of the mind? Wow! How profound!

Jonathan sucks in his breath as the many new realizations fall upon him. It seems that he may not have room in his head for it all.

Yes! Time has progressed, and the voice of Prairie Flower was audible at first ... or was it? ... Anyway, it has become the quiet voice that Sir has often spoken of.

Now as I am about to be eighteen, I realize that my mentor is really a silent, full-time impression; always there to be called upon, and always there to be relied upon for guidance.

Still, as the transition has been taking place, my desire to know the identity of Prairie Flower, and her connection to me has dramatically increased. I know there must be a common thread between us ... Somewhere ... This is really surreal!

I have got to get some sleep, he tells himself as he rolls to his left side. *But my mind won't stop thinking about everything.*

A change of thought comes to the teenager who has more on his mind than anyone should; it seems that his life has morphed into a mission of sorts that is beyond his realm of comprehension.

Jonathan rolls over on his bed again; and with it comes another vein of thought.

My mind is stretched to a point of near popping. I really need to think of matters that are much less serious, or I will never get to sleep.

But, it is only a temporary respite from his memories.

One day about two years ago, during some private time with Ma, I began to ask her a question, "Do the words Prair..."

In a flash I realized it was a mistake to involve her with my dilemma. I suddenly stopped speaking and Ma looked quizzingly at me. I felt caught as though I was committing some sort of fraud!

"Yes, what were you saying?" she wanted to know.

"Oh, nothing. Never mind, it is not important." I am sure that the thoughtful look on my face was less than convincing to Ma ... In fact, it was probably a dead giveaway.

I turned, and walked out of the room. Then I silently chastised myself because I knew that Prairie Flower's identity ... and true connection with me will be revealed by her at the appropriate time.

My inner feelings were really conflicted ... I knew I could talk with Ma about virtually anything, and she would be understanding, but this was kinda heavy,

Besides, I knew that Sir is a better source for the answer. But that seemed totally inconsistent with his personality. Sir would not have any interest in such a question ... Even if he had an interest he would probably not show it ...

He yanks himself back to the present.

"Come on, Jonathan," he speaks aloud, "Get real! Prairie Flower's identity, for now, will have to be set aside."

Set aside, maybe, but not laid aside. She is much too important to be forgotten. Still, I wonder, Who is Prairie Flower and why has she taken such interest in me?

Ohhh ... but for the pains of the mind!

CHAPTER 3 – SIR

Settling back into their rented home near Ponder, Texas, Sir and Ma are meditatively absorbed in their individual thoughts. Their only son is about to reach the age of majority; in a few days he will legally be an adult.

They try to converse with each other, but all they can express are words of concern about their roles in parenting.

"Did we each do the right thing?" is about the extent of their expressed feelings.

Their other commonality is the deep private contemplative mode of each, which renders conversation nearly impossible; only things like, "It is Saturday; the boy will soon be in Krum."

Sir is a troubled man; and he has a lot to be troubled over. In an unsettled frame of mind, and having a heart that aches he leans his head back in his recliner as he simultaneously adjusts the headrest.

Funny, I have never claimed this chair as my private space, but Ma and Jonathan have always deferred it to me ...

As drowsiness approaches and his eyes close, the feelings of distress take front and center in his mind.

What is my true parentage? This is a mental path I have trod many, many times, and the solutions have always been the same and it really distresses me.

The Nation questions my right to share in the tribal windfall: The income that helps provide for our little family. How do I protect the integrity of my own character, such as it is and not leave my son, Quanah's, legacy in shambles. And what is his mother learning about me as we begin to grow old together?

I think however, that my greatest concern is the tribal responsibility that Jonathan is to have placed on him. Ohhh, how I wish I had done things differently over the years ... but ... what would that have been?

Few people in the *Nation* have accepted Sir, whose christened name is Peta Parker. Peta was a name that went way back to his *proclaimed* paternal great-great-grandfather, Peta Nocona. He, with his wife Cynthia Ann Parker, were the parents of Quanah Parker, known as the last of the Comanche chiefs. It is at this juncture that Sir loses his genealogical bearings.

Sir's breathing slows and becomes heavier as his mind enters a dreamlike state. His thought process tries to work through the ancestral questions as he fine-tunes his position in the chair. A quasi-sleep overtakes him as he hears Ma begin to sob in the background. Sir returns to his thoughts:

Some declare that because my last name is Parker I have illegally claimed Quanah Parker is my great-grandfather. A few of them insist that I may not even be Native American.

Quanah had several wives, but I have no proof as to which of them is my great-grandmother. That is the problem. I must have absolute proof in order for the tribal genealogists to accept my pedigree. There are some who do accept my claim, but do so very cautiously. They are looking for evidence to close the gap as to the identity of my great-grandmother. Which of Quanah Parker's wives is my ancestor?

While he sleeps, Sir simply regurgitates the thoughts that have plagued him for many years. He has known that someday he would have to face all of the facts. Facts that are muddled, and that he himself is still trying to clarify. He turns a bit to his left side as his restless sleep continues.

The problem has further magnification. This information is vital in order for Jonathan to qualify for a share in tribal governance and finance. The young man must be able to prove that he is a minimum of one-eighth blood Comanche heritage. I know that Jonathan is entitled to his share, but will he be able to prove it?

Ma, suddenly startled, looks up quizzingly at the sound of Sir's stirring, but remains silent.

To make matters more confusing, I was raised by my father, Daniel, without the assistance of his wife. She had laid a heavy humiliation on her husband shortly after my birth by leaving the tribal culture to join a white man. They moved east and she has never since been heard from. I do not even know my own mother's name.

Family tradition held that Sir was the great-grandson of Quanah Parker, Comanche Chief, and his first wife, believed to be a Mescalero Apache who disappeared in 1875. It was a double-twisted problem … no proof of identity of either his mother or great-grandmother. And the tribal leaders *insisted* on proof.

That proof is not for me to provide; it is to come from the eldest son of the fifth generation. That is Jonathan!

This generational decree came from Chief Peta Nocona, himself. The tribal genealogists know and accept that fact. Peta was a spiritual man who believed that a Comanche's status came through his possession of puha or power. He was endowed with puha because of, and through his pursuit for visionary experience.

To achieve this, he periodically had a three or four-day quest secluded in the place called Medicine Mound. There he engaged in such activities as fasting and praying along with the smoking of peyote.

It was during one of these quests that Peta Nocona received his Fifth-Son Vision. The vision is recognized as a possibility by everyone with puha in the Comanche Nation. The vision is not the problem; the execution of it is! If it is true, many wonder who is the fifth-son?

How I wish I could go back in time! Sir begins to lament the past eighteen years with Jonathan when he could have done more.

There is so much that he is about to learn about my side of the family. Ohhh, how my heart is aching!

He is able to return his thoughts to more pleasant matters, albeit another difficult topic.

To Chief Peta, the vision revealed the loss of some all-important generational identity, thus the loss of family puha until the fifth generation. It is to be restored by the fifth-son. The old chief supposedly buried an artifact that contains the needed proof in or around Medicine Mound. The only evidence of such an occurrence was observed by Peta's young son who had died of small pox at a very young age.

The tribal leaders could neither prove or disprove any of the story. Some call it a Comanche myth, others swear that they know of the story from their own family tradition. The problem is compounded by the lack of just who is the fifth-son? Sir has claimed to the Council that he is the father of the fifth-son.

Sir's ethereal dreamlike state is further disconcerting as he recalls one Tribal Council meeting in which he presented his case.

"The fifth-son is my son, Jonathan! He and he alone carries the puha to restore legitimacy to the family name.

"The Fifth-Son Vision was verified to Peta Nocona as he ended his quest and began the slow walk down the side of the rocky mound. A bull buffalo was standing at the base of the mound close to the foot of the trail; almost simultaneous to the buffalo sighting was a sudden flash of lightning in the western sky. It is said that the lightning bolt was given a special shape.

"Everyone knows that Peta Nocona was always filled with puha, and he had other manifestations even before that: There had been the landing of the eagle and the slithering snake crossing the path ahead of him.

"I, Peta Parker, know that the gods accepted Chief Peta's quest for knowledge and direction. I also know that the Fifth-Son Vision was real, and that my son Jonathan will fulfill that prophecy." I presented my case well!

In a sweat, Sir tries to awaken but is unable. Instead, he is drawn deeper into his emotional search for something; he is not even certain as to the questions.

Tribal fathers agree that proof, if there is any, could come through my son, who is the eldest son of the eldest son, of the eldest son, of the eldest son ... the fifth son. They too, are aware of the verbal history and are willing to accept the Fifth-Son Prophecy; but not necessarily my claim of legitimacy. I don't know what else I can do.

"You, Mr. Parker come to us from nowhere and make this claim. There has to be more, and either you or your son will need to provide the proof. It is your burden," was the response of those in the council.

"In fact," some stated, "what has been your background all of your life? It is said that you may be aligned with the Alliance."

I was more than stunned by that statement! Most of our people are aware of the Alliance but do not know any of the individuals involved.

I know that Jonathan will play an important role in the re-establishment of dignity and puha to our branch of the family. This is an issue that I have wrestled with very often. But I wonder just what my son can possibly learn or even do, that will bring legitimacy to my claim. It is a claim that is repeatedly placed on hold by the tribal genealogists. They have great influence on the Council!

Sir forces himself awake and looks across the room to his wife who is relaxed in her position on the couch. He can tell she is not sleeping, but the expressive smile on her face assures him that she is pleasantly enjoying her thoughts. He presses himself to change the topic of his own thoughts:

One day early in Jonathan's seventh year, I watched as my little boy, whom I lovingly nicknamed Quanah ran with much energy toward his secret place, The Big Trees. Openly, I projected the attitude that it was foolishness to spend any time at all at that place; the place that held so much attraction for the boy. But within myself, I enviously knew Jonathan was being tutored and prepared for what was to yet to come.

I frequently saw a change of countenance surrounding him after a visit to his special place. He was calm, relaxed and energized all at the same time; Ma had noticed it too and encouraged the boy in his desire for private time there. She is such a wonderful and sensitive mother.

Sir only knew that he, Sir, held the key that was to be passed to his son on his twelfth birthday. From there, it would be up to the lad to learn his duty through some source, or sources.

It will take time, probably years for all the learning to come to pass. But I can't help but wonder to myself: Just what occurs at The Big Trees?

I inadvertently learned the name of the secret place when Jonathan accidently referred to it by name; he had mentioned Peta and The Big Trees together following one of his periodic visits to that wonderful place. I decided to keep that information to myself, but I wondered about his use of the name Peta. Interesting combination of words coming from the boy.

Sir moves out of his recliner and retrieves a bottle of cold water from the refrigerator. He gets one for his wife and sets it by her side without interrupting her; she appears now to be sleeping so he is careful to not disturb her.

Is Jonathan alright? What is he doing right now? Has he arrived at Krum yet? What are his thoughts? Sir loves his son, and it is reflected in his own wondering thoughts.

He returns to his chair and resettles himself. Motivation to do anything but sit has left him, and he returns to his thoughts: a combination of The Big Trees, his own ancestry, and Jonathan's tutoring. He takes a long drink, sighs and returns to reminiscing.

Perhaps the boy has been communicating with my great-great-grandfather, Peta Nocona himself, or even Cynthia Ann Parker, my great-great-grandmother. Oh, how I wish for definite knowledge about my heritage. I really wonder which of Quanah Parker's wives is my great-grandmother?

I know that my great-great-grandmother, Cynthia Ann was a white woman, kidnapped by the Comanches when she was about nine years old, and that she grew into a Comanche herself. So much so that she was adopted and considered a "pure" Comanche.

After giving birth to her three children with Peta Nocona, she was "repatriated" and taken back to live with her white family against her will. Cynthia Ann pined for the lifestyle she was familiar with; additionally, her sons Quanah and Pecos had been left behind in the repatriation raid ...

She and her daughter, Topsannah, had tried to escape by horseback but were re-captured and taken again to her white family.

About three years later Topsannah died and Cynthia Ann was so overcome with grief that she died after another six years had passed. Some folks claimed that she had starved herself to death. Certainly Cynthia Ann Parker could be a qualified tutor for Jonathan.

Drowsiness begins again to overtake this gentle, but very private man. He doesn't want to sleep; he just wants to continue in thought. *Maybe I will arrive at answers to my continual questions.*

Sir is in a state of knowing what must be done but feels powerless to do it. Instead, he continues to dwell in anticipatory thought.

Maybe Jonathan is being tutored by the Great Spirit himself; but more likely any tutoring is probably being provided by Quanah, the last great Comanche Chief or his first wife, Ta-ha-yea the Mescalero Apache. In all honesty, I think that she is most likely the tutor. I have always felt that she is my true great-grandmother, and so, who would be more appropriate and faithful to spiritual instruction than she?

Sir makes a self-acknowledgment.

I have always felt it my duty to keep the boy away from evil. That he must remain pure and true in order to be properly tutored and taught by the spirit, whomever it may be. I also feel that Ma and I have succeeded in that endeavor.

Sir needs all of the positive reinforcement he can get, even if only from himself.

It has been important that we relocate our family every few months, although it is difficult. We move partly because it will help protect Jonathan from influences that might divert his attention away from all that is good ... However, the moves have to be strategic in order to meet the requirements of our income for life ... But, how will I be able to honestly justify the methods I have used to gain the money? I know I have been deceitful ... And someday the truth will certainly be exposed.

These thoughts bring a sweat throughout Sir's body. *But this income is crucial for our survival.* He unsuccessfully tries to calm and convince himself.

Sir is deeply troubled over this dual situation: Their income and Jonathan's personal integrity. He is troubled because Ma will ultimately have to be told the truth. He sinks back into deep reverie.

She accepted me all those many years ago because of my promise of adventure and zest for living. She knows of my Native American connection ... but has honored my reluctance to speak of it. She is willing to live openly in the tribal community .. although it has been me who discourages it. She embraces my insistence on our nomadic lifestyle. I know she is putting things together in her mind ... Ohhh, I know I must soon be open with her.

He has made this promise to himself before, and always failed to follow through. But he commits to it again.

I will tell everything to Ma while our son is on his quest ... I cannot allow his integrity to be compromised by my own deceits ... I don't want to face it ...

Sir continues his pondering.

Further, Jonathan is a smart lad, and I know he is questioning our lifestyle and his heritage ... There is no reason to be ashamed of it ... I do not want Jonathan to feel anything but good about his American Indian ancestry ... But neither Ma nor the boy will understand the situation ...

Sir's feelings are running deep; he is then startled by the touch of his wife's soft palm as she brushes it across his forehead.

"Are you alright?," she asks, "You have been moaning in your sleep." Sir is indeed, a troubled man. Ma then walks outside, leaving Sir to himself.

This large, kind man understands that the longer he delays in opening his heart and feelings to the two people closest to him, the more difficult it will become. The nickname Quanah seemed at the time to be a viable way to introduce his son to the strange circumstance, but he is unable to bring himself to the point of discussing it further.

I realized that the lad needed to know some of the story by the time he was twelve years old. But I told myself that I would tell him only what he will need to know in order to prepare himself for what is to come. And that portion will come to him bit-by-bit.

That was six years ago, *and I have not told him anything,* Sir laments to himself.

But wait a minute! Sir suddenly realizes that he six years previous he had processed some instruction given to him by his father, Daniel Parker.

> *When Ma and I were about to be married, my father privately said to me, "Do you remember where we visited every birthday of your life? You will have a son, and on his twelfth birthday you are to return to that spot with him." He then proceeded to tell me the instructions to relay to my son, Jonathan. Father had taught me about the Fifth-Son Vision.*

I succeeded in carrying out my part! Even in my guilt, I have done right! His elation is clearly obvious.

He is glad that Ma has stepped outside.

She has probably gone for a walk to The Big Trees. I hope so because I think it would be good for her.

The fact of the matter is that I know virtually nothing about what the future holds for Jonathan. Will there be danger lying in wait for him? Will the tribal chiefs accept him as the one who brings legitimacy to my claims?

Where will the proof of that claim come from, and in what form? Is it possible that the boy will fail in his duty? How can that be avoided?

Oh my gosh! The problems for my son are greater, and outweigh any benefits of me sharing my own secret life. But still, I must be open and honest with Jonathan and Ma in order to clear my own conscience. What am I going to do?

Sir brings his recliner upright and sits with his head in his hands; he begins to sob. He is clearly distressed as he tries to reconcile his thoughts to his reality.

Yes, there are a lot of things to trouble Sir, and at times he wondered if it will all be worth it. There are so many pieces to the puzzle that he has not been allowed to know, let alone understand. This, combined with what he does know but has not shared, makes him feel profoundly devious.

How can I possibly teach values to young Quanah, when I myself, am being dishonest?

In soundless tears, Sir again reclines his chair and drifts back into slumber amidst feelings of regret and remorse.

His final thoughts as his weary mind closes down are very disconcerting.

What will Jonathan know, and how will he feel toward me when he returns from his quest? I know that I have not been the father and husband that I envisioned of myself many years ago ...

The strength of subdued charm
Brings calm to the troubled mind

CHAPTER 4 – MA

Having just seen her son drive away in the family van, and knowing that he is embarking on a journey that she herself knows little about is very concerning to Ma. All of the motherly fears that are normal engulf her, and she wearily sinks into her old wooden rocking chair while allowing silent sobs to begin.

Will my son be safe? Is he ready for what is to come? What is going through Sir's mind right now? I would like to talk with him but he is in a depressed state; I just don't want to interfere with his feelings. He is suffering the loss himself so I will leave him to his own thoughts, but oh, how I wish he would share his burdens with me.

The thoughts and questions keep piling up in her mind. She reaches for the down-filled pillow that she keeps alongside the rocker, and places it behind her head as she begins to rock in the old chair.

Ma is a quiet woman, at least when she is with Sir. Gazing at him at his time of emptiness, she retraces the emotional attachment she has with this man.

I prefer to give him deference in our matters; in fact we agree on most things, so I am comfortable in that deference. On the other hand, I feel that I am very capable of taking charge when necessary. I have confidence, and I have ability.

When I chose to be Jonathan's school teacher at home, it was a bit of a compromise for me. I had hoped as a teenager to become a school teacher. I received my teaching certificate at North Central Texas College in Gainesville ... then Peta Parker came along ... I am so glad that he did!

I am very happy being a mother; especially when I can also be our son's teacher ... spending so much time with him.

My love for both him and Sir is indescribable; I try to show it in my smiles, my spoken words, and my actions toward each of them. "Ma" is a very comforting name for me from the two men in my family. However, my given name is Elizabeth, and "Elizabeth Finley is a name to be proud of." Gramps said that to me often.

I have to wonder about Jonathan; there are needs and desires that seem quite eerie to me about the boy. I can almost read his mind. Sometimes, I start a new topic while in conversation with him; often, I later learn that I had prevented him from asking certain questions about my mother, Gramps' wife.

Ma looks over at Sir and concludes that he is near full sleep. She smiles as she closes her eyes and resumes her pleasant reflections.

The truth of the matter is, I really don't know a whole lot about my mother. I like to call my dad Gramps because of Jonathan, and Gramps did talk about my mother frequently.

He expressed great love for his "queen." Much of what he has told me is now lost or faded from my memory; except I have been told that she was excited about the birth of her only child.

Also, I understand that she always referred to her unborn child as "her" even though she had no medical proof. She told Gramps that she knew the baby was a girl; a very special one who was to be treated with great respect. She said that this daughter was to be treated as one would treat any daughter of a queen. She appeared to be aware that her own time on earth was about to close.

Ma's life as a youngster had been a happy time, albeit her mother passed away when Elizabeth was a young child. The girl missed the nurture and her mother's touch. Gramps had filled the gap well.

I remember a couple of old photographs of my mother; I looked at them often when I was very young. Hmm, I wonder what happened to them. On the reverse side of one of the photographs was written the name "Priscilla."

She was a beautiful lady with distinct features; she appeared quite dark-complexioned in the black and white pictures. Something in the back of my mind tells me that there was some kind of Native American heritage attached to her.

Ma's mind sidetracks for a moment as she has a momentary flashback.

I know that I must have those pictures somewhere; they may be in the box left to me by Gramps. It is a box that held some old artifacts; That's where I will look! I remember Gramps told me about the negative feelings my mother experienced whenever she looked at the box; as a result, it was never a topic of discussion. The box is in the storage trunk.

Her original thought process continues.

I'm not sure as to the Native American connection with my mother but I'm certain it had to do with Gramps' reference to her as his queen. Gramps had often told me that I should learn about the culture of the Native American people.

In speaking of his wife, he often alluded to "Her Highness," and "My Queen" in very respectful tones. As a youngster I had thought it was simply his love for the woman that he was expressing, but as I grew older, I began to wonder if there were other reasons for such noble references to my mother.

Elizabeth Finley, known simply as Ma, hears Sir open the refrigerator door and remove something, then senses his presence next to her. She decides to remain with her eyes closed. For some unknown reason her feelings were to not interrupt the reveries of either of them.

My mother chose the name for me long before I was born. Gramps said to me several times: "The name she chose was Elizabeth. Elizabeth ... Elizabeth Finley is a beautiful name; a name worthy of a royal lady. You will become an important figure to your own family."

I wonder if all of these goings-on with Jonathan are what he was speaking of. I imagine that it probably is. What a wonderful grandson my parents have in Jonathan!

Ma smiles as her thoughts continue.

Gramps and I lived a comfortable life. We had a nice home in the small community of Krum. His sizable inheritance provided all that we needed, but it did not provide for extravagance. It was when Sir and I were about to get married that Gramps passed away; the already near depleted assets, were quickly exhausted.

Ma lets her right arm hang loose for a moment and feels the cold bottle of water that Sir had placed on the floor just a few minutes before.

Oh that dear man, she thinks, *I just adore him.*

Ma opens her eyes and reaches for the bottle of water. Uncapping the bottle, she begins to rock in her chair, then remembers what

Sir had asked her several years ago: "How can you be so comfortable in that old wooden rocker? It looks so hard on the body."

She replied, "From the time that Gramps first held me on his lap and rocked in this chair, I have loved it. The chair seems to just mold to my body. I am very comfy sitting in it."

She has had so many sweet memories in this chair.

I remember being told that some distant cousin of my father had something to do with the establishment of Krum. I believe that someone in the Finley family donated land for the site of the fledgling town or for the railroad station ... or maybe something else.

But I have to wonder: Is that what my mother meant when she spoke of royalty? Whatever the meaning, I have very warm feelings for Krum, and anytime we move to within a few miles of the town I really glory in the experience, it is so comforting. I so love Krum, Texas!

But, I sure do have a problem whenever we live, or even travel near Quanah. I always feel extremely uncomfortable there. It is as though I have descended into a dark abyss, and I can hardly wait for our next move.

I really do not understand why I feel so heavy when around that town; but I know it is a necessary place in our rotation. Sir clearly has duties to perform in the Quanah area.

Many years ago, I forced myself to accept the location. As miserable as it is, it has come to be a permanent part of my life. But I do try to make the best of it, because that is what royalty does!

I gave birth to Jonathan when I was forty-two years old, and am so very grateful for that wonderful happening. Sir was somewhere around age fifty. I'm not even certain about Sir's age; we are only sure that he is several years older than me. Sir has tried to learn his birthdate but no information seems to be available.

A sudden restlessness from across the room where Sir sleeps brings Ma back into the present. Her own half-asleep, and half-awake mind has driven her into a loneliness for Jonathan. Sir's moving about brings a welcome re-connect with her husband.

"Are you alright? You have been moaning in your sleep," she says.

Ma strokes Sir's forehead as she lovingly rouses him from his own desolating semi-dreams. She decides to stretch her legs and move to the outside of the house.

I will walk to The Big Trees. Clearly, she needs a bit of change.

As much as Ma loves to sit in her old rocker, and think of the mysteries of *her* life, she chooses to change focus and ponder on Sir and her relationship with him as she strolls to The Big Trees.

Our early years of marriage were filled with adventure and the newness of enduring love. I admired Sir's ability to reason through various circumstances, and act appropriately on situations that to me were daunting.

He loved to read the heavens, and recite the genesis of the various galaxies. In fact, much of his magnificence was the telling of what was to come through his reading of the stars.

I actually learned through my studies of America's First that the Native Americans have great faith in the heavens and the lessons to be learned from the stars. However, it seems that as time has passed, Sir's focus has been on other things. He appears to have gradually lost his connection to the heavens; I think that in reality, Sir has become increasingly distant from many matters.

All of these facts led me to question Sir's heritage early in our marriage. When I asked him about his younger life and his family, he refused to speak about it because he claimed to not know anything about his ancestors!

His response was firm, and I soon learned to not push the topic. But deep down in my personal feelings I was certain that he is indeed of Native American heritage, and maybe he has some well-known ancestry; If so, he will surely tell me about it when he is ready.

Patience is one of my virtues, and I am grateful for that attribute. Over the years he has confirmed much of what I suspected; I am proud to have a Native American husband!

As the lady Elizabeth walks toward The Big Trees, two additional questions occupy much of her thought time.

Why does our family need to pack-up and relocate every few months? And where does Sir go for two days shortly after each of our frequent moves? In the beginning, it didn't seem important to me ... and it wasn't important ... at first.

Our first move was about seven months after we were married, and Sir explained that the reason had something to do with his work. That was good enough for me.

Growing up with Gramps, whose livelihood came from his inheritance, I thought little about Sir's explanation in the beginning. But after three years or so I began to observe certain little nuances about this man; there are small distinctions that have intensified as the years passed.

In the early years, Sir was a jovial man who made life enjoyable for me. He liked to go hunting and fishing and he taught me a lot about those sports.

His knowledge of local wildlife was seemingly endless; and as we lay on our backs in our sleeping bags at night, Sir regaled me with stories and folklore about the stars above. His explanations of the alignment of stars fascinated me ... But eventually the stories, and adventures began to change.

I loved those times, and in many respects I would like to have them back. Maybe that is just part of growing old together.

Ma arrives at her destination, The Big Trees, and finds a place to sit and relax; after taking sip of water, her thoughts return.

After Jonathan's birth we continued to take a few fishing trips. But over time they became fewer and fewer until by the time the boy was about seven years old, the outings ceased. Sir's explanation was that the lad has more important things that he must learn because he will soon be a man.

Coming forward to this day, I have learned to notice various changes in Sir's demeanor. I've learned to predict when the next move will be occurring. He becomes withdrawn and agitated; to anyone else it isn't noticeable because it is so subtle. But to me, it signals that a move is coming.

Over the years, the agitation has increased; it is as though there is something on his mind that needs expressing, but for some reason he is unable to share it with me. I hope that he will soon open up with me completely.

Feeling the need to return to the house, Ma takes the bottle of water into her hand, rises from her spot, and starts the short leisurely walk up the path.

Again, she takes up her musings.

Once our large family van is packed and we are on the road, Sir again becomes the man I fell in love with. He is jovial and engaging as we travel to our next location.

Then after settling in our new home, he announces that he has business to attend to, and is gone for two days. Upon his return, our life resumes in normal fashion. I very much want to know more about that part of Sir's life, but my queenly upbringing will not allow me to be so inquisitive. I feel guilty for being so untrusting.

Ma arrives at the house and quietly slips inside. Sir is still sleeping so she settles back into her rocking chair. Placing the pillow on her lap, she clasps her hands together and rests them on the soft pillow as the thoughts continue to flow.

I fail to understand why Sir chose the nickname of Quanah for Jonathan. It is as though the boy's father is trying to instill in the lad some sort of attachment to the Texas community ... I wonder ...

As for me, I want total detachment from the town and the name! I cannot recall anything bad ever happening to me at Quanah, but the recollection of something seems threatening to me.

Until my marriage to Sir, I had little to do with the town of Quanah; even that fact causes some anxiety in me. Oh my gosh! I guess I have my own deep problems, too.

Just the very thought of the name Quanah sends chills up and down my spine. I have never verbalized my feelings because royalty does not do that.

"Royals are strong and able to overcome," I often say aloud to myself. In fact, even my given name Elizabeth brings about feelings of emptiness if spoken in any context associated with Quanah.

Yes, I am most happy and content to be known simply as Ma. Shortly before Jonathan was born, Sir and I decided on this term of endearment, and I am so very glad that we did!

I am thankful for my quality of patience; it has served me well. But I think my greatest attribute may be my faith in what is yet to come. I somehow know that Jonathan's future will be one of honor and accomplishment.

I know the questions surrounding Sir will be answered, and he will rise above whatever it is that troubles him. And finally, I know that royalty or not, I am of great value to my son.

Further, I understand that sometime in his future, Jonathan will have a very important role to play in something, although I have no idea what it might be. I just know that it is up to me to encourage, educate and engage the young fellow in all things good.

Clearly, Sir's insistence on Jonathan's purity aligns itself with my desire to home-school the boy. He has responded well and has grown into a responsible and capable individual.

I chose many years ago, to tutor him at home as part of a protective shield against bad influences, and I am so happy for that choice!

But oh, how I worry about Jonathan and his safety. He is a good and responsible driver, but I fear that there are forces around ... forces that are, or will be working against him.

I am confident that we taught him well, and that he can take care of himself. However ...

Ma suddenly senses something horrid happening. *Ohhh no, what can it possibly be? Jonathan, Jonathan are you alright?*

Her mind probes the air around her hoping to find an explanation of her premonition, but no comfort is to be found.

An open mind, A clear conscience,
An innocent heart: A rare combination

CHAPTER 5 – THE JOURNEY BEGINS

Jonathan, in his hotel room in Denton awakens. Rubbing his eyes and trying to bring his mind and body into sync, he stumbles out of bed. The previous night was one of restless part-time slumber, and heavy pondering of what the next few days may bring.

"I don't want to get up yet," he says aloud knowing that it is an empty and meaningless observation.

Double checking his wristwatch and his calendar, Jonathan confirms that today is indeed the day for his drive to Quanah. He is apprehensive, anticipatory and fearful, but he knows that all will be well because of Prairie Flower's assurance.

I have felt her presence around me almost constantly for the past year. The audible communication from her reduced years ago, but it was replaced with calm, reassuring impressions of my mind. There is no question that she is leading me along the path of something extremely important.

Also, I am sure that my family questions will soon be answered. My parents' obvious concern is understandable, and I want Sir to overcome whatever is troubling him.

Ma just doesn't know much of what is going on. She gives Sir her devotion and trust, but I think she knows that important things are happening. Ma has shown her instincts, because she sure knows when to change the subject during our talks!

Prairie Flower's assurance is the source of Jonathan's optimism and positive actions as he moves forward in what has become known to him as "the quest." There is one uncertainty that is causing some apprehension in his mind right now, however.

Will I recognize the exact spot where I am to turn off of Highway 287? This is the main reason that I made the decision to drive to the area one day early: So as to locate the precise spot. "Nothing must be left to chance," is my motto.

I will stay tonight and tomorrow night in the Quanah Best Western where Sir made arrangements. I should arrive at the designated site shortly after sun-up on Wednesday, my eighteenth birthday. Gosh, I love to feel the "you have made the correct decision" warmth that I feel right now. Prairie Flower, whoever you are, you never fail to make me feel good!

As he drives away from Denton and his original The Big Trees area near Krum, this impression fills his mind: *This will give me an additional day for preparation. I really need it!*

Jonathan smiles warmly as he heads west from the town of Krum. Then, as if hit by a sudden mental slap in the face, Jonathan has his mind turned to yesterday's episode with the fellow in the black Volvo.

That was really scary! For him to intentionally pull out in front of me like that; and then apparently follow me to the hotel is weird! However, he delivered something to me from Prairie Flower that must be important. Oh my gosh, did I put the envelope in my bag or did I leave it at the hotel?

Jonathan quickly pulls over at the first wide spot in the road so he can check his bag to verify that the envelope is there. The spot happens to be a beautiful gated driveway to one of the plentiful ranches in the area.

I had planned to enjoy this drive when I started. It has so many gorgeous ranches, but I am feeling nervous about every little thing.

His hand reaches inside the bag and retrieves the medium sized envelope. *Good! It is here ... Relax, Jonathan!* He tries to *will* himself under control.

I have plenty of time, Jonathan reassures himself as he leans against the van. *I think I will stay on the backroads as Sir always does. Besides, that will give me a lot of time to ponder and speak with Prairie Flower. Perhaps she will be able to clear up many of my questions.*

He looks up as a vehicle passes by at a rather high rate of speed, and his entire body becomes weak. It is a black Volvo SUV!

No! Please, no! He wants to scream aloud but contains his words to anxiety-laden thoughts. *I do not want to be spied on. I need to get to Quanah, and do it peacefully. I do not need this!*

Jonathan again calls upon his inner strength, recalling all of the positive input from Prairie Flower from over the years. He does some deep breathing, and says some positive words aloud for a minute or so, thus putting himself into a calmer state.

He then climbs into the van behind the steering wheel and with one more deep breath, he turns the ignition key and starts the engine. Just the sound of the motor running smoothly brings a calmness and a feeling of security.

His positivity reigns: *I am always calm; I am enjoying this drive! This is my day to see the countryside from a fresh perspective.*

With a heart and mind filled with emotion, and a brain full of knowledge, Jonathan makes some mental adjustments and takes time to enjoy the present.

This is really interesting, I have traveled through this area of Texas several times with Ma and Sir. I've seen most of these sights before, but I have not appreciated them like I do now. There are many things that I believe might be "only in Texas" sights because they are so unusual.

My mind seems almost totally free during this drive. I feel like laughing at some of the names of ranches and the decorated mailboxes. The road sign that I just passed, "Seldom Seen Road" must have a funny story behind its origin.

The other trips I've taken with Sir and Ma through this part of the country have been different; it's been hard to appreciate the countryside. But now, my mind seems truly free for the first time, and I am going to enjoy taking advantage of the freedom.

It seems there are never-ending "Farm-to-Market Roads." They are carefully numbered and cataloged somewhere, I suppose.

I love the roads with self-explanatory names like Seldom Seen Road and Miss Lulu Road. There are so many throughout the countryside, but the one that puts the cap on my wonderful drive is the one I just passed: Big Tree Road.

An hour or so into the pleasant drive, Jonathan experiences, for the first time since he was a very young child, a clear and unencumbered mind. He becomes a receptacle for intensive communication from Prairie Flower.

Audibly he hears his mentor speak, "Jonathan, we need to talk."

Immediately, he pulls to the side of the road while his mind processes the startling turn of events. Taking care to move his van to a safe spot out of any traffic, the young man turns his attention to whatever is to come.

Prairie Flower's voice is clear and she speaks with authority, "It is good that you started your drive early. But do not waste time. You are on the most important errand you will ever experience. Drive directly to Quanah, and check into your room at the Best Western Hotel.

"We have until tomorrow evening to prepare you for what is to come. You have much to learn."

With that directive, Jonathan once again feels both the warm assurance of Prairie Flower, and the worth of her message.

But, doggone it! I didn't remember to ask her about the envelope! She probably wouldn't have given me any information anyway, since all things work according to her time-frame.

On the road again, he quickly completes what would have been a leisurely five hour sight-seeing drive by simply altering his travel plan. Within two hours of highway travel, Jonathan pulls into a parking space at the Best Western. He sits for a few moments reflecting on what is happening.

I have had two hours of wonderful contemplation. I had direct communication with Prairie Flower again! It seems that I will be having a lot of communing with her; that makes me very happy.

But there are a couple of things that I want to try to figure out before she and I meet. Hah! I am thinking of it as holding some sort of a business meeting. Good Grief! Get with it Jonathan ...

While I was on the highway, my thoughts were both pleasant and a bit disturbing. My near lifelong feeling about my ancestry being a puzzlement is starting to come into focus. I believe that the probability of a strong Native American heritage is about to be revealed to me.

But, just who is Prairie Flower and why is she the one to bring the messages to me? Just the name has a Native American ring to it. She must be more than simply a messenger, her earnestness makes it seem as though she has a stake in the outcome of my mission.

The warmth of truth and understanding begins to engulf his body.

****

Entering his room now, there seems to be a familiar odor of trees and brush. He notices a fragrance stick hanging on a closet hook, seemingly placed there just for him. The adequately furnished temporary abode instantly becomes The Big Trees to Jonathan.

He is serene as he places the DO NOT DISTURB notice on the door handle. Jonathan makes himself comfortable in the sizeable armchair, and rests his feet on the ottoman. He thinks of turning on the large television set but feels it might interfere with the purpose of his trip. Instead, he closes his eyes.

"Jonathan, you are about to learn many secrets of your people. You are the fifth-son spoken of by your third-great-grandfather, Peta Nocona, chief of the Comanche Nation." The voice pauses to allow Jonathan time to assimilate this piece of information. Prairie Flower's voice is business-like and direct.

"The, the ... fifth ... son? What does that mean?" The stammer is proof of Jonathan's need to know more. He feels that he has been properly prepared for the meeting and instruction, but this is not what he expects.

"You have Native American heritage from both Sir and Ma. You are the oldest son of the oldest son for five generations and Chief Peta has designated you as the one to restore honor to your side of his family. There is a lost branch descending from Quanah Parker, Chief Peta's first-born son who is your great-great-grandfather."

The no-nonsense voice continues, "Now, think on this tonight. Rise early tomorrow, and drive to the town of Medicine Mound. You will be directed where to stop.

"There you will have much history revealed to you. Right now you must assimilate what you have heard today; ponder it. You will have a coming together of all of your learning in your mind."

Jonathan, taking a long pause in deep thought moves to the bed, and being exhausted, lies down. He has barely closed his eyes in contemplation when Prairie Flower repeats the previously disclosed information and instruction.

In half stupor and half curiosity Jonathan asks hesitantly, "Prairie Flower, who are you and what do you have to do with my quest? And ... and what am I to do with the envelope that was delivered to me yesterday?"

"Jonathan, my young friend, you will know all things when the time is right and you are prepared. Right now, you must keep your mind open to receive and learn, not to ask or doubt." With that, she leaves immediately.

Jonathan has learned to sense when Prairie Flower leaves his presence; there is a void that he feels at her absence. Left to his thoughts he again tries to grasp, and piece together the unfolding story. Fleetingly, he thinks of Ma and Sir and any connection they may have to his quest.

Will they have a role in the story yet to be revealed? What are their thoughts right now? ... I must not focus on these thoughts because I must be focused on the here and now.

Sleep seems impossible, but he knows that he must be refreshed for the teachings of tomorrow. Slowly, sleep does begin to take over, but it is short-lived as he awakens with a start.

Native American heritage on both sides of my family? Maybe that is why Sir wanted me to spend time in Krum; specifically at the museum. He insisted that I leave for this trip on Saturday because he knew that the museum is open only on Saturday afternoons.

Did I miss something by not being more attentive in that rather unique place? Now my mind is playing gotcha games and I really need to sleep. But darn it! ...

"Morning can't get here fast enough," he mumbles to himself as he turns over and closes his eyes.

Jonathan tries to focus his mind on the first action that Prairie Flower instructed him to take tomorrow.

I must find the town of Medicine Mound and drive there. I'm really not sure ... just where ... it ...

He awakes as a shaft of early morning light peeks through the blinds in his room. Quickly Jonathan dresses, moves about gathering his thoughts, and leaves the room.

Arriving in the lobby he approaches the front desk and asks, "Which direction do I go to get to the town of Medicine Mound?"

He pays scant attention to the man who rises from his nearby chair and walks out the front door of the hotel.

The lady looks at Jonathan then glances at the exiting man. She turns her attention back to Jonathan, and gives a nod straight ahead. "Take 287 east and look for the signs ... umm, just a moment, please."

The lady whose name tag identifies her as Anita, quickly scribbles some words on a sticky note and hands it to Jonathan, "Good luck, young man," she says as he walks away.

Interesting response, he thinks momentarily; then hurriedly he gets into the van, and reads the note that Anita had given to him: *Do not take the turn at the sign. Turn right one mile after the rest area.*

Jonathan starts the engine, ponders the words of the note, then heads east on Highway 287. His eyes are peeled for a sign indicating the way to Medicine Mound … *But, Anita's note says to not turn at the sign.*

He tries to settle down and feel secure, but he cannot.

Is Anita simply giving me a shorter route? Or does she have some ulterior motive in mind? She looked at the man who left the hotel just as I began speaking to her. Was there some message sent between them? My gosh, Jonathan, stop with the conspiracy stuff!

Jonathan is able to reset his thinking on what is to come. He knows that Prairie Flower will guide him to the proper place for his continuing enlightenment, as it pertains to his quest.

His trust is well placed as he sees the road sign "Medicine Mound" with an arrow pointing to his right, southbound. He drives past the turn and continues east on 287.

Past the rest area now, Jonathan carefully looks for the road that will take him to Medicine Mound.

There is a road coming up; it sure doesn't look like much! His thoughts begin to trail off into conspiracy again.

Then he laughs aloud at the name of the dirt and gravel road: *Dam site Road – I wonder if there really is a dam or if they misspelled the first word.* He grins at the thought.

A vague feeling of familiarity begins to surround Jonathan; and with his mental awareness increasing, he knows that Prairie Flower is present also.

"This is it!" Jonathan exclaims aloud. Then with a calmer mind, he retraces the drive the family of three had taken six years previous.

This is the same dirt road we took on my twelfth birthday. I recognize the concrete lined wash that I just drove through. Sir had explained to me that during rainstorms this wash carries a lot of water safely out of the area, preventing flooding.

Approaching an intersection, Jonathan's inclination is to turn right onto a paved road. But just before the intersection is a nice looking blue Nissan Titan pickup stopped at a mailbox.

The county worker inside the vehicle is helpful when Jonathan asks for directions to the town of Medicine Mound. The elderly gentleman inside the pickup eyes Jonathan up and down, then begins to tell him how to get to his destination.

He abruptly stops instructing and smilingly says, "Ah, heck! it's a lot easier to just take you there. Follow me."

Jonathan follows the Titan for about five miles until it stops at an intersecting road on the right.

He notes: *The sign says the road is Spur 91.*

The driver of the Titan gets out and points to the intersecting road. "Just take this road for about a mile or so. You will be in beautiful downtown Medicine Mound; the two buildings are on your right."

With a wave and friendly Texas smile, the man climbs back into his vehicle and drives away.

Jonathan is soon approaching the two rock buildings on his right; one is abandoned and the other has a window sign stating it is closed. The painted sign across the storefront identifies it as Hicks and Cobb General Store.

Interesting place for a town, he observes. *It is nestled inside the uppermost point of the triangle created by Spur 91 intersecting Farm Road 1167 at about a forty-five degree angle ... Those hills in the background look familiar .. I think that may be the place ...*

He pulls to a stop when he hears the quiet voice in his mind say, *"Stop here. We will remain alone."*

Jonathan surveys the area around the two buildings.

There is nothing here except huge prickly pears. I sure hope we go inside one of these buildings for whatever is to come.

Nevertheless, Jonathan's heart and mind are transported to his favorite place, The Big Trees. Here, he is free to commune with Prairie Flower and learn from her.

She speaks aloud, "Jonathan, this is the town of Medicine Mound. It received its name from the four mounds a short distance from where we now stand. You will visit the true Medicine Mound at another time.

"For now, remove yourself to the rear of the buildings, and cross the road. Be careful of the prickly pears, they can be dangerous. There you will find a place of comfort. You will be taught the history of the quest you are on."

She further explains, "To fulfill the Fifth-Son Prophecy you are embarking on tomorrow, you need to learn the purpose of your existence. All people have a purpose; yours is very specific. You will understand the reason for being born to the parents to whom you were born. They have taught you very well.

"Your life has been undiluted by outside pressures. Although you and your parents have moved about often, this has helped assist in your purity."

Prairie Flower points out greater influences on Jonathan's life, "There are other matters also, which have been under control of the gods. You have been watched over by your parents, and by divine power."

The past gives reason
To plan the future

CHAPTER 6 – MEDICINE MOUND, THE TOWN

Jonathan finds a good spot in the foliage and underbrush of Medicine Mound, Texas. Then making himself comfortable in a reclining position, Jonathan quizzingly anticipates what is to come. Over the years he has developed a level of comfort within the sphere of the supernatural. Actually, it has become an expectation, and he is openly accepting of paranormal experiences.

"Jonathan, this is Prairie Flower. Please, now hear my father, your third-great-grandfather, Chief Peta Nocona."

The deep but loving voice speaks, "Jonathan, you are chosen to restore honor to your line of my descendants. For now, just observe and remember this day. When you return to your place of stay tonight, write of this account for it is true. It will be important in the coming days and weeks. A record must be kept of what you will now experience. Now look, and see the past."

With that, the great expanse of Jonathan's view unfolds into a vista beyond anything he can possibly imagine. It is as though a scroll is being unrolled, and each complete roll reveals an additional backward span of time.

Jonathan becomes both an observer and a listener as a marvelous story unfolds. There is not only a visual, but also a sort of narration in the process of revealing the episodic events. It is almost as though he is actually drawn into the happenings.

Chief Peta begins the introduction, "Jonathan my son, watch, listen and learn about your people. There has been much said and done that is not good, and is untrue. You are the fifth-son; you must understand in order to fulfill. Know this: You cannot feed others if your own purse is empty.

> *"The children of Peta Nocona and Cynthia Ann Parker chose their mother's last name for their own because of their great love and respect for their mother ... A choice that I honored."*

Three children appear on the scene.

> *Quanah Parker, the oldest of the three speaks, "Peanut, go to the tipi[1] and fetch my fishing line for me. I am going to ..."*

> *"Stop calling me Peanut, my name is Pecos!" The second of the siblings shouts back. "And go get your own line!"*

> *"Peanut, Peanut, Peanut, Peanut," the oldest sibling continues to taunt his younger brother. "What's the matter? Can't you take it?"*

> *"Leave me alone, you big bully! I hate you! I hate you!" yells the youngster running away in tears. "I hate you!"*

> *"Stop fighting, stop fighting!" screams Topsannah, their sister, the youngest of the three siblings.*

> *In tears, she is clearly disturbed by the words and vile actions between her two big brothers. "Can't you just get along for once?"*

> *"Peanut, Peanut, Peanut,"* continues the fading taunt as Quanah skips away from the other two.

---

[1] teepee

The vision unfolding in front of Jonathan shows a very husky lad, Quanah Parker with his younger brother Pecos, who is frail and sickly looking. The youngest of the three siblings, Topsannah their very fair-skinned sister, completes the group of children.

Because Quanah is older, larger and stronger than his brother and sister, he carries an air of superiority about him, and he isn't bashful in demonstrating it.

"I'll get even with you some day, you are horribly mean! Just you wait and see. I'm gonna get even with you!" Pecos continues to scream at the top of his lungs.

Jonathan tries to grasp the significance.

****

The scroll rolls up, and a new scenario unrolls.

"Jonathan, cite your mind forward, and you will soon understand," intones the voice.

"Run, run!" calls the look-out from his perch atop a tree. "The Rangers are coming!"

Pecos Parker finds a hiding place behind some brush on the side of a shallow ravine. "Why aren't Chief Peta and Quanah here. We need them?"

He watches in horror as his little sister and his mother are swept up on the invader's horses and are soon out of sight. Others were abducted also, and the camp is left in massive disarray.

The scene slowly fades away, then just as slowly, it reopens indicating the passage of several hours in time.

Quanah and Chief Peta Nocona ride into camp hours after the raid by the Texas Rangers, and are extremely distraught by the chaos among the tribe of Comanches.

"You deserve the name Peanut!" is Quanah's exclamation upon seeing the youngster hiding in the brush. He cannot believe that a son of Peta Nocona, and his own brother would be so cowardly, no matter what his age.

"You could have done something to protect your mother and sister! All you did was hide yourself over there!" he said pointing to the ravine where Pecos had been hiding. "What kind of a peanut are you anyway, ... Peanut?"

Pecos vows to himself: I am going to leave at the first chance I get. As soon as the time is right I will go to the white man's camp and live with my mother and sister.

Quanah goes about trying to help establish order among the tribe, focusing on the young braves of his generation all the while making Pecos the butt of his deriding comments. At the same time he is building up his leadership stature among his peers. Some see him as their future leader.

"He has puha, and puha will make Quanah a great chief," many of the braves claim.

Peta Nocona tries to calm his youngest son, "Pecos, your brother is only trying to have some fun with you. He knows that using the name Peanut makes you angry, that is why he does it. You must not let it be so."

"No! He does it because he thinks he is better than me. Quanah is just being a cruel bully. Someday I will show him!"

****

With the unfolding of a new scroll, the calm, deep voice of Peta Nocona continues.

"Several months after the abduction of Topsannah and her mother, my wife Cynthia Ann Parker, our Comanche tribe was overcome by an outbreak of smallpox. Many of the children were seriously affected."

"Bring all of your sick children to the big tipi. We will take care of them," is the instruction given by the Medicine Man. His directive is followed; Pecos Parker, recognizing the opportunity, voluntarily places himself in the man's care.

Chaos and confusion become issues as the tipi is soon overrun. Pecos takes advantage of it. He makes certain he is counted among the sick; then lying on his makeshift bed in the big tipi he recounts his plan.

"This confusion will be my cover. There are too many sick children for them to count. I will not be missed, and I do not feel at all sick. I will leave!" Pecos says to himself.

Late on the first night, Pecos slips out of bed and silently leaves his confines. He is a smart lad who realizes that he must be very careful as he moves about. Pecos knows the area well, and is able to care for himself for a few days as he collects supplies for his journey to the white man's territory.

Two days later the announcement comes: "We have lost many of our young people to this sickness called smallpox. Their bodies are to be destroyed by fire to prevent the spread of the sickness."

The communication from the Medicine Man is heeded, and Pecos Parker is counted among the dead.

Pecos, being nearby, but still in hiding in the area overhears the lamenting cries and later, under cover of darkness he creeps close to the big tipi.

"Chief Peta's son Pecos is one who died, and one who's body we destroyed by fire," the Medicine Man says sadly to a small group of tribal leaders.

But Pecos sees it as good news because his strategy is working even better than planned.

****

A fresh narration begins as a new vision depicts Pecos in his search for his mother.

"Jonathan, watch, listen and learn."

Pecos lies under cover of darkness as he watches the activity in the white man's camp. He deliberates: I am sure that this is where my mother and sister are being held. I want so much to see them, but I am scared to go in. The white man might hurt all three of us, and Quanah will probably learn that I am here. I think I will go and live with another band of my people to keep all of us safe.

Pecos finds another band of Comanches to associate with. He then claims to be an orphan, having been left behind when his former band moved out.

Jonathan watches as Pecos grows in age and physical stature. His slightly built body adds mass, and he becomes virtually unrecognizable as Pecos Parker.

The voice continues, "As Pecos's mind develops, his thought process plots revenge against his brother. He becomes increasingly irritated as Quanah receives attention and praise as the great Comanche leader and warrior. The praise is noted in both the Native American nations and among the white man."

Jonathan is entranced as the narrator opens the mind of Pecos who is recalling an experience he had as a youth:

I remember an experience I had with my Ape,[2] Peta Nocona, who prefers to be called Peta, or Chief Peta. In one way, it was a strange experience ... and yet ... Peta had been known for his reliance on the communications he had with the Great Spirit at Medicine Mound ... so it was not so strange.

On this particular day, Chief Peta invited me to join him and stand guard as he ascended the tallest of the mounds. He would be at the top for about four days cleansing his internal body by drinking a water and gypsum mix.

This was to be followed by the smoking of peyote and receiving instruction from the gods. My job was to stop anyone else from climbing that special hill while Peta was there in meditation. I really felt that something extra special was about to take place.

About mid-day on the second day, it began to happen. The sun was high in the sky, the air was beginning to get hot and I was beginning to drift off to sleep. Suddenly I heard some noise as Peta came hurriedly through the brush. "Pecos, Pecos my son," I heard Peta calling, "I need for you to do something, now!"

Peta appeared almost as a ghost, his body being covered in white gypsum powder. He had been rolling in the abundant mineral as a vital part of his ritualistic cleansing and healing.

---

[2] Comanche for Father, Phonetically: Ah-pay

Immediately I arose and stood at attention waiting for his instructions. "Pecos, ride as quickly as you can to my tipi and get my secret box. Bring it to me; I need it now."

This really surprised me because that box is very sacred; no one besides my ape and I know that the small chest exists. Besides, Hardly anyone is ever allowed to enter the chief's buffalo hide tipi by himself.

The rustle the flap makes when opened can be heard easily; and I had learned to slip through the buffalo hide flap quietly when I had to get away from Quanah.

Once, when I entered, it totally surprised Chief Peta as he was saying a prayer over the partially open box. After committing me to an oath of secrecy, the chief placed the box beneath a pile of buckskin. Everyone knows it is not to be disturbed.

"Hurry my boy, the Great Spirit atop the mound is waiting for you," encouraged Chief Peta. I was already on the move, anxious to do what he wanted. Besides, I loved to ride my sorrel pony, Dot; I named her Dot because of the white mark on her forehead.

I grabbed a handful of Dot's long heavy mane and swung myself up onto her back as quickly as I could. I had to stretch to kick her flank, but I did it and we were on our way.

I love to feel the wind blowing my hair when I'm leaning against old Dot's mane. I am proud to be Comanche because horsemanship comes natural to the Comanche.

The camp was a mile or so away, and as quietly as possible I slipped into Peta's tipi and retrieved the treasured box. I was on my way back to the mound in a few minutes, and arrived in time to satisfy Peta's desire.

It was two days later as the two of us leisurely returned to our home camp, that Peta fully confided in me. It seemed that he felt a strong need to share his experience.

"Pecos, my youngest son, I will soon be gone to the earth, and you should know of my experience. Inside the secret box is what will someday become the key to the restoration of honor to a branch of my family. It will be from Quanah's line because he is my first-born son."

Just bringing up the name of Quanah makes me upset, let alone the recognition of him as Peta's first-born. It seems that everywhere I go, Quanah is right there!

"The key will be delivered into the fifth-son's hands when he reaches manhood. Because you already know of the box, you are allowed to know that I have put it in a special place. It is to rest there until the coming of the fifth-son.

You are never to speak or share this knowledge with anyone. It is now part of our oath of secrecy, the one we have already made." I simply nodded in agreement, and although I was just a lad I understood the heavy nature of what I was allowed to know.

At that time, I also began to wonder how much longer my beloved ape, Chief Peta, would remain alive. Greater weight on my mind however, was what sounded like more publicity for Quanah. The more I think about it, the more my blood boils. I will get my revenge.

This entire episode with Peta has become very important to my plan to destroy Quanah! I immediately added this experience to my plan. Quanah will be held responsible for many bad things, and I am glad his line will lose their honor. I hope I am able to be a big part of that destruction!

****

The scrolls roll together and the vision ends. Jonathan tries to keep mental order to the story that had unfolded before him: He had watched as the hatred toward Quanah grew within Pecos; he saw it as Pecos matured.

Jonathan observed as Pecos's physical appearance changed; he saw Pecos morph into a very dangerous individual. And he watched as the actions of Pecos became increasingly more devious.

But, in a weird sort of way, Jonathan thinks to himself, *I seem to be able to understand Pecos's feelings.*

Chief Peta Nocona gives final instruction to Jonathan, "Jonathan, return now to your room, there you are to write, ponder and meditate on what you have learned. It is important to know the past so you can understand the future as it happens."

With that instruction from Chief Peta, Jonathan rises from his comfortable spot in downtown Medicine Mound, strolls across the road, and past the prickly pear plants to his vehicle.

Oh boy, do I have a lot to think about; and I am instructed to write all of this. How can I possibly get it all done? Fortunately, I have a recorder on my phone; sure hope I have enough space! I wonder if that would be alright to do. Hmmm ...

Oops, No ... Not a smart idea ... I have been instructed to keep my phone in the off position. Come on, Jonathan, stay with the program!

He is startled, and his attention diverted by the loud roar of an engine. He looks up, and to his left as a dark colored pickup is disappearing from his view.

A jigsaw puzzle is only a random group of pieces
Until they are put together – much like life

CHAPTER 7 – FINDING THE PARTS

Back in his room at the Best Western, Jonathan's mind tries to decipher the points of the astounding messages he received earlier today.

The time at the town of Medicine Mound has been really good! I must write ... making an audio is not an option ... besides, it would not be in total keeping with Chief Peta's instructions ... I will do as I am told and use pen and paper to make the record of today's events.

Actually, as he begins to write, he feels a great deal of relief.

Interesting, this is much better than recording, because it will be easier to re-create and prioritize everything that I witnessed in the vision today. It was so very overwhelming!

He is sensitive in his recollection.

Gosh, the history of Cynthia Ann Parker and her daughter in their capture and recapture must have been horribly traumatic. What a different world that was.

Jonathan momentarily sets his notes aside.

I wonder about Quanah Parker and what seems like unfair treatment of his young brother. Why did he have to be that way? Just bigger and older, I guess.

He pulls himself back into sync with his duty. Systematically, Jonathan then writes all that he witnessed in the vision today.

He wonders much, as he writes.

What is the importance of my learning these things? And it is interesting that I am instructed to write it all down.

Wearily, Jonathan sets his pen and paper aside, lays his head on his arms which are stretched across the desk, and marvels at the magnitude of it all.

Today I witnessed the shaping of a young mind. Pecos allowed the infiltration of evil; it appears to have totally taken control of him.

But in Ma's America's First class ... What about Quanah Parker? Quanah was admired by so many people those many years ago; not only by the Comanche but also the white man ... In fact, he had ultimately gained access to, and favor with national political figures in the white man's government ... Quanah seems like a real contradiction ...

What damage could Pecos possibly have done to the last and great Comanche chief, Quanah Parker? This is the question on Jonathan's mind as he drifts off to sleep in his awkward sitting position at his desk.

A mental view of the overabundance of tasks ahead of him moves through his dreams. First and foremost is the command that he be at his appointed place early tomorrow morning.

What will it be all about? Will I be prepared? What will I be expected to know and do? Will it all be finished after tomorrow ... or is there more to come?

These are among the perplexing questions besieging Jonathan's mind as he struggles to take a short nap.

Trying to sleep under the circumstances is an exercise in futility.

A cold Dr Pepper with a Subway sandwich seem like a good idea at this point, and it is only a short walk to the sandwich shop. I think that the physical activity will help clear my mind and stretch the joints.

Leaving the hotel he hurries to the street and turns right. Walking along the side of Highway 287, he is deep in thought.

The Subway shop is on the other side of this main road through Quanah. It is connected to the Love's Truck Stop, right over there. It should be only a few minutes before I'll be back at the hotel.

He reaches the traffic light which is flashing yellow. Jonathan looks both ways assuring his safe crossing, then begins the trek across the wide highway.

The entire area is quiet and beginning to close down for the day.

What a nice peaceful evening. Maybe I should also take a walk before returning to my room; he considers doing so.

Screech ... roar ... screech! The sound is terrifying and Jonathan is startled out of all thoughts. He quickly jumps aside, and a rapidly moving pickup truck narrowly misses him. Shaken and white faced, he finishes his walk across the street and finds a place to sit.

Jonathan tries to figure where the dark pickup had come from so suddenly. *I know that there were no vehicles on the road when I began to walk across.*

He reflects: *There was a pickup parked in a parking lot with its motor running when I walked past. Could it be the same? ... Dark pickup ... Medicine Mound ... What is going on around here?*

He turns his eyes toward the hotel.

I just came from there; and a dark pickup was in the parking lot when I left. I don't see it anywhere. What in the world is happening? Seems that turning my cell phone to off isn't helping in others not knowing where I am!

Hmm ... Dark pickup ... Medicine Mound today ... Is there a connection ...

Still shaking and nervous, Jonathan returns to his hotel room with his drink and sandwich.

Now I have another thing to be concerned about, he laments. *And to make matters worse, I have this pesky fly trying to eat my sandwich.*

Chuckling, he shoos it away with the back of his right hand as he sits in the comfortable room chair. Accepting the notion that there will be little to no sleep tonight, Jonathan returns his thoughts to the happenings of the day.

He reviews and adds to his notes, writing questions as they come to his mind. Meanwhile, he attempts to forget the near-miss on Highway 287 just an hour before. However, that episode begins to fill his mind disproportionally.

None of it makes sense. What are the connections? Sir gave me some instructions six years ago and I am simply following those that guidance.

Prairie Flower has taught me a lot about myself. I now know I am from Native American heritage, and I am proud of that. She has tutored me in tradition and faith. Her presence has comforted me and let me know that I have an important role in the future of my people ... but what is it?

Why was I shown the vision this morning? It must have been to prepare me for tomorrow and whatever is to come.

What about the pickup, was it an accident? If so, why didn't the driver stop to see if I was alright? If it was on purpose, what was the purpose? Is it related to my quest, my mission? And what about the envelope that I received back at the Super 8 Hotel?

Disconcerting little scenarios move through his head like tiny firecrackers, exploding at every thought.

The pickup incident was surely a coincidence ... but Prairie Flower taught me that there is no such thing as coincidence. She explained that there is always something that triggers a coincidence.

He can find no rationale. *Oh, Prairie Flower, where are you?* he mentally pleads. *I really need your advice. This is getting to be overwhelming!*

"What?!? Whoa ... Wait ... Wait a minute!" Jonathan exclaims aloud. His startled body jumps from his chair, and his mind is suddenly activated, alert and confused, all at the same time.

Prairie Flower introduced her father, Chief Peta Nocona, as the one to give me further instruction. That would make Prairie Flower the sister to Quanah Parker. That means ...

Jonathan's thoughts trail off.

The possibilities are much too deep to be considered at this time.

His head begins to swirl as he struggles to process all of this newly acquired data.

The whole family is the sum of its parts
Wherever they may be

CHAPTER 8 – THE RETURN

Rising on this Wednesday morning, Jonathan begins to sing to himself, "Happy birthday to me. Happy birthday to me … Happy birthday dear Jonathan … Happy birthday to meee." He moves swiftly to get on the road to his appointed place: Medicine Mound. His thoughts are positive: *This is exciting … I can hardly wait!*

The sun is just high enough in the eastern sky to be a hinderance to Jonathan's vision while heading an easterly direction on Highway 287. Lowering the sun-visor, he leaves the town of Quanah. He is en route to the special destination defined exactly six years ago today. At the same time, he spots a dark pickup eerily similar to the one that almost ran him down last evening.

It is parked on the right side of the street as though the driver knows which direction Jonathan will be driving.

Just for the sake of safety, I must be aware of anyone following me, he thinks to himself, *caution, Jonathan, caution.*

With that, he watches through the rear-view mirror as the pickup pulls out of its parking place.

About a mile out of town the pickup pulls around to pass Jonathan. When the vehicles are parallel, the pickup slows, allowing Jonathan to look briefly at the other driver who is looking at him. The tinted window obscures the other drivers' facial features.

After a moment of looking at each other, the fellow in the pickup smiles broadly and waves to Jonathan, then speeds off and disappears over the horizon.

Momentarily setting his paranoia aside, he continues toward his destination.

I will take the same road that I took yesterday because of things I recognized ... Surely Prairie Flower will redirect me if I take a wrong turn ... Wonder what would happen if I turn off of 287 at the first sign to Medicine Mound ... No. that is not a good idea ... or is it? ...

Arriving at the point where on the day before, he had considered turning right. He is tempted to turn.

"No Jonathan, do not turn here. Go to the road you took yesterday." He hears the voice of Prairie Flower.

This is the road that Anita at the hotel told me to not take yesterday ... I'm sure that there must be a good reason for staying off of that route.

I will turn right at the road with the funny name; it is a mile past the rest area. I am certain that my special voice will let me know where to go from there.

Jonathan successfully turns onto Dam Site Road and drives past many recognizable spots, including the same wash that he drove past yesterday.

Oh yes, I remember now. The road coming in from the right ... where I was tempted to turn yesterday ... I'll bet that is where I am to turn today.

There it is, just ahead! I am impressed to turn right onto the paved road.

He does so, and travels just a mile or so westward.

I know this place; this is near where Ma, Sir and I stopped ... Oh gosh ... I can almost hear my heart beating ... Six years ago I didn't pay a lot of attention ... until we stopped ... I think I recognize the landmark that is ahead of me! I drove past these mounds yesterday ... but the perspective from this side is different.

Jonathan's heart beats rapidly, and his body feels the warmth that he has felt so very often when he has made a correct decision; the feeling when he has followed the promptings from Prairie Flower.

Driving a little further, he exclaims aloud, "This is it! This is the real Medicine Mound!"

In a moment, he turns left onto a dirt road that leads to the base of Medicine Mound, the northernmost and largest of the four mounds.

I'll pull up to this little clearing and stop ... This is almost exactly where we stopped six years ago ... I recognize the spring to my right ... I remember that it flows very slowly ... and there, just to the other side of the spring is the narrow draw!

These are some of the landmarks he identified and memorized six years ago. Jonathan leans his head against his hands which are clenched to the steering wheel.

Quietly he pleads with Prairie Flower, "I need you now, more than ever. I know you have given instruction over to Chief Peta Nocona, but I still want your guidance. This is overwhelming!"

After spending several minutes getting his thoughts and emotions under control, Jonathan gets out of his van. He feels weak in his knees; he is impressed to stay right in place for several moments. Leaning against his van at the base of the tallest of the four mounds, Jonathan waits while strength returns to his body.

I just know this is where Peta Nocona buried his special box over one-hundred-fifty-years ago. This is sacred ground, and I must honor that sanctity.

His feelings now are similar, but much greater to what he has experienced many times over the years.

I have never felt such a depth of feeling as I am feeling now. This is much deeper and more intense than being in The Big Trees having Prairie Flower visit me. I wonder if the Great Spirit is here now ... I feel that ... I feel that it is very possible!

"Jonathan ... Jonathan, come to the top. Meet me at the top of the high mound." Jonathan recognizes the voice of Peta Nocona. It is deep, reassuring and quietly piercing; he follows the command.

As he follows the promptings, he locates what appears to be the most practical route to the top.

There is a lot of overgrowth, and the climb looks to be difficult. The hike will probably drain some strength. It's kinda' hot, but I am healthy and know I can do it ... so sacred!

He makes his way through the juniper brush.

I've got to absorb many things so that I can focus on what is to come. My memory must work perfectly ... Such as: How I will be used to re-establish honor to all of Chief Peta's family ... How I love being with that man ... and ... I will do my best for him ... Whatever that is!

Achieving the final distance to the flat top of Medicine Mound, Jonathan takes in the panoramic vision of the countryside below. He has a commanding view of acres upon acres of ranchland.

But, being physically exhausted and emotionally drained, his mind wanders freely.

How has it changed over the past many decades? What was it like when Peta Nocona spent those four days of fasting ... and communing with the Great Spirit ... Burying his special box?

"Jonathan, come forward to me. Over here near the silver bush." There in the view of Jonathan, the area becomes bright. In the midst of the brightness stands a man, his lengthy hair in braids, and his clothing is of muted colors.

He continues speaking, "I am Chief Peta Nocona, your third great-grandfather, and we are at the top of Medicine Mound. You have learned much thus far, and you have much more to learn. Sit and observe."

Peta's tone is reassuring but Jonathan senses some urgency as he hears the Chief speak.

"Listen carefully my son, you are in grave danger. There are those who would have you fail in your mission. You must be on guard at all times; but you will be protected if you take precautions."

Then it dawns on Jonathan.

I am not a new eighteen-year-old boy; I am a new eighteen-year-old man! And I have taken on a mammoth-sized responsibility!

Years ago, I accepted Prairie Flower's tutoring and Sir's insistence that my life remain pure. I guess that has moved me into the realm of one who can be trusted and relied upon.

Truth-Honesty-Integrity: These are words that carry honorable acclaim in Prairie Flower's world; she has made that very clear to me over the years. If I had known ... Probably wouldn't have ... But maybe I would ...

"Jonathan, you must focus on my words and the things you see. Do not allow your mind to wander. Your life and the honor of your family name is at stake." Jonathan is brought out of his reverie into Chief Peta Nocona's world.

"Now, my son, I will first show to you the contents of my special box; the box that you saw in your vision. It holds the key to all that you are working for. Come here."

With those words, Jonathan moves to a boulder that is protruding from the ground by only an inch or so. Under instruction from Peta, he brushes the leaves and dolomite soil from the top and around the protrusion, allowing him access to the finger-grip on the side.

Lifting on the grip he removes the rounded boulder. It reveals that it is the lid to the container Jonathan had witnessed in his vision. Inside is another, smaller box.

This is the secret box that I saw Pecos deliver to Chief Peta. Wow! I am so very humbled to be involved.

"Jonathan, open the smaller box and remove what it contains," directs Peta.

Jonathan does so, holding the artifact gently in both of his hands.

"You are now holding the key that will return honor to your line of my family," Peta begins. "Hold it and examine it carefully. I will explain its meaning.

"It has a name and a purpose. The name of the crescent shaped object is Quanah Bananah. It is the key to everything that our family deserves; but it is incomplete, and is of no use until joined with its companion piece."

Peta pauses, allowing Jonathan to observe and internalize what is being revealed to him.

The teaching continues, "The outside edge of the crescent is smooth, representing goodness and compatibility. The inside edge of the crescent is rough-shaped; there are protrusions and indents, all representing dissention and the bad. In total, when joined with the missing part, it represents all of my family, past, present and future.

"Your duty will be to join the other section with this section, thus bringing completeness to the Peta Nocona family."

Continuing, Chief Peta Nocona says, "Return the key to its box now, and place it back into the stone container; replace the cover and restore all as you found it."

Jonathan does as instructed, then Chief Peta continues, "You must leave now, my son. It is important that you return to your place of stay before the bad is aware. Return tomorrow, about mid-morning and be prepared to stay the night here. Write your thoughts and bring all of your written notes with you tomorrow ... be vigilant."

Peta fades from view and Jonathan is left alone ... Except, the presence of the divine power remains.

So powerful ... The time has passed so quickly, but the sun is beginning to go down in the west. How could that be ... I don't want to leave ... But I must ...

His thoughts continue as Jonathan begins his descent from Medicine Mound.

I am feeling very weak, but oh so grateful! What is the purpose of the key ... And what about the pickup truck and it's driver ... That has me really concerned ... Is that the bad? ...

Suddenly his attention is drawn westward.

There, in the sky is a sharp bolt of lightning. It looks almost like the shape of the key! ... That is what Chief Peta saw after he buried the box! Wow, this is so very satisfying ... I feel extremely close to both Prairie Flower and Peta Nocona.

Jonathan continues to think and to ponder.

Who or what is the bad? Did Peta mean the driver of the vehicle or something much larger? How am I to take precaution?

Heading back to his hotel in Quanah, he comes to where the dirt and gravel road ends at 287. He chuckles at a new thought.

Well, I didn't see any dam anywhere so it must be a misspelled word on the sign.

After turning westward onto Highway 287, he repeatedly looks in his rear-view mirror. He is watching for any sign of something out of order.

There is a vehicle on the side road just ahead. I need to be aware of anything out of the ordinary.

As Jonathan passes Mud Road, a white Chevy sedan pulls onto the highway behind him.

He wonders, *Shall I pull into the rest area just ahead to see if they will continue on? Oh, come on, Jonathan, paranoia is taking over again! I'll just continue on toward Quanah.*

He watches in the mirror as the car quickly closes the gap between the two vehicles. Jonathan slows a bit, and hopes the car will pass him.

There is no reason it shouldn't, since we are on this 4-lane highway. But it is slowing in unison with me ... Oh, my ... Just settle down, Jonathan ...

I've slowed three times, and sped up three times; the guy behind me has done the same thing. Oh good, here he comes; the white Chevy is moving to the left lane to pass. Thank goodness!

The car pulls alongside, and just as the pickup had done earlier today, it slows and the drivers of both vehicles look at each other. The driver of the Chevy smiles broadly at Jonathan, waves and speeds ahead. The car and driver are soon out of sight.

Jonathan rehearses the words of Peta Nocona several times.

You will be protected but only if you take precautions ... protected, precautions ... protected, precautions ...

The two words: *Protected* and *precautions* become embedded in his mind.

I will add a third P word, proceed. That combination will become my personal slogan: Protected – Precaution – Proceed, is now my motto!

Arriving safely at the Best Western in Quanah, he parks the van in front of the hotel and exits. As he does so, he sees the familiar dark pickup pull away from the curb in haste. It is as though the driver *wants* to be noticed.

Jonathan leans against the side of his vehicle, his hands shaking, and his head beginning to swirl.

I think I am going to be sick. I'm feeling nauseous and weak. I must get inside, and into my room ... Quick! ... I am tired and hungry ... So much ... Knowledge ... Spiritual stuff ... People spying on me ... Or ... Maybe not ...

He swallows uncomfortably as he hurriedly makes his way to the hotel lobby.

I've got to get to my room before I lose total control ... Easy, Jonathan ... Just take it easy ... You have had a very remarkable day ... Peta ... Medicine Mound ... Great Spirit ...

As Jonathan enters the sliding doors to the hotel, a man with an angry sort of look is leaving through the same doors.

Something about him makes me uncomfortable. I'm sick ... and paranoid ... This is absolutely awful!

"Are ... Are you alright, young man?" Anita, the lady behind the hotel desk asks of him. She appears flustered and a bit anxious.

"Did you find Medicine Mound yesterday, without any difficulty?" She eyes him curiously, awaiting Jonathan's reply.

"Yes, yes I'm fine," is his reply, but he knows better. She had given him the curious send-off yesterday; this makes Jonathan even more uncomfortable.

Is there some connection with the man who left just as I was coming in? What in the world have I gotten into? he rhetorically asks himself.

I don't even know for sure what I am supposed to be doing. I've got to get to my room before I get really sick!

Jonathan hopes he can get inside before the nausea takes its toll.

He continues to the elevator and pushes the up button. The door is almost closed when an arm reaches through, and the door reopens. The open door allows a rather large and burley man to enter. Jonathan notices the man's Native American features.

I wish he would stop looking at me. Maybe he thinks that I am going to be sick all over him ... or maybe ... Maybe he knows who I am ... Is he part of the bad? ...

The elevator stops at the second floor.

Whew, I'm almost there and I can relax ... My room is just one door to the left, across the hall ... Oh for heaven's sake ... He is following me ...

As Jonathan arrives at his room the large man comments, "I hope you have a good evening."

He moves past Jonathan ... to the next room. Giving Jonathan one last lengthy look, he unlocks his door and enters.

Jonathan has a sudden sense of recognition.

The man leaving when I entered the hotel ... He looks a lot like the man in the elevator ... That is strange ... Oh my gosh ... I am probably just imagining things ... Or maybe not ... Hurry ...

Knowing the past gives one understanding of the present.
Understanding the present gives one confidence
And power for the future

CHAPTER 9 – ALLIANCE

Jonathan opens the latch to his room and pauses. *Precaution,* he reminds himself as he slowly enters and looks around. Finding all things in order and undisturbed, he plops onto his bed hoping that the nausea will quickly dissipate.

Rest, being alone, and knowing a change of focus will help his sickness, he begins to recount the day's happenings. Spontaneously he begins to chuckle as he remembers the other *P* word: *Paranoia!*

I must not let paranoia take hold. If I take precautions, I will be protected so I am going to proceed, he reassures himself. Allowing his overloaded mind to relax as he pulls the blanket over his shoulders, Jonathan drifts off to much needed sleep.

"Jonathan ... Jonathan," she whispers. "Jonathan, awake and listen. This is Prairie Flower. I have been sent to you with important information. It will help you protect yourself and your family."

My family ... Ma and Sir? Immediately, Jonathan is awake and giving full attention to Prairie Flower. He moves to the chair.

As he is about to ask his long-time friend about Ma and Sir, she speaks first, "They are fine now. There is no danger from without, but there are some things you must know. This knowledge cannot come to you on the sacred mound. You will be taught here."

Prairie Flower continues, "This must not be written. It is given to you for your personal understanding. Watch and listen."

Her voice as always, gives Jonathan calming feelings of peace and assurance. Today is no different. The room becomes light as the panoramic life of Pecos again unfolds for Jonathan's view. He wonders, *Why must this occur here rather than on Medicine Mound?*

The vision opens with Pecos's thoughts.

> *I have carried my ape's secret with me for a lot of years, and I have had serious mixed feelings. I am confident and proud to be the only person alive to share in the secret box matter; but on the other hand I just cannot bear the thought that Quanah is gaining in popularity throughout the Comanche Nation.*
>
> *It seems that every plot and strategy that I have used against him has failed! I have tried robberies and thievery; and they all got botched up. I even contacted Jesse and Frank James about teaming up with them but they just laughed at me.*
>
> *But I am determined to get even with him, even though he is my brother. He is callous to me and helpful to everyone else. They all think he is mighty and good. I will disprove them all.*

Jonathan now comes to the realization that Peta Nocona is not the one to bring messages of hatred or vile behavior. He is above that; it cannot be delivered on the sacred ground of Medicine Mound.

Pecos's life remembrances continue.

> *I am acquainted with people from other nations, the Apache, Kiowa, Shawnee, Pottawatomie, and others who have been cast out for various reasons. We have become good friends, and have actually formed an alliance.*

Really, I am rather prominent, and I am counted among the leaders of the Alliance. This has made it rather easy to drive hatred toward established nations.

We created the rightful government for all Indian nations. "We are the rightful leaders of all Americans Indians, and we will bring us together under one nation" is our theme and purpose of our alliance. This is the message we share among ourselves.

I have taken for myself the new name of To-sah-wi; my influence and puha is impressive. I am known for my ability to deal with people, and for my friendly nature. In fact, we are known as the To-sah-wi Alliance!

One day by chance I learned of an Apache lady by the name of Ta-ha-yea. It was said by some that she had once been the wife of a Comanche chief. That was good fortune because she is the perfect person for me to work with. I asked Ta-ha-yea about her story. She was happy to share.

Jonathan moves closer to the edge of his seat as the puzzle is beginning to form a clearer picture in his mind.

These are the words spoken by Ta-ha-yea to me. "It was said that I simply disappeared from my life as the wife of Quanah Parker. The truth is that I was driven out by tribal leaders.

"They did this because of my allegiance to my native Apache blood. When I left the Comanche, I was pregnant and no one else knew about it ... not even Quanah Parker, the father of my son-to-be.

"I am preparing to go back to the great Comanche Chief Quanah Parker, with my now twenty-four-year-old son, Bodaway Parker. Once there, we will make claim to the

wealth and privilege Quanah is enjoying. When we have accomplished this, my revenge against my son's father, who is your brother, will be complete."

I am To-sah-wi who was known as Pecos Parker, Quanah's baby brother. I devised and presented another plan to Ta-ha-yea; it is a much better plan. It is a plan that will make the Fifth-Son Prophecy impossible to fulfill. Ta-ha-yea has seen and accepted the wisdom of my plan; we now have a common purpose, an alliance within an alliance. The To-sah-wi Alliance will rule."

The vision ends and the scroll closes. Prairie Flower speaks, "That is all for now, Jonathan. There will be more to come, but you are to spend time in contemplation, absorbing this information. The meaning of your quest will soon fall into place. My father, Peta Nocona will await you tomorrow. Be cautious."

Jonathan opens his mouth to speak and ask some questions but she is gone. In slight despair, Jonathan mumbles aloud, "What am I to do about those who are following me?"

Protected – Precaution – Proceed, he reminds himself. With that final instruction to himself, Jonathan confidently moves back to his bed, lays his head on the pillow, and closes his eyes for sleep. Exhausted, somewhat perplexed, and filled with wonderment he settles in for a wonderful night of sleep.

The parting words of Chief Peta Nocona flow peacefully through his mind: ... *Return tomorrow, about mid-morning and be prepared to stay the night here. Write your thoughts and bring all of your written notes with you tomorrow ... be vigilant.*

Suddenly, he hears muffled, but excited chatter coming through the wall above his head. It is from his elevator neighbor's room, and is followed by laughter and a stern, "Shhh!"

If I had known what I know,
I wouldn't be as I am

CHAPTER TEN – AWAKENING

That same night, back near Ponder, Texas, Ma and Sir are each having a very restless night. Sir rises from his prone position and walks to the living room. He goes to the front door, pauses and peers out the window before beginning to open the door.

This large, usually unflappable man then changes his mind; instead he paces back and forth across the expansive living room floor. Ma watches from the open bedroom doorway.

"Is there anything I can do for you, Sweetheart?" she asks.

Sir shakes his head, "No … No one can do anything … Not now," he softly answers.

This loving father sits on a straight-back chair, places his elbows on his knees, and buries his head in his hands. He begins to weep.

"Oh, what have I done to the boy? Jonathan will never trust me again," he speaks through the sobs.

"I am not even sure that he is safe. I have been so torn, and now I think I have lost my son. My most treasured Quanah! My baby boy." Sir begins to wail and to shake.

Ma is totally startled. She has never seen Sir in such a condition, and does not know what to do. Her maternal instincts take over as she kneels beside Sir, strokes his flowing hair and places a kiss on his cheek. "Please talk to me, Peta," she gently pleads, her voice is soft and loving.

That is all it takes; Peta Parker, respectfully known by his family as Sir, turns toward his dedicated wife and buries his face in her shoulder.

"I want to talk with you, but ... but you will hate me for what I have done ...who I have been ... and what I will tell you," his tears interrupting almost every word he speaks.

Moving to the nearby couch where they sit close together, their hands are clasped tightly. Sir begins to share the secrets that have been a menace to his mind ever since Jonathan began his almost daily sojourns to The Big Trees.

As he speaks, Ma's gasps become increasingly audible. She tries to hold back her own tears as she squeezes Sir's hands tightly. Elizabeth Finley, the gentle lady with the queenly name who prefers to be known simply as Ma, is drawn into a mental world that she does not want to enter.

Long forgotten and hitherto unfamiliar episodes in flashback form, begin to attack her rapidly. Her own life starts to unfold a bizarre parallel to Sir. It is as though they are singing different verses to the same song.

Ma tries to shake off the thoughts of her own life in order to focus on the words being spoken by Sir. It seems an impossible desire.

She thinks: *This is the time for me to learn, then reveal my own history to Sir.*

Her memory is becoming a reservoir of previously unknown events; or events that have been deeply hidden in her mind. Ma's head seems filled by rapidly dispensing flashbacks.

Ma commits to herself that she will share all of her feelings with Sir.

But first I must gather all of the facts from my thoughts of this night, so that I can know and understand everything to tell him. I need more time, but it must happen before Jonathan returns home to us.

I do not think our son's life is in danger, but I do think he is under great pressure from another source.

Ma tries to consider all of her alternatives and options in her upcoming talk with Sir.

Sir's discourse ends; he sits back on the couch and leans his head on a pillow. This is a clear signal to Ma that he wants to be alone. She takes this as an opportunity to leave the room and walk outside.

I must have time to myself ... I need time to figure out these mysteries in my life. I don't understand what is going on in my brain!

In one respect I am happy to have answers about Sir ... but in another respect I am afraid for our little family. Is there something actually true about my reputation of royalty? Do I have an important part in Jonathan's quest in addition to being his mother?

The inside of her head is an emotional swirling vortex: *This is not anything like I have ever experienced in my life.*

She is suddenly overcome by a feeling of very deep depression, a feeling of being suffocated in an immobilizing paralysis of the mind.

Abruptly, Ma is mentally surrounded by the singular word "Quanah," repeated time after time after ... . It is as though bells are ringing in her brain; she is driven to her knees in anguish.

"Stop! Stop!" she cries aloud as her body writhes on the ground. "What is happening? Please stop! I cannot breathe!"

Ma's anguish is genuine, and just as suddenly as it started, it ends; the image of a very young Native American girl appears in her mind. The girl is on the floor with her arms defensively over her head.

A large Native American man holds a belt in his raised right hand as he towers over the cowering girl. "Where is it? Tell me now!" he demands.

The young girl's mother is standing off to the side, her head in her hands, and tears are flowing profusely. The verbal threats coming from the man are directed to the mother.

"I want the box! I want the box NOW!" he demands. "Give me the box or ... or .... " He unexpectedly drops the belt and hangs his head in shame, then drops to his knees,

"Ohhh, I am so sorry, so very, very, sorry. Please forgive me, my little Priscilla. And you, Chenoa, my wife, can you ever please forgive me?"

Then in total change of demeanor, the large man sits lifelessly on a convenient three-legged folding leather stool.

He speaks, "You must leave! Both of you must leave tonight! You must disappear and create new lives for yourselves. Oh, I am so very sorry and I will love you forever.

"I do not want you to leave, but you must; and take the box with you. I ... I do not know what it all means, but you must

leave now! Chenoa, you are the princess of our band and you will be missed, but you have a greater mission to fulfill.

"I will be alright. There will be a price that must be paid, but I will pay it. Now go! Quickly go and do not attempt to make contact with me or anyone else here, ever! Carry my love in your hearts forever. Good-bye, My Loves."

He turns and walks away, his head hanging low; his sobs are the only sounds heard. The Queen and her daughter disappear softly into the dark of the night.

The flashback ends as Ma struggles to regain her breath. She sits on the ground with her back against the lone backyard tree; she tries to comprehend what just happened ...

Sir emerges from the house and calls to her, "Ma, Ma ... Elizabeth, where are you, My Love? Are you alright? Please speak. It is dark and I cannot see you," he pleads. "I really need you. Elizabeth, where are you? Are you alright?"

He hears a stir near the only Red Oak tree in their back yard, "Here I am, over here."

Ma's voice is weak, subdued and barely audible, "I am sitting under the tree. Please come to me." Sir settles beside Ma as they both sit in blank limpness.

Simultaneously they turn to each other and begin to speak, "Sweetheart," they both begin, then slight laughter breaks out and some relaxation is felt by each.

"Please let me go first," Ma says; Sir's silence is a signal for her to go ahead and speak.

"I ... I don't know what all is going on, but I do know that Jonathan will be alright. I also know that there is much that you and I must learn about ourselves before his journey can be fully complete … whatever that journey is.

"We must be one, unified and open in order to be of the greatest benefit to our son. He needs us to be there for him, no matter what.

"I have a feeling that there is a dark side to our lives that goes beyond what either of us has said." Ma pauses, awaiting a response from her husband.

Sir sits silently for several seconds trying to find the appropriate words.

Finally he speaks, "Yes, yes, of course you are correct. Where … where … no, not where! How do we begin?" he asks.

Ma opens with these words, "You already began with your story earlier. I am certain that there must be more, but that will come.

"Tonight, I learned for certain that my mother's name is Priscilla. She was a Native American who was in serious danger. I do not know why she was in danger, but I am sure it will be shown to me.

"I feel that if we will be open to impressions, and search for resolutions to obvious problems, answers will come. It will not be easy but it will be worth it, and our son will be able to complete his pursuit with honor and dignity.

"I do not know the extent of what he is engaged in, but I think we are both involved deeper than we can imagine."

Interest begets desire
Desire begets preparation
Preparation begets success

CHAPTER 11 – REVELATION

Back in his hotel in the town of Quanah, Jonathan is struggling. He struggles with focusing on writing his notes as instructed; he struggles with the idea that all may not be well with Ma and Sir; and he struggles with the increasing knowledge that danger is lurking around him.

He hears Prairie Flower, "Jonathan, you do not need to be concerned about your parents. They are fine at this time. It is wise however, that you be aware of possible danger, but as long as you are cautious, you need not be worried.

"Just let your mind recall the messages you have received from Peta Nocona. Now pick up your pen and write all that you have learned from him. I will stay for a while."

"Thank you, Prairie Flower," Jonathan says, "You are awesome! Thank you so very much."

Picking up his pen he begins his writing. The recall is thorough, but the message is condensed; it is written topically, and in outline form. He uses bullet points to be certain that all pertinent information is included. The process lasts for about two hours.

I need a change ... Leave the room? ... No don't think so ... Just open the curtain ... Peer outside ... Mind will be refreshed ...

As he pulls the drapery aside he surveys the area in front of the hotel; his eyes become fixated on where his van is parked. It is dark outside, but illumination comes from the lone overhead light in the parking lot. Additional glow fades in from the streetlamp along Highway 287.

Did I just see what I think I saw?!? There was a man running from my van across the lot and going behind the Dollar Store! Oh, noo! I just don't think I can continue doing this. My life is threatened, my parents must surely be in danger. What am I going to do???

Exhaustion, fear and frustration are taking an enormous toll on this young man who is only trying to do the right thing.

Suddenly he hears the deep mellow voice of Chief Peta Nocona, "Always remember this: When you go for the good, the bad will try to intercede."

Jonathan is overcome with emotion and confusion; he sits in the armchair at his side. Tears form in his eyes as he considers if he really heard Peta's voice or if it was an impression in his mind.

I am not certain how I heard it, but I must consider the meaning of that statement. Going for the good means progress; the bad interceding means to stop the good, and try to destroy it!

Thank goodness that I don't need to be at Medicine Mound until mid-morning tomorrow. I need all the sleep I can get.

He nervously turns down the bedcovers. As he does so, a humorous thought that carries a tinge of paranoia goes through his mind: *Maybe there is a snake under the covers ... I am scared spitless of snakes!*

He chuckles at himself as he thinks of his four Ps, only out of the normal order: *Paranoia, Precaution, Proceed, Protection. Why am*

I so very paranoid when I have Prairie Flower and Chief Peta with me?

When you go for the good ... go for the good ... for the good ... be prepared to spend the night ... how do I prepare to spend the night? ... spend the night ... Quanah Bananah ... The thoughts bring pleasant sleep to Jonathan's weary mind and body ...

"Jonathan, Jonathan, wake up now. It is early but you must leave quickly." Prairie Flower speaks distinctly and firmly.

"What? Why? It is dark outside and I don't need to be at Medicine Mound until mid-morning," Jonathan says aloud, trying to clear his head. His night had been pleasant, and he didn't want to give it up.

"Jonathan, get dressed and gather your things. You are to leave your room quietly, and exit the hotel through the door at the end of the hallway on the ground floor. A car will be waiting for you.

"Remember to bring the envelope with you." Prairie Flower's instructions were crisp and very clear.

In thirty minutes Jonathan was exiting his room. *Be quiet, take precautions* are his thoughts as he heads to the elevator.

Off the elevator now and on the ground floor, he turns right, then makes a quick left out the exit door. Dawn is just barely breaking, and he spots a dark vehicle on his right. It is backed into a parking space immediately to his side.

A familiar male voice says, "Here Jonathan get into the rear, just behind the driver's seat."

The guy is outside of the vehicle holding the rear door open for Jonathan to enter. Looking into the vehicle, and then at the fellow holding the door, Jonathan realizes why the voice is familiar.

He asks, "You … you are the man who delivered the envelope to me in Denton, aren't you? This is the same black Volvo, right?"

"This is no time to chat! Get inside and lay down on the seat. We can talk later," the man instructs. The male voice is calm, yet direct and commanding.

What in the world is going on? Am I being kidnapped? This is not the way things should be going! Jonathan begins to panic. *Ughh, I think I might be sick again.*

The man closes the door behind Jonathan, places himself behind the steering wheel and calmly pulls away from the parking space. They turn left onto the side street, then right, and left onto Highway 287; there is no appearance of urgency, only a normal car traveling a normal speed.

"Keep laying down on the seat, Jonathan, until I tell you differently. After we are past the city limits we should be fine," comments the driver of the black Volvo SUV.

****

"Sir, Sir, wake up! Sir, wake up, now!" Ma shakes the shoulder of her husband early in the morning. "Peta, wake up. Jonathan is in trouble! I have this horrible feeling deep inside of me."

"What are you talking about?" Sir responds groggily as he turns to his left side, struggling to open his eyes.

His wife is sitting straight up in the bed, half speaking and half screaming.

"He is in terrible danger! I had this dreadful nightmare … we must do something … Oh, what can we do? Peta, we must do something!"

"Please, Elizabeth, please try to be calm." Sir's comforting voice is reassuring and pleasant to hear. "Tell me about your awful dream, Sweetheart. Please, let's talk."

Between sobs, Ma tries to speak, "Jonathan ... he was being ... he was being followed by someone ... someone who looked like ... he looked like a demon ... the person who was following our son looked like a demon who wanted to destroy our Jonathan."

Sir wraps his arms around his beloved wife, drawing her close to him. *No! Not her too. This is terrible; I must keep her calm ... And at the same time keep my own wits about me ... We must be totally honest, and ... and ... divulge our full stories. Strength, please, strength!*

"Darling, please keep talking and you will soon be alright," he tells her in his usual calm, uplifting voice.

Ma pulls herself away from the loving arms of her husband and repositions herself on the bed so she can look at him.

I love this good man so very much and I know there is a lot that we both must share with ... but I don't want to have to do it ... but I must ... and so must he.

"The sun is coming up now, and it is going to be a warm day. I want to fix some breakfast for us, then I feel that we should walk to The Big Trees and spend some time there," she says. "How does that sound to you?"

"I think that is a good idea, except I want to help you with the breakfast. We make a good team when we do that," Sir tries to lighten the mood.

They decide to prepare Jonathan's favorite breakfast: Sausage and scrambled eggs with small pieces of dill pickle included.

Their morning meal finished, and the cleanup completed, Ma and Sir join hands and begin their relatively short walk to The Big Trees. It is about an eighth of a mile away, which gives them time to casually stroll while holding hands. They alternately put their arms around each other's waists as they walk.

Little is said verbally, but each is preparing how they might begin the conversation. It is both a loving, and a fearful stroll.

Ma thinks of her previous visits to The Big Trees. *I have only spent personal time at The Big Trees once and that was this week. It was a comforting place for me; I was searching for understanding and some meaning to all that is going on in our lives.*

Other than that visit, I think that neither of us has been to this special place for any reason, other than to bring Jonathan back home.

Sir is having similar thoughts. *I believe that being there together will be very helpful for each of us.*

Arriving at the trees, they look for a place to get comfortable, agreeing on an oval shaped area with little underbrush. They sit on the ground against a large oak tree, each turned slightly allowing them to face each other.

Their thoughts are unified. *The feeling here is really special. It is serene, peaceful and ... and tranquil. It is no wonder that Jonathan always looked uplifted after a visit to this place.*

Ma speaks, "It was my suggestion that we come here. I don't know why, but it was an strong impression that this really is a very special place. I think I was correct."

"I agree," Sir answers. "In fact, I know that Jonathan was receiving special tutoring in preparation for the quest he is now on.

Someone, I do not know who, has been visiting him in The Big Trees wherever we have lived over these many years."

Sitting in meditative thought for several moments, they hear a voice, "Please listen carefully. This is Jonathan's mentor and tutor, and I am still with him. I am known as Prairie Flower. Jonathan is safe now, but there are forces that would do him harm. His quest is honorable and you can help him.

"I am here to let you know what you must do to help and protect your son. Open your hearts to each other; be honest and forthright, leaving nothing out.

"Jonathan's safety, his success in his quest, and the honor of your family name rests upon you.

As you share what is in your hearts with each other, Jonathan will also be taught, and he will know of these things. I will now leave."

****

In the black Volvo, the driver turns to Jonathan and speaks, "It is safe for you to sit up now, Jonathan." Continuing from the driver's seat, he says, "My name is Michael and I have been instructed to be of help to you."

"How ... wha ... who ... gosh, I don't even know what to ask or think," Jonathan says. "Who are you besides Michael? Are you a friend of Prairie Flower? What is your interest in my quest? Why did you pick me up at the hotel?"

Michael answers, "I am taking you to Medicine Mound where you will receive further knowledge concerning your quest. All other answers will come at the appropriate time.

"Right now, you are to focus only on your errand; you are to focus your mind and actions only on the quest that you are engaged in."

The drive continues quietly as Jonathan is deeply engrossed in the sudden turn of the day's events.

I quietly exited from the hotel – leaving through the side door – riding in the same SUV that delivered the envelope – I have to trust the driver. Ohhh, myyy!

The sun is rising above the horizon, and Michael lowers the sun visor. He has been vigilant in watching his rear-view mirror and everything seems in order.

"We will be at Medicine Mound in about fifteen minutes. Are you feeling OK back there?" His voice is clear and seems sincere.

"Yeah, I'm alright. I just want to know what is going on, and you're no help in that department," is Jonathan's acerbic response.

Michael laughs a bit, then says, "Sorry, but my job is as a courier. I don't ask questions, but I do know that you are one very special person!"

Jonathan has his own comeback, "If special is what I am, then why am I so darned paranoid?"

"I think paranoia can be a blessing when it results in caution. Precaution results in Protection," responds Michael.

"So I will proceed," Jonathan whispers to himself.

The car turns to the right off of 287 and heads south on the road now familiar to Jonathan. He relaxes with a feeling of peace and security. His trust in Michael the driver, is being validated.

Jonathan settles back in his seat and enjoys the Texas scenery.

I am to be prepared to spend the night on the mound. I'm mentally prepared, but have no sleeping bag or any such thing. There are so many things to remember and now I have this issue to deal with. Maybe Michael can help ... But he's just a courier!

He decides to ask, "Michael, I may be required to spend the night tonight, at Medicine Mound. I have no sleeping bag with me. Do you have any suggestions?"

"That, I can help you with. In the back of the car is a backpack for your use. It contains a sleeping bag and some snacks. I guess I am good for something besides being a courier, aren't I?" He laughs at his own remark which sparks a good chuckle from Jonathan.

Jonathan offers a good-natured challenge, "Betcha can't answer this question: I am supposed to arrive at Medicine Mound at mid-morning. We are very early. My question is: What am I supposed to do in the meantime?" Jonathan expects the courier excuse again.

"You will have no difficulty in being occupied. If Prairie Flower is not there to fill your mind with wisdom, your entire being will be overcome with the sacredness of the place. That is nothing for you to be concerned about." Michael's already good reputation just moved up a notch in Jonathan's mind.

Stopping at the base of Medicine Mound, near the very slow running spring, they both get out of the vehicle and Jonathan asks Michael, "What are your plans, now?"

"I will help you with your backpack, then I will move on to my next assignment. I wish you the very best in your quest, whatever that may be." He gives Jonathan a fist-bump, and returns to the Volvo; then with a wave, he drives away.

"Jonathan, welcome to the mound again. Please come to the top where you will learn much. I am sorry that you had to rise early, but it is for your own protection.

We have much to talk about, so it is good that you are here early."
The mellow voice is unmistakably that of Chief Peta Nocona.

Chief Peta continues speaking with an unusual sense of urgency,
"Your mother and father are greatly concerned for your safety; and
they must also learn as you learn. Together you will all understand
your purpose. Today is a day for understanding, love and
acceptance."

Where there is no vision, the people perish:
But he that keepeth the law, happy is he.
(Proverbs 29:18)

CHAPTER 12 – ANSWERS

Jonathan moves quickly to the top of the high mound. The urgency he felt from Peta Nocona's voice, coupled with the mention of Ma and Sir, prompts his sense of resolve.

Nearly out of breath from the rushed hike up the three-hundred-fifty-foot tall mound, Jonathan plops down in the same spot he had occupied yesterday.

"My son, for several years, you have held a lot of questions in your mind about Sir. Ma has had many of the same concerns. While you have been away from them on this quest, they have been on their own personal journeys of self-discovery.

"You are about to witness their internal struggles; but as you do, you will be required to be understanding and forgiving. Your parents have been told that what they share with one another, you will also learn and know what is in their hearts."

Jonathan attempts to assimilate all that he is being told. *I am not sure just what I heard ... How will I witness their internal struggles? ... Yet, I will learn and know ... Incredible ... What can ... Will it? ... I don't understand ...*

"I know you are very perplexed now. However, as you experience this day, you will receive the answers you have sought. Today will be the culmination of learning and the beginning of restoration for our people, our family.

"There are feelings, cultures and actions that will be disappointing to you; this day will not be easy. You can withdraw from this quest now, if you choose. But if you continue, you will restore honor and puha to all descendants of Chief Peta Nocona."

Chief Peta pauses his instruction to allow Jonathan to assimilate what has been said.

He continues, "However, if you choose to not continue, the Fifth-Son Prophecy will be broken. You, Jonathan, are the only fifth-son to be prepared; there is no other. But you do have the choice.

"You need to rest now. Let your mind ponder on what you have just heard, take some nourishment for your body. You will be alone for a while. Decide if you want to continue … or if you choose to abandon the quest."

Peta Nocona withdraws; Jonathan feels the absence of his instructor.

I am very tired and I really need to absorb what I have been hearing. I was told to be here at mid-morning, and instead, they picked me up early. Now I am required to make a decision over something that I thought was already decided. This is bizarre!

Thirty minutes later Jonathan hears Chief Peta speak to him, "Do you have questions for me, Jonathan? Are you going to continue with your quest?"

"Yes, I am. I have been preparing for this all of my life, and I know that if I do all things correctly, my quest will be successful." Jonathan's voice was strong but soft as he responded to his friend, the father of Prairie Flower.

"Good," says the chief, "be alert, and we will visit The Big Trees."

****

Jonathan is visually and audibly transported to The Big Trees.

Ma is speaking to Sir, "Last night I learned for certain that my mother's name is Priscilla. She was an American Indian, a Comanche girl who was in serious danger. I do not know why she was in danger, but I am sure it will be shown to me.

"I feel that if we will both be open to impressions, and search for resolutions to obvious problems, answers will come. It will not be easy but it will be worth it, and our son will be able to complete his pursuit with honor and dignity.

She continues, "I don't know the extent of what he is engaged in, but I think we are both involved deeper than we can imagine."

Sir answers, "Yes, I know our Jonathan will be alright, but I must cleanse my soul before we go any further. There are more things about me that I must share."

"Yes, Sweetheart, you go ahead." It is a typical response from Ma, the lady who's sweetness belies her strength and determination.

Taking a long breath, Sir says, "I told you earlier that the reason for our frequent moves, is because my income requires me to be available to the tribal leaders where they live. That is only partly true.

"I have been living a double life ever since Jonathan was born. The family from which I come belongs to the To-sah-wi Alliance ... I am one of them. We ... we are sworn to the overthrow of all Native American self-governance. It has been that way since the days of Quanah Parker."

Sir hangs his head in shame and embarrassment. After a long, and very uncomfortable pause, he raises his head and looks at his wife in a cautious manner. He has no idea what to expect from her.

He speaks softly, "My father, Daniel Parker said that the day would come when I must place my life in serious danger; today is that day. In order for our special son to succeed in his quest which was given by Chief Peta Nocona many years ago, I must be willing to be exposed."

In gulping sobs, he continues, "They will come after me for being a traitor to their cause. The To-sah-wi Alliance is a brutal enemy to the Nation. Even though they certainly must know that their cause is lost, they continue in hate for all but themselves.

"They surely know the Alliance will collapse because of the great respect for Chief Peta Nocona, and his great spiritual background."

Ma looks at Sir with much sympathy, and disbelief at the same time. She speaks, "First Peta, tell me what you mean about your income. What do you mean that it is only partly true?"

"Ohhh, it hurts too much! I don't want to tell you. I ... I thought it would be alright; that this day would not come. Our son is in so much danger, and now he will never trust me again ... And I don't know about you!" Sir's sobs have turned to full-fledged crying.

Struggling, Ma tries to be sympathetic. She says, "You must be totally open and honest, My Love. Jonathan's success rests on our actions. We have to be completely clear, honest and open."

****

Jonathan cannot contain his own emotions as he witnesses the scene being played out before him. He turns his head away from the view and buries his face in his arms. He sobs and sobs as he pictures the deceitfulness of his father.

"Oh, Sir," he exclaims aloud. "What have you done? You are my father and you have taught me that honesty – truth – integrity are what I must always believe in! I have learned everything from you about integrity and honesty. I am nothing if I am without honor!"

"I don't want to see any more of this! Chief Peta, please … can we stop … now?"

"Jonathan, my son," the chief speaks, "you are of my flesh and blood. You are chosen to restore what has been lost. In order to restore the lost, you must understand what was lost, how it was lost, and why it was lost. You cannot accomplish unless you understand. You must learn what is being laid before you.

"Again, remember this: When you go for the good, the bad will try to intercede. You have been doing a lot of the good; what you are witnessing now, is much of the bad. Please, turn back to the scene."

****

With wet, red eyes, Sir looks up at Ma and he sees a princess, the one he married so many years ago, Princess Elizabeth Finley. She strokes his forehead softly and with an empathetic touch. He wonders how she can continue to love me.

He wipes his eyes, looks squarely at Ma, then after swallowing hard, he says, "I have been paid for information every time we move, and every place where we have lived. I have been selling information about Jonathan to the Alliance leaders. They know all about his visits to The Big Trees. They know he has been tutored, and … and worst of all, they know of the quest he is on right now.

"At first, in the beginning it didn't seem important; it was just some sort of game. I tell them about Jonathan's trips to The Big Trees, and that he is always very happy and peaceful afterwards.

"They pay me, and a few months later we move. After we move, I go through the ritual again. It seemed harmless ... For a few years ... And now this ...

"When I tried to quit ... when I tried to pull out, they threat ... they threatened ... they threatened to harm you ... and to harm Jonathan. They have threatened to stop paying me, they have threatened to spread horrible rumors about you!

"Oh, Elizabeth, I cannot explain my turmoil. I just want to disappear out of your life but that would not solve anything; it would be very selfish of me.

"What am I going to do? What can I do to make things right? How can I take care of you? Most of all, will you ever forgive me?"

Ma hesitates, begins to speak, then stops. She moves away from Sir just a bit; then having readjusted her position she says boldly, "Peta Parker, you are known as Sir! This is because of the love and respect that Jonathan and I hold for you!

"Remember what the voice said to us earlier? I think she said her name is Prairie Flower; and that she has been Jonathan's teacher. She said, that you and I are to be totally open with each other, that as we share our hearts with each other, Jonathan will also learn and know.

"I am not certain just what that means, but we must place our trust in what she says to us. Also, we have been promised that Jonathan will be safe; she said that we need to communicate and be totally open with each other. That means no more secrets.

"The paths ahead of us may be rough; and we must travel them for the sake of our son! I still do not know what his quest is all about, but I think you can tell me."

Sir shifts about, and very uncomfortably looks at the ground as his large hands fidget nervously. "I know a lot from experience, and I was taught much by my father, Daniel and my grandfather, Bodaway. They were respectable men, but were also very troubled. They lived within the practice of the To-sah-wi Alliance as have I.

"I have been taught that the Alliance was started by Ta-ha-yea Parker, an Apache woman who had been the wife of Quanah Parker for a short while. She is supposedly my great-grandmother; it is through her that I was born into the To-sah-wi Alliance.

"She was cast out from the Comanche, and apparently began the To-sah-wi Alliance with Pecos Parker. Pecos Parker was the younger brother of Quanah, and there was great animosity between the two young brothers."

At the mention of Quanah, Ma feels the familiar darkness surround her. "I feel terrible but it must not show ... I am royalty ... I am"

Sir continues, "It was reported that Pecos died of smallpox as a child, but that is not what happened.

"He left the Comanche tribe and found his way into a group of other outcasts. He came to be known by the name of To-sah-wi. He and Ta-ha-yea shared a hatred for Quanah Parker; together they formed the To-Sah-wi Alliance to destroy Quanah, as well as all of the traditional Indian governments. They became a rogue government in and of themselves.

"My grandfather, Bodaway Parker was the son of Ta-ha-yea and Quanah Parker. When Ta-ha-yea left her husband, he was unaware of her pregnancy. Quanah Parker never knew of this son.

"Bodaway, his son Daniel and I have all grown up in the Alliance culture. We have lived it as though we believed it; however, we have also lived as true Comanches.

"My second great-grandfather, Peta Nocona received the Fifth-Son Vision. He ..."

"Whoa, wait a minute!" His intrigued wife has a delayed reaction; it takes a moment for Sir's latest comment to register in her mind.

Ma demands, "What do you mean, you have been living as a true Comanche? You have been living with Jonathan and me!"

Sir attempts to explain, "You know that I have attended tribal meetings all of our married life, don't you? I have done that in order to qualify for the annual income from casino investments."

Ma blurts, "And all the while trying to overthrow it!? And what is this Fifth-Son Vision all about?"

"Overthrow?" Sir contemplates the questions, "Not exactly, The Alliance is committed to not let the Fifth-Son Prophecy come about.

"If the Fifth-Son Prophecy is allowed to come about, all of Chief Peta Nocona's family will be reunited; and that is not to be permitted! Quanah Parker fraudulently usurped the leadership!"

Sir quickly notices the tone of his voice has become belligerent, and he tries to calm himself. "You see, Peta Nocona buried an artifact of some sort many years ago. It is to remain in its burial place until the fifth-son is led to it, and retrieves it.

"The fifth-son is the first son of each male descendant down to the fifth generation. Quanah is the first son, Bodaway is the second son, Daniel is the third son, I, Peta am the fourth son, and ...."

Again, Ma interrupts, "And Jonathan is the fifth son. He is to be led to the artifact, whatever it is. That is the quest he is on right now? Is that the story?"

"Yes, it ..." he is cut short by Ma.

"And you have been willing to sacrifice our son so that the artifact cannot be found, right? You have been selling him, piece by piece for most of his eighteen years!

"And just what is the so-called purpose of the artifact?" she demands to know.

Reduced to shame and surprise at Ma's strength of character he answers, "I do not know, but it has been said that it is to be joined with another piece, and is symbolic of the unity of all of the Comanche.

"Peta Nocona was told in the vision that a branch of his family would lose their identity. Maybe that is what this is all about."

Sir further tries to assuage his conscience, "This has been my demon; the knowledge of Jonathan's magnificent calling, and my duty to the Alliance to keep them informed.

"Also, our ability to survive financially has depended on me keeping the Alliance informed ... Oh ... Oh, Elizabeth, it is such a huge relief to share this rotten weight with you." Again, tears swell in Sir's eyes as he looks for approval from his princess.

****

Up on Medicine Mound, Jonathan cannot withhold the tears as he lays his head on his arms which are folded across his knees.

He speaks aloud as though Sir could hear him, "Sir, my father, you have carried such a heavy responsibility to everyone. Somehow I have known ... it has been obvious that you have had serious matters on your mind. Thank you for being a man of integrity.

"I cannot imagine the weight of it all. I forgive you for anything, and everything you have done against my quest. You have been a wonderful father. I forgive ..."

His body shakes uncontrollably as the tears flow freely. Jonathan tries to roll his body into a ball as his mind is actively working.

I am beginning to understand the purpose of my quest, but there are so many questions, so many unknowns. I wonder about the artifact and its companion piece. What is in the envelope delivered to me by Michael? And when will I be allowed to open and view its contents?

"Jonathan, let's return to The Big Trees," counsels Chief Peta.

****

Sir speaks, "Ma, you and Qua ... You and Jonathan ... You both mean every ... Everything to me. I have tried to justify ... To justify my actions to myself ... But that ... That has not work ... Has not worked at all." Being distraught, Sir cannot seem to organize his thoughts or words.

"Elizabeth, do you think that Jonathan ... Elizabeth ... I know you prefer to be called Ma, but you are so much more than that to me ... Will you forgive ... Will my son ever be able to underst ... understand and ... and trust me in the future?

"What am I going to do about the Alliance? How can I ever get ... get out of this mess that has been put on me? What ... and how?"

His wife understands that Sir needs some type of validation but she is also apprehensive about his forced, but strong attachment to the To-sah-wi Alliance.

She attempts some consoling thoughts, "Yes, Peta, I feel that everything is going to be good. He will forgive. We raised a good son ... And as we move forward with our part ... I know he ... Oh no! ... Oh my gosh ...

"I just thought of something ... Tell me all you know about the artifact. Does this have anything to do with his twelfth birthday? Does it have anything to do with our trip to the Quanah area, and the adventure you sent him on?"

Suddenly a faint feeling overtakes Ma. I think ... I think ... that ... My mind is traveling backwards ... My mother, Priscilla ... The box ... Give me the box ... You both must leave ... Now!

"Oh my beloved Peta, take me in your arms, hold me, please ... please hold me tight ..."

One leg in heaven; one leg in hell
Which leg will triumph?
The one with the most exercise

CHAPTER 13 – RECKONING

"It's alright, my darling," Sir takes Ma into his arms and gives her the protective hug that she is in need of.

He softly inquires, "What is happening? What has gone through your mind? It sounds like there are more flashbacks."

Ma pulls away from Sir and looks him in the eye as she speaks, "Do you remember that I learned the other day about my mother's name being Priscilla?"

Sir nods his head and replies, "Yes."

Ma continues her story, "I also learned that my mother's parents, my grandparents were Comanche. There was something horrid going on; my grandfather was threatening to beat his daughter, my mother, if my grandmother did not give him some sort of box. My mother was a very young woman."

Sir looks into her eyes and asks, "Ma, how did you learn all of this? Where did the information come from?"

She thinks for a moment about how to begin, "There have been pieces of information from my childhood ... I think they must be memories from my mother ... memories that I may have overheard her speak about before she passed away. Piece-by-piece these thoughts have accumulated in my mind.

"Since that awful evening outside of our home, I have had flashback after flashback; they have been hurtful and they have been enlightening. But mostly they have been very releasing to me. I have learned about my aversion to Quanah. I think that I should share these flashbacks with you, but I am afraid that you may not understand."

Sir holds up his right hand and says, "I have just bared my entire soul to you. We have been told by the voice to be open, and complete with each other. Are saying that now, you do not want to be open and complete, yourself?

"Elizabeth ... Ma, You must do the right thing and tell me everything! Leave nothing out. Together we will be able to work through anything. Do you understand?"

Ma wrings her hands trying to be comfortable speaking, "Sir, I think ... I think ... No, I am sure that my grandfather was a member of the To-sah-wi Alliance. Do you remember that I told you about one flashback where he was threatening to beat my mother because of a box?"

"Yes, of course. That was just a moment ago," Sir answers, then seems to hold his breath while waiting for her to continue.

"My grandmother Chenoa, and her family lived in the town of Quanah. I recall my mother saying that we were never to go back to Quanah, that it was a dark place. She said that evil lived there, and that we would be punished if we ever went to Quanah.

"I am certain that this is the reason for my depressed state of mind whenever we have been in the area, and whenever the word is spoken around me.

"Chenoa was not associated with the Alliance, and my grandfather forced them to leave the American Indian world. Grandmother

Chenoa took my mother and they left it all behind. Chenoa was a princess in her tribe; and when she and my mother, Priscilla disappeared, the tribe mourned their loss for many days.

"They secretly came to this area, living somewhere near Krum where they entered the white man's world. This is where Priscilla met and married my father, Gramps.

"All of my horrible flashbacks have brought my memories to the surface. My mother's influence in my childhood has remained with me, totally forgotten except for the fear and evil feeling regarding Quanah."

Sir begins to show some impatience and sharply says, "Ma, you have mentioned a box two or three times. What is that all about? Tell me about the box."

Ma becomes white-faced as she works to find a suitable response, "I do not know what is in the box. Gramps kept it hidden because it represented the beating which my grandfather threatened to give my mother.

"It also represented the town of Quanah, and he kept it away from her. He loved her too much to watch her suffer in anguish and emotional pain."

"Elizabeth," Sir's voice is showing some frustration. "Listen to me! Where did the box come from? I know that you do not know what is in it. But where did it come from and where is it now?"

"Grandmother Chenoa had the box; it had been passed to her by her mother who received it from Chief Peta Nocona. It is known simply as the treasure.

"When Gramps died, it was among his belongings, and I did not like what it represented; so it is still in my trunk of old stuff.

"I am scared, Peta ... I am really scared, I am afraid of what is in the box."

Sir is stunned but asks, "Why didn't you ever tell me about the box? Don't you understand that our own very lives could be in serious danger?" His voice is demanding and threatening.

Shocked and shaken, Ma pulls away from Sir but he grabs her arm and pulls her back; back into his control.

"Sir ... Peta! Do you have any idea what you are doing!?" Ma is equally demanding in her question. "You have given up the life of the Alliance ... You have, haven't you? Tell me, tell me now!"

"What I know is that I must know what is in the box!" Sir is beginning to raise his voice, "They will make our lives miserable when they find out that we are holding back information!"

Standing her ground, Ma says, "You don't have any idea what is in the box! You are not married to me ... You are married to them! You are married to the To-sah-wi Alliance!

"Leave me alone! Leave me alone until you have come to your senses!" Ma is now red-faced and shouting. She turns her back to her husband and takes a couple of steps away.

Sir stops his aggressive behavior and drops his arm to his side. He begins to pace; back and forth, around in circles, and finally steps outside the small confined area in the trees.

His thoughts are of surprise. I have never, ever seen Ma act like this. She is standing up to me; I don't understand what is going on!

Ma is equally amazed at herself, and her willingness to be demanding. This is a new experience for me. My mind seems to have been taken over by some strange impulse; my son is in danger, my husband is not being rational and it is up to me to bring order to this chaos! I must maintain control; that is what royalty does.

Ma returns to her place on the ground and sits against the tree. She stares into the mass of trees surrounding her.

I will not let Sir destroy all that we have built together. He will not place Jonathan in further danger; I will see to that!

Sir comes back into the small haven in the trees and walks toward Ma with his arms outstretched. Ma stands, walks past him without a glance, and begins her return home in haste.

In Sir's confused state he sits, then stands and sits again. His mind will not focus on any single issue; and he struggles to find rationale in his own actions.

Oh, what am I doing? I have just lost my family, the only ones who really care for me. The Alliance will surely punish me if I don't let them know about the ... the ... I am being a traitor to both sides ...

Ma walks hurriedly toward their home in a determined fashion, then her pace slows as her mind seems to accelerate.

Why is the box so ... What could possibly be so important ... Peta is just ... Jonathan ... Fifth-Son ... Grandmother Chenoa ... Give me ... Box ... Gramps ... Oh, Gramps, how I need you ... I am so lost ... What can I do ... What am I supposed to do?

She reaches their home, and after entering Ma plops onto the couch in the living room ... and erupts in tears.

Exhaustion takes its toll and Ma is soon asleep. Her dreams are both comforting and unsettling.

Look in the box, Elizabeth. The contents will help soothe your mind, it will help provide relief – No, Elizabeth, the contents will harrow up your mind – Do not believe the demon, look in the box and find the good – The To-sah-wi Alliance is in the box – The great Spirit is in the box.

After an insufferable hour, she awakens in a profuse sweat. Her mind is muddled, everything is awhirl around her, and dizziness takes its toll. Ma collapses to the floor; then she hears the voice.

"Elizabeth, This is Prairie Flower. You must do the right thing. Look in the box, you will then know what action to take."

Moments later, Ma recovers slowly. Rising, she goes to the refrigerator and reaches for a bottle of water, her mind questioning what she had just heard.

Was it real? I don't want to look in the box. I don't even want to find the box!

In her quandary, she knows that the right thing to do is as Prairie Flower instructed. Ma goes to the garage in the backyard, walks inside and stares at the place where the trunk is buried; it is under many rarely-used items.

I have hesitated long enough and I must get on with it!

Determinedly she attacks the job ahead of her.

I put it in the bottom of the farthest corner of the trunk after Gramps died because I just did not want it around. In fact, I thought about destroying the box and its contents, but for some odd reason, I was prompted to not do so. I just did not want to ever see it again.

Oh, my! I am getting so sick just thinking about the box, and what it represents to me; and especially what it represented to my mother. I do not want the box! But if it means success to Jonathan, I must go through with this.

In fifteen minutes the trunk is uncovered and opened. Ma moves things aside and burrows to the bottom of the left side of the trunk; she lifts the lightweight box out of the trunk.

Holding the box in her two hands, Ma begins to quiver; her mind is half-terrified and half-curious. She places her right thumb on the latch and begins the twisting motion. Tears form in her eyes, she hesitates, then begins again to open the box. Despairingly, she sets it aside and simply stares at it.

It is an attractive-looking container, the top has beaded designs and the sides are a pretty blue-green color. I am sure it is a very useful jewelry case. I want to open it ... but ... but ...

Ma picks it up again and places her right thumb on the latch. Closing her eyes, she lets her thumb flip the latch and raise the lid. Slowly, she opens her eyes and allows them to see into the box.

As Prairie Flower said to me: I now know what action to take; I must go back to The Big Trees, and to Sir.

****

Ma arrives at the trees and quietly steps to the edge of the oval area she had earlier abandoned. She is numbed by what she sees.

The man is just sitting there on the ground. He looks like he is suffering in deep despair, his knees are bent up, his arms folded across, and his head buried in his arms. He should be suffering!

She stands looking down at her husband in silence for several seconds, then he senses her presence, and looks up warily. In the crook of her left arm is a paper bag.

He remains silent, watching her every move. Without expression, Ma reaches into the bag and retrieves its content. She pushes it toward Sir.

Her words are sharp and caustic, "Here ... Here is your precious box. Two of the contents are pictures of my mother; one item is what I believe to be her wedding ring.

"I do not know what the fourth thing is."

With sheer surprise Sir stares at his wife, his Elizabeth, in disbelief and amazement.

Wha ... What is she ... What does she expect me to do? ... How ...

Ma continues, "If it is so important to you to give up your family, including Jonathan, then do so.

"I have learned for myself why I am so uncomfortable around the town of Quanah. In addition to that, I have learned that my family, my Comanche family, has suffered immensely; and it is because of your stupid Alliance!

"As of right now, I will not move away from the area of Krum again. You do whatever you want to do. I will forgive and accept you back, but only if you make the right choice! Here! Take the box!"

Ma's thoughts tell the story: He must sort out his own thoughts, actions ... And the remainder of his life.

Sir looks blankly his wife; he instinctively reaches for the box that she has thrust in his face. Ma turns and walks away from the area, leaving Sir to himself ... And with the box.

Learn to see, not just look
Learn to listen, not just hear
Learning to do both is success

CHAPTER 14 – RECONCILIATION

"No! … No! … Sir! … No!" Jonathan jumps to his feet and tries to leave the mound, but is drawn back by the sudden realization that he cannot leave the area.

"Sir," Jonathan screams, "what are you thinking? That is my mother, your wife, your princess!" Little does he realize that no one can hear his screams except himself and Peta Nocona.

Chief Peta Nocona speaks calmly but resolutely, "Jonathan, Jonathan, my son, now is a time for your understanding. Remember what happens when one goes for the good? The bad tries to intercede.

"You have just witnessed what a lifetime of teaching by the bad can do in one short moment of forgetfulness. You have also proven by your own action, that a lifetime of learning the good will not tolerate a moment of the bad.

"Your father will be alright. It takes time for an eagle raised in a cage, to learn to fly after being released. Sir has just been released from a lifetime of being caged."

Jonathan is so aghast at what he just observed in his beloved sanctuary, that he fails to hear. "Chief Peta, I think that I must return home to my parents. They need me now more than ever. Sir *is not* being the man I grew up with; he is not thinking clearly!"

The wise old chief speaks, "Jonathan, you are an extremely sensitive son. Your parents love you very much, and each wants you to succeed in your quest.

"However, neither of them fully understands the impact that your victory will have on them or the entire family of Peta Nocona. They are each experiencing two demons fighting inside of them.

"The Alliance knows you are on the mound at this very moment and they lie in wait for a vulnerable time. This is the reason you must stay tonight on Medicine Mound."

Jonathan sits in silence; disbelief fills his mind and animosity attacks his heart.

Sir is willing to give me up to the Alliance ... his love for me is false ... he is a fraud. I am beginning to hate him. How can he do this to our family?

All of a sudden Jonathan's mind takes a sharp turn.

The box ... What's in the box? Does it have anything to do with my quest? Oh my gosh! Is it important to Sir ... and to Ma? This is awful!

Chief Peta interrupts Jonathan's thoughts, "Let yourself take a break for a while. Walk the top of the mound, discover new perspectives of the world around you, and listen to the quiet voice of your mind. Now go, you will know when it is time to return."

Jonathan knows he cannot argue with the wisdom of Chief Peta Nocona. He stands, turns about, and surveys the mound's terrain.

I have never thought of exploring the mound. It has seemed that the only purpose of this place is for me to be tutored and led. Getting another perspective is an idea that seems a bit odd, given the circumstance.

Perplexed yet hopeful, he begins to stroll away from the small spot that he has occupied atop Medicine Mound. He has filled his space for several hours, but now as he looks around he sees a rather large expanse; probably the size of a football field.

The change of posture, and some physical activity will be good for me.

He recalls: *The quiet voice of the mind; Sir has used that phrase in the past. It rings true; I really need it! Prairie Flower, where are you? Please help me know what I am to do.*

Walking slowly through the Redberry Juniper brush that surround the flat area, Jonathan observes much that he has not previously noticed. All of his other visits have been for shorter periods of time, and for a singular purpose; the purpose of furthering his quest.

He sees the Pincushion Cactus which also carries the name of Horse Crippler Cactus.

I can certainly understand why either name would apply to this treacherous plant.

Other various shrubbery and small wildlife bring a new perspective of the mound to Jonathan.

I am walking on the same sacred ground that for scores of years has been the holy place for probably hundreds of people. This is no place for bitter feelings, anger or hatred. I must learn patience, understanding and forgiveness. Prairie Flower, I want you with me.

Prairie Flower speaks as the quiet voice of his mind.

Yes my friend Jonathan, I am here, in your mind, and I know your anguish. Sir is suffering his anguish also; it is important that you

135

know he loves you and Ma with all of his heart. He has had a lifetime of subservience to the other side. What you witnessed was a momentary relapse into the dark world of his To-sah-wi Alliance background.

Sir needs your love and support. He does not need your anger or revenge. Think on this as you wander the mound. This is a sacred place; let your mind dwell in those thoughts that bring happiness and joy to your inner self.

Somewhat breathless, Jonathan sits on a nearby boulder and looks around. For some reason there is a freshness in the air that extends to everything within his sight. An overwhelming brightness fills his three-hundred-sixty-degree panoramic view from the top of Medicine Mound.

It is almost as though I can see forever. This is so very inspiring; it is no wonder that this mound was used as a special place.

I remember a conversation that Sir, Ma and I had on one of our trips through Quanah. It was with the owner of Old Bank Saloon in Quanah. Someone had suggested to Sir that we visit the bar and grill for dinner.

I believe the owner's name was Steven; he and his wife Torey own the place together. He was a very nice man, especially when Sir brought up the topic of Medicine Mound ... Sir seemed to know a lot about the place, and that made me even more curious about his heritage ... and my heritage.

Steven said that he had been told that on a clear day, a person at the top of the mound can see the Wichita Mountains, the farthest point being up to forty or maybe even fifty miles to the east.

Today, I can see several towns and a lot of productive ranch land. At the south end of Medicine Mound is the mound next in size; it is known as Cedar Mound. After that, the third larger mound is known simply as No Name Mound. Of course, the fourth and smallest of the four mounds has the name of Little Mound.

Sir and Steven both know a lot about the area. They talked about these historical landmark mounds. I really enjoyed that visit..

Wow, this change of perspective is really working! Just a re-focus for a short period of time is marvelous.

Jonathan feels an enthusiastic beat of his heart; this special young man reverently speaks aloud, "I can do it! Whatever it is, I know I can do it!"

The weighty load of just a short while ago is gone, and he knows it is time to return to Chief Peta Nocona. The relief surrounding Jonathan is almost palpable. His face is showing release and new-found respect.

"Thank you, thank you, thank you," is all he can utter. "Thank you Prairie Flower, and thank you Chief Peta."

Chief Nocona's voice is heard by Jonathan, but it seems distant and secondary to the release of all the pain and drama Jonathan has just been experiencing.

Peta Nocona speaks, "I think you are now ready for the difficult part of your quest, Jonathan. But first, it will be to your safety and protection to spend an additional night here on the mound. Michael will deliver additional supplies for your extra day's needs."

Suddenly, Jonathan realizes that the Chief is speaking, "Huh? What did you say? I am sorry, my mind was on other things; the new perspective you told me about, and how much better I feel."

His teacher replies, "Yes I knew it would help. Now Jonathan, hear me carefully. The difficult part of your quest is about to begin.

Thus far you have been learning the all-important history. Tomorrow you will hear what you need to do; the action part of your quest. And I repeat, you are to spend an additional night here.

"Opposition is going to be strong; you have just witnessed the power of the Alliance in your father. You will now need strategy in order to succeed."

Jonathan is giving Chief Peta Nocona his rapt attention.

I know that I must not let anything escape me, but wow, what a lot for my mind to absorb! I want to ask about the box, but ... but ...

The chief comes close to Jonathan, speaking in a soft, confiding voice, "The To-sah-wi Alliance is very active right now, and you need to prepare for their actions also.

"Your upcoming training is to consist of two parts: The first part will take place tomorrow, it will be focused on the strategy you must use to be successful in your quest.

"You will have time to study it out, planting it firmly in your mind. A night of rest then, will help adapt it to your mental planning.

"The second day will be a day of learning how to deal with the bad works of the To-sah-wi Alliance. They are cunning and devious; they must be dealt with in a very careful manner.

"You will spend tonight and tomorrow night here on this most marvelous mound. We will meet early tomorrow morning shortly after sun-up, and you will receive instruction on the actions you are to pursue.

"You are safe while you are here on Medicine Mound. But when you are elsewhere, it is of utmost importance that you keep yourself alert. Remember to take precaution in all you do.

"If you will do that, you will be protected."

Jonathan hears all that is said, but his mind continues to return to the last scene from The Big Trees.

What about the box? Do I need to know? I want to ask Chief Peta but my quiet voice says no. I will ask Prairie Flower. Yes ... that feels better. Chief Peta is here to teach, Prairie Flower is here to guide. But ... Is it even important to my quest?

DENNIS BOYD CALL

If you want the hide,
You must first have the buffalo

CHAPTER 15 – STRATEGY

It is early on the morning after Jonathan's first full night spent atop Medicine Mound. The air is fresh and cool; the sense of autumn is in the north Texas air, and Jonathan awakens. His mind is clear and alert.

Chief Peta Nocona speaks first, "Jonathan, it will not be good for you to put the strategy in writing. It must be committed to memory; the reason should be obvious to you."

"Yes, Chief Peta I understand," Jonathan responds. "But I did bring my notes about the past history with me, as you instructed."

"Good," replies the chief, "that is important for two reasons: First, to be certain that it is under your control at all times; second, because you will be required to provide it to tribal leadership at some time in the future. It will serve as secondary proof that you are the fifth-son."

Jonathan is eager to discuss the strategy with the chief, but first he has a question that has intrigued him for most of his life. He takes a deep breath, and draws on all the courage he can muster.

"Chief Peta, before we get started on strategy, I have another question for you. May I ask it now?"

"Yes, my son. I know you have questions; you have been patient throughout your entire quest. Together we have built a lot of trust and respect for one another. You are blood of my blood, and I am proud of you. What is your question?"

Jonathan straightens his shoulders indicating his respect and honor for the chief. "Prairie Flower introduced you as her father. According to my reckoning, that would make her the sister to Quanah Parker and Pecos Parker. Is that correct?"

"Yes, Jonathan, that is correct." Chief Peta further explains, "Her name is Topsannah which means Prairie Flower. She passed from this earth at a very early age, after she and her mother Cynthia Ann Parker were kidnapped and taken to the white man's life."

"So that is why she has taken such a special interest in me?" Jonathan further asks.

"Topsannah always hated the bickering between her brothers, and she did everything she could to bring them together. She has been planning for this quest for four generations. Finally, her wish is about to be fulfilled." Jonathan thinks that he can see a hint of a tear in the old chief's eyes.

"Do you have any more questions, my son?" Chief Peta lovingly asks.

"No sir, I think I am now ready to plan and move forward. Your explanation and answers have given me much strength and determination." Jonathan is humbled by this very personal dialogue with his third great-grandfather.

"To plan the strategy we must know what we want to accomplish," is Chief Peta's opening remark. "Jonathan, do you know what you are to accomplish?"

"Yes, Chief, I am to join the Quanah Bananah piece which you buried, to another piece; a piece that I know nothing about."

The chief's rejoinder is short and direct, "That is only part of your duty. You are to bring the two sides of my family, our family, together. Never forget that!"

Continuing the tutorial, Chief Peta says, "Here are the facts that you have to work with: You know that you have access to only a part of the key. The complete key is both parts of the Quanah Bananah. You must locate the other part of the key.

"After locating it you are to present the two parts of the key to the tribal council. There will be a question asked of you. That question is: 'What is the key?' You must give the correct answer. Do you know the answer?"

"Yes," Jonathan answers, "it is: The Quanah Bananah is the key."

"No, Jonathan, that is incorrect. You must think back, and give me the exact words."

Jonathan is bewildered as his mind retraces the episode of six years ago.

Sir told me that the Quanah Bananah is the key. That I must always remember it because he would never say it to me again. Oh my gosh, have I forgotten part of it? It has been on my mind a lot all of these years.

Chief Peta speaks, "When you go before the tribal council, it will consist of only a few of the leaders and medicine men. But one or two of them are secretly members of the To-sah-wi Alliance.

"They will want you to fail. You will have only one opportunity."

He pauses as Jonathan absorbs what he hears. Then, "If you fail to say the exact words in the correct order, they will cancel your request to be recognized as the fifth-son. The Alliance will have permanently succeeded in their quest of destruction.

"But if you state the phrase correctly, the entire council will know that the Fifth-Son Prophecy has been fulfilled."

Mesmerized by the exactness and the precise language to be used, Jonathan asks, "But, how do they know what the key is?"

"The oldest and wisest medicine man of the council will be able to read the inscription written on the Quanah Bananah. When you state the key correctly they will all know."

"And if I state it correctly, what happens to the To-sah-wi Alliance?" Jonathan asks Chief Peta.

"The To-sah-wi Alliance will fail. It will dissolve and cease to exist because their purpose will have been defeated. Their sole purpose has been to destroy the Comanche Nation's governing body, and replace it with a counterfeit government."

Again, Chief Peta pauses momentarily, "They will not be able to succeed because the two factions will have been brought together.

"There are some who have lost their inheritance and freedom, because they chose allegiance to the Alliance. But many have been born into the Alliance; they are just waiting for you, the fifth-son, to expose the bad so they can escape the captivity.

Jonathan is gaining a knowledge that he had certainly not expected.

So, the bad exists because some will voluntarily choose to belong; they make secret oaths to destroy the good at all costs. They chose evil!

Others are born into the bad, and they are held captive to it because they are taught that bad is good! I am beginning to understand ...

Oh, my gosh! I just described Sir! He wants to be released but cannot succeed because he is held captive. When I finish my quest, he will be freed along with countless others who are in the same situation!

"Chief Peta, I get it! I am beginning to understand!" Jonathan cries aloud. "My father, Sir, is one who is trying to escape the captivity of the To-sah-wi Alliance isn't he? I must succeed in order to free him."

The Chief displays a brightened countenance, "Yes Jonathan, you are correct. You have caught the vision and meaning of your quest. If you multiply your personal connection by thousands, you will begin to understand the magnitude of your mission.

"Now think back, what is the key?"

Jonathan opens his mouth to speak, then hesitates and thinks for a moment, then answers, "Quanah Bananah is the key."

"That is right," says Peta. "You must not add or take away from those five words. The Medicine Man will confirm that you have stated it perfectly. There will be other questions, and it will be important that you have the notes you have written, with you."

Jonathan makes his commitment, "I understand, Chief Peta. I will remember the key, and never leave the notes behind. They will be with me wherever I go."

Peta Nocona continues, "That is good! Now let's talk about the artifact. Each piece of it contains a portion of the inscription. The pieces fit together with interlocking protrusions. When together, they form an oval shaped object."

"But ... but where is the other piece," Jonathan asks. "Does the Medicine Man have it already?"

"No, it is for you to obtain. And therein lies the most dangerous part of your quest."

"Then how do I get it?" Jonathan's face shows concern and doubt as he asks the question.

"When this visit to the mound is finished, getting the other piece will be the first objective to your quest's completion.

"You see Jonathan, I gave it to your mother's great-grandmother when she was a very young girl. The youngster became like a daughter to me after my wife, Cynthia Ann and my daughter Topsannah were taken from me.

"The box was known as the treasure, or the treasure box. Your mother came into possession of it legitimately."

Chief Peta takes a break as he observes Jonathan's countenance. In a few seconds the student looks into the eyes of the mentor; Jonathan displays an appearance of understanding, disbelief and horror all merging into one expression of rejection.

Jonathan exclaims in an escalating tone, "Am I to understand that my mother, Ma now has the box? Are you telling me that she is also a member of the To-sah-wi Alliance? Is that what you are saying? Is it!?"

"No, my son. That is not what I am saying," Chief Peta replies calmly. "But I am saying that I think your mother knows where the box is kept. Also, I am saying that the Alliance too, knows that she has knowledge of the treasure box.

"You have a two-fold challenge of protecting your mother. and at the same time safely obtaining the box. Once you have the box in your possession, you must quickly meet with the tribal council. Listen to the quiet voice ... always.

"The To-sah-wi Alliance is on the move now. They know their time is short, and will stop at virtually nothing to obtain the box. They are closing in as we speak."

Jonathan is shocked and shaken, "Wha … wha … How do I find and … And get the … Treasure … The box?"

Chief Peta Nocona looks intently at the young man and says, "You are to trust Michael. He will know when to make a move; he will be your guide, your messenger and your friend.

"He will be here at the end of tomorrow's session, and will take you where you need to be."

Jonathan sits in wonderment and awe.

I am to protect Ma, all the while trying to find the box without creating trouble with Sir. In the meantime, the Alliance is out to get me … and any cost! Ohhh …

Chief Peta concludes his instructions, "You and your parents are in much danger. Sir is a troubled man, and must be approached carefully. The bad, that is the Alliance, is close to accomplishing their evil design. Be ever on guard!"

DENNIS BOYD CALL

The Great Spirit provides
Nature gives us substance to live
Mortality gives us opportunity to succeed

CHAPTER 16 – ADVERSARY

As the second sun rises on Medicine Mound for Jonathan, he is enthralled by the crispness of the air and the clarity of the sky. His experience of two days ago awakened him to the value of a change in focus.

It is early, and I think I have time to walk around the flat top of Medicine Mound again. I want to consider all that I have learned regarding Ma and Sir.

Their connections to the To-sah-wi Alliance is disturbing to me, and maybe the newness of the day will help with my perspective regarding them.

Shedding the comfort and warmth of his sleeping bag, Jonathan slips into his denim jeans and long sleeve shirt. When camping, he had learned to sleep with his socks on; so he adds his heavy sneakers, and is ready for a casual walk around the large clearing.

Jonathan, taking a bag of trail mix from his backpack, begins a counter-clockwise stroll. He looks to his right, westward out over the expanse of flatland below the mound.

It is so beautiful and clear today; I think this is a good sign. It is a sign that the things of the earth are organized, which means that the things of my mind can be organized also.

I need to sort out the roles of Ma and Sir in regard to my quest, and their possible activities in the Alliance.

I think that Chief Peta said yesterday that Ma is not involved with To-sah-wi Alliance but how could that be? She has a connection with the treasure box, she has ... or had possession of it ... That does not necessarily mean she is a member ... Or does it?

She clearly has inner conflict that she is dealing with ... Passed down from her mother ... She told Sir about it ... Sir has the box ... Ma gave it to him ... What will he do with it? ... The Alliance will get it ... I must stop him ... Change focus ... Walk around ...

He stops and looks at the plant life by his side.

The prickly pear is such an interesting and deceiving plant. On the exterior it is dangerous; it could do extensive damage to anyone who is careless or unaware ...

But I remember Ma making prickly pear jelly; it was delicious ... How could that be? I have read that the skinned prickly pear can be sliced and eaten ... that it can even help treat diabetes.

Jonathan turns to his left, and continues his casual early morning stroll. His thoughts return to his parents.

Can Sir be trusted? His entire life has been controlled by the Alliance. However, when he has had to come face-to-face with our family, he has done what is right for us. Is he sincere? What is he doing at this minute? Is he being kind to Ma?

Walking close to the overabundant brush in the area his mind is once again taken over by the plant life.

I wonder about the redberry juniper. Sir knows a lot about it. He told me that it thrives in the dry rocky soil here on the mound. I guess that is why it is so plentiful. It isn't very tall; I would guess about eight or ten feet high. After climbing the mound, I would have to say that it is difficult to walk through. The thought brings a smile to his face.

Having walked the west then the south sides of the top of the mound, Jonathan turns north, toward his campsite and today's meeting with Chief Peta Nocona.

Within his sight is the low growing horse crippler cactus, a type of barrel cactus.

One could certainly be crippled by one of these small plants. They are only a few inches in height as well as across.

It is important when walking these mounds to be aware of this small cactus that could do so very much damage. Sir has said that they produce the blooms in late spring and early summer. I can see a few wilted blossoms still.

Jonathan is approaching the end of his very pleasant little journey, so he steps up his pace; he doesn't want the chief to wait on him.

"Welcome back from your morning walk, Jonathan." Chief Peta's voice is light and cheery. "I have been watching you with great interest. What have you learned during your hour-long stroll? Surely, you gained some knowledge."

"Learn?" Jonathan gets a quizzical look on his face. "I was just going for a walk and enjoying the nice morning."

The wise old chief asks, "What were your thoughts as you pondered the prickly pear cactus?"

"Well," started Jonathan, "I thought about how it can be dangerous but at the same time if dealt with correctly, by removing the spines and skin, it can be made into a delicious jelly."

"So," begins Chief Peta, "the sharp spines may be there for protection, not for malicious deeds, correct?"

"Ahh ... yes, I guess so," Jonathan answers slowly.

"You see," explains Peta, "mankind is much like the cactus. We are not always what we seem to be on the outside. Some people are rough looking on the outside or appear mean because they have been mistreated. In reality they are really nice and sweet people, when you get past the exterior ..."

"And," continues an enlightened Jonathan, "some people are nice on the outside and are very bad on the inside. Correct?"

Chief Peta smiles and nods.

"But," says Jonathan, "there are people who look nice and are nice ... and there are people who look bad and are very bad ... so how are we to know which is which?"

"You have just stated the dilemma that you will be facing beginning tomorrow, and lasting until your quest is finished." The chief is deeply serious and his concern is notable.

"You see Jonathan, you know about all of the plants around you here on the mound, and you know what they are like. If you only knew the people you will meet as well as you know the plants, you would have no problem. But that is not so."

"But ... but ... there has to be a way ..." Jonathan states.

"My boy," replies the tutor, "you gained much of your plant knowledge because you were taught by your father. You trusted what he told you because you know him. The same can be said about people in general. When someone whom you know as well as you know Sir speaks a word about another person, you can usually be sure it is good information."

"But Sir has not been honest in everything with me ... and with Ma. He has deceived us both."

"What is your attitude now, right this minute, toward Sir?" Peta asks.

"I ... I feel good. He has been going through a lot of trouble and seems to be wanting to do the right thing. I do ... I feel good," is the answer offered to the hief.

"Jonathan, did you notice how you answered my question?" The experienced man reasons with Jonathan, "Two times you said the word, *feel*. Those are words from the quiet voice of the mind. It is important that you understand that.

"When you are honest yourself, you can trust and count on the quiet voice of your mind to guide you correctly.

"Sometimes, the voice will tell you to ask questions and search for confirmation. Sometimes, the voice will leave your mind confused and muddled; this is also a message for you. It is a message of caution."

Jonathan sits in deep thought, then speaks, "I have had Prairie Flower speak to my mind often. Will she always be the quiet voice of my mind?"

Thoughtfully, the chief says, "I cannot answer past the completion of your mission, Jonathan. Beyond that, it matters not who the voice is. The important thing is that you should always be prepared to hear the quiet voice of your mind.

"You are prepared now to proceed with your quest. Michael will be waiting for you when you return to the base of Medicine Mound. Remember that he will be your guide, and that you can trust him."

Chief Peta Nocona concludes the discussion with these words, "This will be our final meeting and communication until just before the council meeting.

"I wish you good fortune from the Great Spirit. I leave you with two thoughts that you are already familiar with: Truth – Honesty – Integrity are to always be your guide; and the second is to always listen to the quiet voice of the mind.

"Goodbye Jonathan, goodbye. Michael awaits you."

Practice with Principle
The man with both has but one face

CHAPTER 17 – ALLEGIANCE AND LAW

Back at The Big Trees, Sir sits in silence; his body is as though anesthetized. His mind tries to bring reason into reality and logic to his senses, but only mental incoherence is the result.

The box ... To-sah-wi Alliance ... I don't want ... What is the purpose ... My son ... My life, my Quanah ... Elizabeth hates that name ... Evil place ... The Alliance ... Evil ... What's in the box ... Who is ... Why do people ... Please, please, please ... Oh, why, why, why ...

His brain is in a whirl, and his body begins to shake. Tossing the box into the underbrush, Sir attempts to stand and walk around the small space amidst the trees, hoping to rejuvenate both his mind and joints. His legs are weak but he does succeed in moving about.

I don't want the box nor do I want whatever is in it. But I must report it to the Alliance ... However if I do, I will be destroying Jonathan, my Quanah, and I will not do that!

But if I don't tell them, the To-sah-wi Alliance will surely destroy us all.

Sir turns and looks toward where he tossed the box. As he does so, he is overcome with blackness; a splitting headache causes him to collapse to the ground. He softly implores, "Elizabeth, Elizabeth ... I need you, Elizabeth, please ..." His voice is muffled in the leaves beneath his face.

****

Having returned to their home from The Big Trees some time earlier, Ma is trying to busy herself with the mundane. Her thoughts are wrapped in Sir and his incomprehensible allegiance to the To-sah-wi Alliance.

Can't he see what he is doing to our small family? Doesn't he understand the evil that is being spread by them? I know he cares for us, and that he is worried about Jonathan.

Sir has to make a decision! It is either that Alliance or us. What does the box have to do with anything? It must be important; my mother and grandmother left their home because of it.

Ma turns the pillows on the living room couch for about the tenth time and adjusts the window blinds ... again. As she surveys the room for something else to alter, she hears a voice, it is coming from the direction of The Big Trees.

"Go to Peta. Go to Sir ... NOW!" She reacts immediately and is on her way to The Big Trees.

Rushing into the special haven of The Big Trees, Ma reaches her husband as he begins to stir. She kneels beside the large man and reaches to touch his forehead.

"Peta, are you alright? Can you tell me what happened?" She pleads, "Did you fall? Peta, Sir, please speak to me."

"I ... I don't know ... I have a terrible headache. Ohh, it hurts so much. What can I do? What can I do about Jonathan? How can I be true to everything?" His questions come haltingly, but they reflect his inner state of mind.

Sir continues, "Jonathan, Jonathan, we must protect Jonathan. We don't even know for sure where he is."

"Can you get up? Can you stand so we can get you to the house? Peta, are you able to get to your feet?" The voice of Ma is soothing and brings warmth to this troubled man.

Leaning on Ma, Sir is able to stand, and together they succeed in completing a long slow walk to their home, mostly in silence. Ma, however senses some sort of urgency from Sir; she becomes anxious to get him seated and comfortable, so they can talk.

"Peta, please tell me what happened after I left The Big Trees. Did you faint? ... Oh ... Oh my gosh, where is the box? We left the box in the trees!" Ma has gone from curious to anxious.

"I threw the box into the trees," Sir answers. "I don't want the box and I don't want to see what's in the box. No matter what I do, it will be the wrong thing for all of us."

His headache subsides significantly, and he continues, "Elizabeth, I honestly don't know what to do. If the box is valuable to the Alliance, I am bound by oath to tell them. If I even *think* it is valuable to them, I am bound by oath to tell them. I don't know what to think or do."

Ma begins to speak, stops as though to reconsider and then starts again, "Sweetheart, I understand you are under more pressure than I can imagine. But you must consider what means the most to you, and then make your decision. I cannot do it for you. Just know that I will not stay with you, and be married to you *and* the Alliance.

"It is beginning to get late, and we both could use some sleep. Stay here with me tonight and tomorrow you must either leave Jonathan and me permanently, or break with the Alliance permanently. It is a decision that must be made tonight." Ma is firm in her statement and solid in her resolve.

****

BAM! BAM! BAM! ... "HELLO, HELLO, IS ANYONE HOME? HELLO!" The noise reverberates throughout the house.

"Sir, wake up, wake up. Someone is banging on the door. Peta, please get the door!" Ma is shaking his shoulder and pleading for Sir to awaken.

"Huh? What is it?" He half asks and half states. "OK, OK, I'm coming." He looks at the bedside clock and sees that it is only 10:15 pm.

Groggily he stumbles to the door in his pajamas and opens it a crack. He peeks at the caller then opens the door wide, admitting two uniformed officers into his home.

Ma's anxious voice is heard from the doorway to the far side of the room, "What is it? Is our son alright? Is it Jonathan?"

"I am Deputy Herring, and this is my partner Deputy Anderson. We are from the Denton County Sheriff's Department. May we be seated?" It is the older of the two men who is speaking.

The four of them are seated in a conversational pattern, and Deputy Herring asks, "Is your son's name Jonathan Parker?"

"Yes! Yes!" Ma responds in a near scream. "What is wrong? Where is he?"

"I am sorry, Mam, but we need to verify some information before we proceed. Is your son on a trip to Quanah? And is he driving a dark green, nine passenger GMC van?" This time it is Deputy Anderson speaking, he glances at Herring, seeking approval.

Putting his large arm around his wife and drawing her close, Sir tries to be calm in answering the deputy's questions. "Yes, and yes to both questions. Can you please tell us what is going on?"

"Was ... Was ... Is your son staying at the Best Western hotel in Quanah?"

"Yes! Now please tell us what has happened!" says Sir in an increasingly demanding tone.

The two deputies look at each other; Anderson defers to his senior. Deputy Herring speaks, "I am sorry Mr. and Mrs. Parker, our office has been notified by the Hardeman County Sheriff's Department that your son seems to be missing. Jonathan has not been seen by the hotel personnel for two days ..."

Herring looks at Anderson in an apparent signal for him to speak, "His van is in the parking lot, and all four tires have been flattened. We are wondering if you could give us any reason someone would want to hurt or disrupt your son in any way?"

As his partner speaks, Deputy Herring surveys the room, his eyes seeming to penetrate every minute detail. Sir watches as Herring's head turns, taking in all that can be seen from his vantage point. He spends considerable time focused on the bookcase at the far end of the room.

What is he looking for? Does he think we have something to do with Jonathan's disappearance? Sir is becoming uncomfortable with this man's strange interest in their home.

Both men are brought to listen to Deputy Anderson as he concludes his dialogue, "We do not have any sure knowledge if your son is in danger, or if anything has happened to him. We will let you know as the investigation proceeds.

"As we said, the hotel people reported the van being parked there for two days without being moved; they have not seen Jonathan for those two days. It may be nothing. Be assured that you will be kept informed."

Ma is in tears and left speechless as she allows her mind its freedom.

Our son is in danger ... or even ... maybe ... something worse ... much worse!

The two officers of the law stand, and move toward the door to leave. They turn, then Deputy Herring says, "We will be in touch with you. If you hear from your son or learn anything about him, please call us immediately. Here are our cards with contact information."

With their hands extended they offer handshakes to the distraught parents. Herring shakes Sir's hand and holds it in a lengthy tight grip as his eyes fix searchingly into his host's eyes. Sir feels a sick, dark sensation at the non-verbal interchange.

Herring speaks to Sir, "I am sure we will talk again ... soon."

Choose your friends wisely
They are your second family

CHAPTER 18 – MICHAEL

On Medicine Mound, Jonathan feels the loss as Chief Peta Nocona bids him goodbye.

How can I ever get along without Chief Peta? He is my third great-grandfather, and he has taught me much. I will miss him for a long, long time. Will he have reason to visit me again someday? I hope he returns during my quest.

He rolls up his sleeping bag, attaches it to his backpack then places his other camping items inside. After making certain that the area is clean, he puts the pack on his back and begins the trek down the northwest side of the mound.

His mind is now free for reflection.

I still have Prairie Flower, or Topsannah to help guide me. Let's see, she would be my second great-aunt ... I think. My great-great-grandfather is Quanah Parker and Prairie Flower is his sister ... Oh no! I just thought of something!

Jonathan stops and turns to look back up the short distance he has walked.

I wonder if I will ever be able to return to the top of this wonderful, spiritual mound. I sure hope so, but Chief Peta may not be here to talk with me. I feel very lonesome already.

He turns back to continue his hike to the base of the mound where Michael is to be waiting.

From what the chief said, I think Michael will be with me almost constantly throughout the rest of my quest. I think that will be good. I like Michael, besides he seems to have a neat sense of humor ... Gosh, that is something that I really need!

The black Volvo is parked on the flat area near the natural spring that flows at the base of the mound. Michael and Jonathan spot each other almost simultaneously, and their arms go up in a wave of recognition.

"Hey, it's good to see you, my friend," calls out Michael.

"The same backatcha," responds Jonathan in a shout. "How are things?"

Michael laughs, gives Jonathan a high five and a fist bump then says, "Things are good and we have a lot to talk about. But first: it is good to see you, and I am happy to be assigned as your guide."

Inside the SUV now, Jonathan is sitting in the front passenger seat. He asks the obvious question, "So, what's next? Where are we going and what are we going to do?"

"I thought we could stop at Medicine Mound Depot Restaurant for something to eat," answers Michael. "Do you like fried pickles?"

"Never had'm before, but sounds like something I might really go for." Jonathan's interest is piqued, "I like'm cooked in my scrambled eggs! Cut up into little pieces, that is."

"Ok, we'll be there in a few minutes," says Michael, "In the meantime, let's recap what you need to get done, and how soon we need to do it. Especially since we know there will surely be problems."

Jonathan thinks for a short moment then begins a brief outline of the tasks as he sees them. "First of all, I need to find and get my hands on the other par ... Oh good grief! I don't have the first part. The part that is buried on top of Medicine Mound! I totally forgot about that!"

Michael laughs and says, "Rest easy, Bud. It would be foolishness for you to be responsible for that too, right now. You will probably come back during your quest. You shouldn't be concerned."

He continues, "Carry on, my friend."

Jonathan restarts his overview, "I need to get the second part of the key and arrange to meet with the tribal council. Then, as you said get the buried piece and after that, meet with the council. That's all there is to do. Sounds pretty simple, doesn't it?

"Of course," he backtracks, "I do not know where the second part is. I think it may be in the possession of Ma, my mother that is. The problem is, my father is a member of the To-sah-wi Alliance and I am not certain about Ma. I really don't really think she would be a member ... Gosh, I hope not!"

Michael nods his head, "Yeah, I kinda get the picture. We need to figure out how to approach that problem, alright." He slows the SUV, beginning a left turn into the parking lot of Medicine Mound Depot Restaurant, located just inside the eastern city limits of Quanah, along Highway 287.

Stopping the vehicle, and switching the ignition to the off position, Michael turns to Jonathan and says, "We will not talk about anything to do with your quest while in the restaurant. Our conversation must consist of only everyday things for everyday people. Any questions?"

"I have no questions!" says Jonathan, "I will follow your lead, sir."

Michael chuckles and replies humorously, "And don't you ever forget the *sir* part."

Entering the restaurant, Jonathan looks around at the patrons inside the place. Everyone seems involved in their own conversations and not interested in new customers coming inside. A good feeling of peace and security give him comfort.

They take seats fairly close to the door, and Michael positions himself to be able to observe the comings and goings of patrons.

They quickly place their order; then both of them place their elbows on the table, and lean in so they can speak without being overheard.

"So, Michael," Jonathan begins, "who are you, really?" Jonathan queries.

Michael shows a large grin on his face and answers, "You are getting a bit personal, I would say. But since you were brave enough to ask, I will tell you this: I am your guardian angel. Now, let's change the subject, okay?"

They continue their friendly exchange until their food order is placed in front of them. The fellows had ordered a fresh salmon salad for Jonathan and a mushroom and swiss burger for Michael, with an order of fried pickles to share.

"Wow!" exclaimed Jonathan, "That is a lot of pickle on that plate. It could probably make a meal all by itself!"

The man and woman in the table closest to them look over at the two young men and laugh. The man speaks, "They taste every bit as good as they look, too."

Jonathan turns toward the couple and chuckles. Suddenly, a loud clap of thunder startles the friends, drawing their attention to a window. An abrupt downpour of rain comes as a surprise to both of them, and apparently to most if not all of the other customers in the restaurant.

People begin to chatter across tables making it seem as though they have all been lifelong friends. Their comments all have to do with the suddenness and intensity of the storm outside. The lightning strikes are close, immediately followed by claps of thunder that shake the building.

"This is crazy!" exclaims Jonathan. "It was beautiful and clear this morning up on ... err ... when I woke up." He looks apprehensively at Michael, then looks around to see if he had been overheard.

The older couple who had spoken to them earlier look at Jonathan and glance at each other in a sort of raised eyebrow expression. The man slides his chair sideways to be closer to Jonathan.

In a voice that can barely be heard above the din of the outside storm, he asks, "Up? The only up around here are the mounds south of here."

The lady, having moved closer to the table of Jonathan and Michael says, "Can you tell us about the mounds, young man?

"We are from Longmont, Colorado and are doing research on Native American cultures and practices. Our purpose here is specifically focused on the Comanche; we understand that those mounds play a significant role in their lives, is that correct?"

"Uh ... Uh, I don't know much about that ..." Jonathan stammers as he looks at Michael for relief.

Michael jumps into the conversation saying, "We are from *down* near Fort Worth. I think he means *up here*, don't you Bruce? Not up on the mounds, right?"

"Bru?? ... Uh, yes. Yes, of course, that is what I meant. Sorry I guess the sudden storm kinda rattled my brain," replies Jonathan.

The man laughs while looking askew at his partner, "That's alright, It came as a great surprise to everyone. Looks like it is clearing up almost as quickly as it came. I understand that sudden storms like that are common in this part of the country."

"Yeah, they are," quickly responds Jonathan. A sharp kick under the table brings Jonathan to mental attention. He adds, "We have them during late summer down where I live."

"We need to eat and leave right away, Bruce," comments Michael. It is important that we get moving." He then turns to the server and asks for boxes to hold their food.

"Oh yeah we do, sorry Michael." Jonathan is embarrassed that he has been so open to the strangers who had moved close to them.

The man remarks, "Yes, we must be on our way soon, also. Which direction are you two headed?"

Michael jumps into the conversation and answers, "We must be getting back to Fort Worth soon."

The lady attempts to restart the conversation, "Before you go, can you tell us anything about Comanche history? I mean Quanah Parker was a famous Indian chief in his time wasn't he?

"We heard that he used to visit those mounds out there, is that true?" She points her arm to the direction of Medicine Mound.

"I'm sorry, Ma'am but we must be on our way." Michael is up and out of his chair, as he gives an urgent nod of his head to Jonathan.

The couple watch as the two quickly exit the restaurant ... they exchange a disdainful smile of understanding with one another.

Jonathan and Michael hurry to their vehicle, the rain-washed air is refreshing; the afternoon sun is again shining.

Being seated inside the SUV, Jonathan leans his head back against the headrest and moans, "Ohh, I feel sick … how could I have been so stupid. My mind was just not functioning at all. Prairie Flower and Chief Peta have both warned me to be cautious, and I totally forgot!"

Michael quickly turns the ignition switch, and the engine starts. They back out of their parking space then turn and head west toward into the town of Quanah.

Leaving the restaurant parking lot, Michael glances through the rear-view mirror, "Oh great! That couple is outside the place and watching us leave. Fort Worth is the other direction!

"I sure hope you learned something in there, Jonathan. You cannot afford to make those kinds of mistakes! Understand?"

"Yes! Yes, of course I understand," Jonathan answers his friend in a very subdued tone of voice. "I really blew it back there, and I know it. I am sorry, Michael."

"That's alright, let's just get on with your tasks and hope that nothing comes of it." Michael is once again using his gentle friendly voice, but with a renewed sense of urgency.

"We need to get to your hotel room, and map out a plan to complete your quest."

They drive in silence for several minutes until Jonathan comments on the *Welcome to Quanah* sign.

He says, "I wonder if they knew how true that statement is, when they put it on the sign."

"Huh, what are you talking about?" Michael asks.

"That statement under *Welcome to Quanah*: It says 'The Place Where Puha Lives.' I doubt they knew how very true that is! Power has two sides, hasn't it?"

Michael chuckles a moment, then the Best Western hotel appears on their right, and they make the turn into the parking lot.

"Well," says Jonathan, "at least my van is still where it was when we left the other morning."

Jonathan suddenly recalls the image of someone running away from his van.

I have totally forgotten about that. Did it really happen or is it just a figment of my paranoid imagination?

He says, "Michael, let's park as close to my van as possible. I want to make sure everything is okay."

Pulling alongside the green GMC van, Jonathan's heart sinks, "Oh, nooo! The tires are flat, I think all four of them are flat!"

He hurriedly exits the SUV and walks to the far side of his van; he becomes faint and leans against the vehicle.

Jonathan exclaims aloud, "NO, NO, NO! It was real. I saw someone running away from here the other night. This is what he must have been doing!"

White-faced and shaking, Jonathan returns to his place beside Michael in the SUV.

He speaks, "Michael, this is bad. Really bad. The bad guys are getting closer, and closer. What are we going to do? I am concerned about Ma and Sir. Are they alright?"

Michael replies with a reassuring voice, although he himself is feeling the pressure, "Things are going to be alright. Remember this, when you go for the good, the bad will try to intercede.

"The extension of that statement is this: When you are near the end of your good quest, the bad will accelerate its efforts to stop you!

"Jonathan, it is clear that you are nearing the end of your quest. You must not give up. Instead you must remain calm, keep yourself under control and move forward quickly."

"Yes, certainly, you are right," says Jonathan. "Let's hurry up and get to my room so we can figure out what to do."

Michael takes charge saying, "You go in now, I will park my car and come in shortly. I kinda' want to scope the area out before I join you."

Jonathan walks to the hotel's main entrance. Just as the automatic door opens, a slight squeal of tires is heard. Turning to see what is going on, he is shocked to see two police cars rapidly enter the parking lot. Jonathan is further taken aback as he also sees the familiar dark pickup parked outside of the Dollar General Store. It is in the expansive parking lot just across the street to the east.

Anita the hotel clerk is on the telephone, "Yes, just now," she pauses then says, "oh, about ten minutes ago, I would say. Okay, goodbye."

She hangs up the phone and welcomes Jonathan, "Well, hello there, young man. You have been gone for a couple of days. Didn't you think we would miss you?" Her voice was lighthearted and merry.

Jonathan replies, "Yes, I am fine. I had some out of town business to take care of."

They both look toward the door as two police officers enter the hotel lobby. The lead officer nods to Anita then turns to Jonathan.

"Are you Jonathan Parker?" he asks.

Jonathan timidly responds, "Yes, what is going on? Do you know about my tires?"

"Come over here and talk with us, please. We have some questions to ask you," says the younger officer. The three of them take a seat across the lobby, Jonathan dropping his backpack to his side.

"I am Deputy Chapman, and this is Deputy Wheeler. We are with the Hardeman County Sherriff's Office." It is Chapman, the older of the two officers who is speaking.

"Young man, the hotel reported your absence yesterday after seeing your van's condition ... I mean the flat tires. They checked your room and you were nowhere to be found.

"We have kept in touch with each other and you didn't return last night either. It is good that the hotel personnel show their concern."

Deputy Chapman leans forward and continues, "We would like to know just where you have been for the last three days, and two nights. Will you please share with us, what you have been up to?"

Jonathan sits in silence, searching his mind for an answer to the question; he wants an answer that will not compromise the quest.

What is your treasure?
That depends upon your need
Your need depends upon your heart's desire

CHAPTER 19 – THE BOX

Ma and Sir have spent an extremely uncomfortable night. The deputies left their home around midnight, and the distressed couple didn't even try to go back to sleep.

Their new day is made up of repetitive moving about, attempts at diversionary distractions and mundane conversations. Everything they say and do has been done several times during the day.

"We don't have a second car for us to go to Quanah," says Sir stating the obvious for about the sixteenth time.

"What would we do even if we did have another vehicle?" Ma is again the voice of reason. "We would probably get in the way of the investigation, and might even cause more trouble than we already have."

"We've got to hear something soon, or I will go crazy," comments Sir as he tries to fix something to eat.

"I cannot eat anything, why am I doing this?" he ask himself as he puts the slice of bread back into the plastic bread wrap.

Ma has much the same problem; she states, "Sometimes I think the clock is broken. The hands seem stuck and do not move. Oh, my Jonathan, where are you? Please, please get in touch with us. I think that I cannot deal with this much longer. "

"Well," says Sir, trying to lighten the mood a bit, "it says it is now six o'clock in the evening, so the clock is doing something."

She replies, "Yes, I know, but I just cannot focus … I have no more tears … Oh, please … please … " But her tears do flow again, freely.

Sometime shortly after six-thirty, a knock is heard, followed by a ring of the doorbell. Ma and Sir look at each other then they both rush to the door. Ma gets there first and opens the door wide. It is Deputy Herring from the night before.

"Good evening, Mrs. Parker. May I come inside?" He offers a polite tip of his hat as she steps aside, allowing his entrance. The deputy seems eager and reticent at the same time.

Ma says, "Please, please have a seat," motioning to the easy chair. She and Sir sit side-by-side on the well-used couch.

Ma continues, "Have you heard anything about our son? Is he alright? Where is he? Where has he been? Wha …".

The deputy raises his left hand, palm forward and says, "I do have some information. First, your son is safe, so please relax about that … There are other things we must talk about."

Sir, recalls the previous night's handshake, and the accompanying dark feelings he experienced. He looks at the officer with doubt in his mind.

"Jonathan is at his hotel in Quanah. He is being interviewed by the sheriff's department in Hardeman County as we speak."

Deputy Herring shuffles his feet and adjusts his position in the padded chair where he is seated. Then glancing around the house he hesitates; he wants to start a new conversation, but vacillates a bit.

Sir notices the somewhat uncomfortable hesitation of Deputy Herring. He knows that he and Ma must be extremely careful in the talk that is about to begin.

Sir asks, "What is it that you want to talk about? It's not about Jonathan ... is it?"

Herring clears his throat and begins, "There is something about a box. It is apparently very important to your son. What do you know about a box?"

Ma is startled, and looks anxiously at Sir. He places his hand on her forearm and gives it a squeeze; Herring notices the action. Sir then speaks, "Box? Did Jonathan say something about a box? What kind of box?"

"I only know there is something about a box. I have no information other than that," answers Herring.

"Well, we have several boxes around. Some have not been unpacked since we moved here. There are storage boxes as well. You need to give us more information for us to be of help." Sir shows some sarcasm in his comments.

"Does your son have some sort of treasure box?" Herring presses for information of some sort as he looks at Ma.

She responds, "I am not aware of Jonathan having any such box. He is not a collector, or anything of the kind."

The deputy turns back to Sir and asks, "And you Mr. Parker, do you spend a lot of time with your son?"

"Sure, our family spends a lot of time together. We enjoy each other's company, and do as many things as we can together. Why? Is that unusual ... or important?" Sir is getting impatient, and it is beginning to show.

Ma reaches over and pats Sir's leg as a sign to calm himself a bit. Herring takes note of the gesture and continues his questioning of Sir.

"I mean just you and Jonathan. What do you do together: I mean ... like ... do you go hiking together? Do you take drives together, and just talk? The real question is this: What kind of relationship do you have with your son?"

Sir looks at Herring straight in the eye, "We have a great relationship! We are best buds. Is that what you want to know? Or are you saying that he is involved in something that we do not know about? If that is what you mean, it is not true!"

Sir's impatience is growing, and Ma is becoming increasingly uncomfortable with the questioning; and with Sir's changing attitude.

"I just want to learn if there might be something that you do not know about your son ... or ... if there is some secret just between the two of you. Is there any such thing?" The question is pointed and somewhat accusatory.

"NO! Of course not!" Sir plants his right elbow on his knee, and points his finger at Deputy Herring.

Herring changes his posture, and looks at Ma, "And you, Mrs. Parker. Is there anything between you and your son that Mr. Parker is unaware of?"

Ma straightens her back and glares at the deputy, "Absolutely not! Our relationships with our son are honorable and good. And I think you have gone far enough in this interview!

"If you think we have done something wrong, then say so! What does all of this have to do with a simple box, anyway?"

"Thank you," Herring says coldly, "I certainly hope that Jonathan is not detained because of a *simple* box." He then stands and offers the customary goodbye handshake.

He says in conclusion, "I am sure we will be speaking further."

Ma, accepting his offer, takes his hand and says, "Well, at least I can thank you for letting us know that our son is safe."

Releasing Ma's hand, the deputy turns to Sir and offers the same gesture. Sir shakes his hand and looks Herring deep into his eyes.

Sir, having taken some control of his attitude, remarks, "Yes, thank you for the information. Do you know when we will be hearing from our son?"

Herring responds, "I think the Hardeman County officers will want to get a clear picture of all of your son's activities before he will be released. I will probably see you tomorrow. Goodbye."

Deputy Herring's parting look at Sir is penetrating, intended to send a message which Sir understands, but tries to not acknowledge.

The officer stands at the open door, then turns to face the troubled couple. He says, "I may be required to search your home with a search warrant ... unless, of course you will allow me to conduct the search now. Would you be open to that?"

"For a box?" they reply in near unison. "You don't even know what kind of a box you are looking for."

Herring gives his response acerbically, "I will know it when I see it."

Sir looks at Ma and Ma looks at Sir; it is clear that they both are thinking the same thing. "Well yes, if it is important, and if it will get our son home to us sooner. Come on back in, and conduct your search."

Deputy Sheriff Herring heads straight for the living-room bookcase and begins shuffling things about, all to no avail.

He seems disappointed, then gives this instruction: "You must not leave the house, in fact you are welcome to be with me as I go through each room. But if not, you must stay in this room while I complete my search."

"I will stay with you," states Sir. He looks at Ma who indicates she will remain in the room.

Forty-five minutes later the two men emerge from the final room; Herring is sweating and frustrated. He says, "Is your garage the only out-building? If so, is it locked?"

Sir answers, "Yes and yes. I will get the key." He glances at Ma who gives him a slight nod of approval and reassurance.

Herring leads the way to the garage; his gait indicates urgency as well as irritation. The two men arrive at the side door to the garage; Sir unlocks and opens the door, motioning Herring ahead of him.

"Hmm, not a whole lot in here is there?" The officer is both relieved and disappointed.

This won't take very long, but I probably won't find anything of interest, either.

Surveying the nearly bare floor of the garage, Herring's eyes focus on the pile of goods against the far wall.

That trunk over against the wall, underneath a pile of storage boxes is a good place to begin. I am sure that there is nothing suspicious on the shelves; just tools.

This stack of goods is made up of mostly plastic containers with a few small cardboard boxes. This won't take long.

After about fifteen minutes Deputy Herring is opening the trunk. Sir watches, and despite the fact that he knows the box is not inside the trunk, he is still a bit wary of Herring's action.

"Hmm," affirms the officer, "nothing here. I apologize for the inconvenience. Do you have any storage units anyplace?"

"No, what we have, you have seen," is Sir's response.

"Well, the department will advise you of any developments regarding your son. Actually, I have been assigned to the case and so it will probably be me who keeps in contact with you. Remember, if you learn anything further about him, let me know."

They exit the garage as Ma exits the house and joins them. She shows signs of relief at the apparent conclusion of the search.

"Okay, but you did say he is safe and in custody of Hardeman authorities, didn't you?" Sir is taking control of the conversation.

"Uh ... no, I think I said he is being interviewed right now," comes the reply.

"So, he is free to come home, if he chooses, correct?" Sir's further queries cause some discomfort within Deputy Herring.

"I think that will be the case unless there is some unexplained reason for his two-day absence. Well, I must be leaving now. You folks have a good evening." Herring quickly moves to his black Chevy van.

Sir and Ma watch as this officer of the law turns his unmarked vehicle around and leaves the premises. Once the van has been out of sight for few moments they look at each other and heave concurrent sighs of relief. They fall into an embrace; it is a mutual need that they each carry.

"Ohhh, I need to get inside and sit down!" Sir is in an exhausted condition, and Ma is overcome with a good feeling of liberation.

Shortly they are inside and seated in the living room. Ma is the first to speak, "Wow! Just what was that all about? Jonathan doesn't know about the box … does he? I have never mentioned it to him, at least not to my recollection."

"I don't think so. I didn't know anything about it until after he left last Saturday on his quest. There is no reason that he could have known." Clearly, Sir is pondering along the same thought line as is his wife.

Silent for about two minutes, Sir releases what he has been feeling ever since the first visit from the deputies. "Elizabeth, Deputy Herring is a member of the To-sah-wi Alliance. I saw it in him yesterday, and his action here today confirms it to me. That is the only way he could know about the box."

"Peta," Ma says, "do you realize what you have just done? You have made your choice … permanently. The allegiance you have held to the Alliance all of your life has just been broken. You are now a free man! There is no going back. Do you understand that?"

Sir replies, "Yes, Elizabeth, I do understand that. I also understand that we are now marked people. The scrutiny will be intense.

"Jonathan will be followed and hounded mercilessly. Further, you and I must never return to The Big Trees … at least not until Jonathan has completed his quest."

"Yes," confirms Ma, "I understand that. I am so thankful that you threw the box into the trees. But … But how will Jonathan get …"

Sir interrupts, "I am certain that all of the tutoring over the years, and whatever he is doing now will give him all he needs to know about getting the box ... that is, if he needs it."

Ma thinks about the whole situation briefly then states, "I will be so glad when this is all finished and we can be a happy family again."

She looks at Sir straight in the eye and continues, "We will be happy again won't we?"

Sir's hands begin to fidget; then a sudden realization hits him for the first time since Deputy Herring left. "I ... I hope ... I hope so ... I just gave up almost all of our entire income. I have no idea how we will survive financially."

Ma, in an attempt to lessen the bleakness of Sir's comment, says, "I have my teaching certificate, remember? I think that I will be able to get a job locally. It would mean no more moves, however.

"But I have already said that I will not move away from this area again .. of course ..."

Sir catches Ma's subtle little jab at herself and smiles.

She is so much fun and I love her with all of my heart. But, I still must carry the primary burden of providing for her. Actually, Jonathan will be able to take care of himself soon, so that will help.

He straightens his shoulders and speaks, "I know you will be willing to take a teaching job if necessary, and I will honor that. But I must fulfill my responsibility also.

"There will be some work that I am able to perform. Actually, it will be a huge relief to settle down and be normal human beings, I think!"

They hear a car pull into the graveled driveway; in a few moments the doorbell rings again .. twice. Hesitatingly, Sir rises and walks to the door, opening it slightly.

Privacy can be achieved
No matter where you are or who you are with
But it helps to be alone to fully enjoy the experience

CHAPTER 20 – THE ROOM

In Quanah, Deputy Chapman's query of Jonathan's whereabouts puts the young man in an awkward position.

The experience in the restaurant this afternoon was bad, and I handled it poorly. I must be on my guard all of the time. But I still must be honest.

"Well. I did some hiking and backpacking with a friend," replies the nervous young man.

"And your friend, where is he now?" Deputy Wheeler steps into the conversation.

"I don't know, he just dropped me off and left. Can we talk about my van and the damaged tires?" Jonathan wants to get off the topic about himself, but has difficulty getting it done.

"Yes," comments Wheeler, "we do need to address that issue, but right now ..."

Jonathan interrupts, "I am uncomfortable with the increasing foot traffic through this place; through this lobby. May we go to my room where we can have some privacy?"

It is Deputy Chapman who responds, "That is a good idea. We shouldn't take very long with this. You have not been officially reported missing, and as far as we can see you are not guilty of any criminal activity. The problem besides your tires, is your room. We do need to address that issue."

Jonathan is jolted by the comment, "What? What did you say? What is going on with my room?"

"Let's head on up there now. We can talk a bit on the way up," says Chapman.

They reach the elevator just as the door is closing. Deputy Wheeler grabs onto Jonathan's arm, stopping him from reopening the door.

"We want to ride up alone," he whispers into Jonathan's ear.

Giving the elevator button a moment to reset, Wheeler pushes the button that will call the elevator back to the main floor. It appears quickly, the three men enter the confined space as soon as the door opens.

Pushing the up button, Chapman looks at Jonathan and says, "So, Jonathan, where wer ..."

An arm reaches through the almost closed door. It automatically reopens, allowing a large man to push his way into the limited space. He makes eye contact with Jonathan while giving him a smile of recognition.

"Well, hello there young man," he says. "Where have you been? Your absence caused quite a stir around here. Are you alright?"

Jonathan swallows hard; he recognizes his next door elevator companion. His stomach suddenly becomes roiled which makes him want to throw up. But he responds, "I'm good ... A bit tired."

The group reaches the second floor and the door opens. Deputy Chapman asks the interloper, "What do mean, his absence caused quite a stir?"

"I mean just that. It seems his absence created quite a stir." The hotel resident from the room next to Jonathan, sounds a bit miffed at the deputy's query.

"I'm sorry," says Chapman, "I am Deputy Chapman and this is Deputy Wheeler. We are from the Hardeman County Sheriff's Office. I'm just curious what you mean, and what you know about his absence. Please tell us your connection."

Jonathan is deep into his own thoughts. *I am getting to really like this Chapman fellow and his buddy, Wheeler. Oh, wow! This is what I have just been taught about who I can trust. I must be listening to the quiet voice of my mind. This is cool!*

"And what is your name?" Jonathan hears Deputy Wheeler ask the man following their short conversation.

"My name is Herring, Louis Herring. I'm sorry I couldn't be of more help. I guess I am just a friendly old gadabout. I kinda took a liking to this young man when I checked in the other day."

Louis Herring pauses before going past Jonathan's room to his own. He looks at the deputies, and says, "Actually, I feel kinda close to you fellas, my brother is with the Denton County Sheriff's Office. Deputy Richard Herring is his name; you guys wouldn't happen to know him would you?"

Chapman laughs lightly and answers, "No, 'fraid not, Denton is light years away from here. At least for us it is. Well, good to meet you, Louis. Have a good evening."

The deputies exchange glances, and at the same time Jonathan has a fleeting thought about his friend and chauffeur, Michael.

I wonder where he is right now ... I sure hope he doesn't show up while the deputies are here. It would be very tough trying to explain who he is! Probably saw the deputies come into the hotel and is waiting for them to leave.

The deputies and Jonathan move into Jonathan's room. Instantly, Jonathan realizes something is dreadfully wrong; some of the drawers are pulled open and the bed is in disarray. He is frozen as he stares into what has been his home for several days.

"What in the world … What is going on?" He looks first at Chapman, then Wheeler. "Is this what the guy next door was talking about?"

"You didn't hear him?" asks Wheeler.

"Well, yes, kinda', but I … I was absorbed in some thoughts of my own, I guess," was the only answer available to Jonathan.

He continues, "Please, gentlemen, have a seat."

Deputy Chapman speaks, "This is what we started to tell you about in the elevator when the fellow caught the door and stepped in.

"The housekeepers found your room in this condition. It was the morning after your first night away. We had them leave it as is."

Wheeler continues, "It was then that someone reported your tires had been flattened. City police were called in, and it was decided to turn the matter over to the sheriff's department. Here we are!"

"Okay," says Jonathan thoughtfully, "so what am I supposed to do? I am really confused … I have never been involved in stuff like this before."

Chapman is ready to take charge of the conversation, "First of all Jonathan, you are *not* under suspicion of doing anything. We believe you are purely a victim.

"While you and Officer Wheeler were speaking, I notified a local service to come and put air in your tires; they will be here shortly. In the meantime, the three of us need to work on solving the mystery."

I know these men are my friends! The quiet voice of my mind is telling me so. But I cannot reveal my quest. Jonathan is finding his comfort zone.

"Jonathan," asks Wheeler, "can you tell if anything is missing from the room?"

"Well, I really don't have anything. I took my wallet and some papers with me; nothing was left behind. So nothing could be missing." Jonathan is thoughtful in his response.

"How did anyone get into my room, anyway?" he asks.

"Good question!" It is Chapman who is speaking, "We believe that the perp stole a master cardkey ... or worse yet, an employee of the hotel may have done it. It is our opinion that someone has an illegal copy of a key.

"The real question is this: Why? Why would someone want to do this to you, that is the question. Do you have any idea?"

Jonathan tries to come up with a reasonable answer but his mind seems scrambled. "Maybe ... Maybe it is a case of mistaken identity? Could that be the it?"

"That is possible. In fact, that is pretty much what we have decided." Chapman looks at Wheeler who nods in agreement.

"Our report will be written that way, but if anything happens or if you think of anything else, you are to call one of us. Okay?" Deputy Chapman hands a business card to Jonathan; Wheeler does the same.

There is a knock on the door. Deputy Wheeler walks across the room, and peers through the peephole. He opens the door, allowing the automobile service technician to enter.

Chapman smiles and says, "Howdy, Marc. Is everything alright? Was any damage done or did someone just let the air out?"

"No nails or slit tires," comes the answer from the young husky man. "Looks like a simple case of minor vandalism … Or maybe not minor …"

He glances at Jonathan before addressing the deputy, "Sorry, there is no such thing as *minor* vandalism, is there? You have told me that a million times!"

They all chuckle as Chapman laughingly says, "And I suppose I will still be saying it to you for the next ten years, won't I?"

"Do you have a bill for our friend here?" Deputy Wheeler is asking the question, motioning toward Jonathan.

"No," says Marc, the good natured mechanic. "I think I owe him a freebie because I called the vandalism *minor*. I will just charge the next guy twice as much."

They all shake hands and Marc leaves the premises. Jonathan says, "What a nice guy. I like him."

"Yes," says Officer Chapman, "Marc is the kind of man you can trust. He is honest and reliable. Plus, he helps us out a lot."

Sitting quietly for a few seconds, Chapman breaks the silence, "So, what will you be doing next, Jonathan? Will you be returning home or do you have other plans?"

Oh boy! Those are sideways questions; and now comes the hard part. Or at least the questions that will be hard for me to answer.

Jonathan tries to brace himself for the onslaught of personal interrogations.

"Well," Jonathan begins, "I'm not sure. Have my parents been told anything about this stuff? I mean, do they know I was reported missing?"

Chapman, with compassion says, "Our department has kept it to ourselves intentionally. We have done this because your room has been reserved indefinitely, and the hotel has told us that they believe you are working on some sort of project.

"For you to be gone was not a concern, until the flat tires on your van were discovered. That is when the hotel notified the authorities."

Wheeler adds, "We saw no reason to place undue concern on your parents. But given another day or so, we would have called them."

"So, what can you tell us about your project? And your immediate plans?" Chapman pursues the question again.

He sure seems determined to get something out of me. Somehow I need to get them out of here, find Michael and figure out what we are going to do.

Jonathan makes a quick decision on the answer to Chapman's question.

"I think I will return home tomorrow. My little reason for being here probably isn't all that important anymore. I just needed to get away and make some personal decisions.

"My parents love me a lot, but I am now eighteen and need some personal time and space." Jonathan feels pretty secure with his answer; it was quite direct and truthful.

Deputy Chapman nods, smiles and answers, "Yeah, I think that is a good idea. Parents need to know that their kids are alright. How about you call them on your cell phone … or the hotel phone right now while we are here? Let them know you will be returning home tomorrow. Will you do that, please?"

"How many children do you have, Officer Chapman?" Jonathan almost feels like he is being instructed by Sir.

The sense of responsibility is so very familiar. I can hear Sir saying the very same thing to me! In fact, he reminds me of my father in so many ways.

Chapman laughs and says, "Dead giveaway wasn't it? We raised a family of five; three girls and two boys. They are the very best! Of course that is a parent speaking!"

"Now, here is the phone, Jonathan, please make the call." It is Wheeler who is speaking, "I too am a father, and what Deputy Chapman has said is true. They need to know that all is well."

"Sure," Jonathan responds, "I am most happy to talk with Ma and Sir."

Seeing the mystified look on the faces of the deputies, he quickly adds, "That is how we have always addressed each other. My father is Sir, my mother is Ma and I am Jonathan. Sometimes Sir calls … Oh, never mind. It's just a nickname."

Before either deputy has a chance to ask about the nickname, Jonathan takes the phone off the hook and dials "9," waits for a tone then punches in Ma's cell phone number.

He is not required to wait long. It seems the phone barely rings and Ma answers.

"Hello, Hello," her voice is hurried and anxious.

"Hello, Ma? This is Jonathan. Are you alright? You sound like something is wrong. Is Sir alright? What is going on?"

"Oh, oh! SIR, PETA! It is Jonathan! It is Jonathan! Here I will put it on speaker phone. Hurry Sir, it is Jonathan!"

Jonathan hears Sir's strong voice, "Jonathan, are you okay? We were told that you were missing, and then we were told that you are safe! What is happening? We need to know."

"Wait … Wait a minute! Did you say you were told that I was missing?"

"Yes, that is what we were told. Two deputies visited us with the news; then one deputy returned, and told us that you are safe," the parents answered simultaneously.

Deputy Chapman is now hovering close to Jonathan who looks up at him in disbelief. Chapman motions with his hand to keep asking questions.

"Ma, who told you that? Did you say some deputies were there?" he pauses, waiting for an answer.

"The main one's name was Herring. He and another officer came the first time, and then Herring was alone the second time." Ma's voice is still excited but filled with relief.

"You say the deputy's name was Herring?" Jonathan is getting the rhythm of asking questions.

Deputy Chapman turns to Wheeler and says, "Get over to Louis Herring's room next door NOW! Do not let him leave! NOW,GO!

Deputy Wheeler was already on the move. He knew just what to do without being told, but Chapman needed to say it anyway.

"Ma? Are you still there? Are you alright? I will be coming home tomorrow sometime."

Sir answers, "Jonathan ... Quanah ... Ma is alright. She is so relieved that she cannot stop crying. She will be alright. Please hurry home, we both need you, Jonathan. We love you, Son. Thank you for calling."

"Thank you, Sir. I love you too, tell Ma the same. Goodbye."

Deputy Sheriff Chapman looks at Jonathan and gives him a thumbs up. He says, "Don't leave until I tell you it is safe. I am going to help my partner."

Chapman is gone to the room next door for several minutes, then returns with a sense of urgency. "Jonathan, did you say you have been with a friend who dropped you off here?"

"Yes," replies Jonathan, "that is correct."

"Can you get in touch with him to pick you up tomorrow?

"For your safety we are going to impound your van as soon as our friend Marc can come get it. That way, no one can get to it.

"We will hold it overnight, but you will need for your friend to pick you up, and bring you to the county impound lot tomorrow. Do you think you can arrange that?"

"Yes, I can do that," is Jonathan's reply, confident that Michael will be in touch very shortly.

"Good," says Chapman as he scribbles an address on a business card. "Here is the address of the lot. Please call me at my office in one hour to confirm your plan. By the way, what is your friend's name?"

Oh no! That is a question I cannot fully answer. Jonathan is panicked momentarily.

"His name is Michael, that is all I know him by. But he will be contacting me soon, he said he would do that."

Whew, that was close! Jonathan breathes easier.

"Okay, that will do for now. We have more important matters at hand. When you come to the impound lot tomorrow, plan to spend an hour or so with my partner and me; both you and your friend."

Deputy Chapman is clearly onto something that involves me, but he is not going to take time today to explain it.

Jonathan is fully engaged in two matters: The immediate possibility of danger, and the quest that he is on; the quest he has been in training for, for almost his entire life.

Prairie Flower, where are you?

DENNIS BOYD CALL

True friends are there when needed
True friends are willing listeners
True friends are rare

CHAPTER 21 – THE FRIEND

Jonathan sits wearily in the overstuffed chair in his room, and wonders just what is going on next door.

There is definitely a connection between the Herring brothers, and any message to my parents that said I was missing. Louis may have told his brother that I was missing ... but why?

Then it dawns on Jonathan.

Both of them must be members of the To-sah-wi Alliance. They are trying to extort something from my parents. Does that make any sense? Wow! This is heavy stuff!

Prairie Flower, I need your help. I need Chief Peta's advice. And I need my friend Michael ... I really need a rest ... And so does my mind ...

Moving to the disheveled bed, he fluffs a pillow and lies down. Just as he does, there is a knock on the door.

"I sure hope this is Michael," Jonathan says aloud to himself.

He opens the door and instead of meeting his friend eye-to-eye, he looks down a few inches at a lady holding some sheets and towels.

"They said that your room can be made up. Shall I do that now?" asks the lady from housekeeping.

"No, no thank you. I am good. Tomorrow morning will be just fine," he responds a bit perturbed. "I only need some sleep, thanks very much."

Jonathan returns to his bed, and makes himself comfortable again. He begins to enter a sleep state when another "knock, knock" occurs.

"Alright, alright, here I come. Seems a person cannot get a good night's rest around here." His grumpy side is now showing.

This time he remembers to look through the peephole; he is pleased to see his friend Michael. Gladly, Jonathan opens the door wide; he ushers the fellow he has come to consider his partner, into the room.

Jonathan exclaims, "Am I glad to see you! What took you so long?"

"Sorry Jonathan, but I had to wait until the officers left, then I had to be certain that they were out of range. But, your van was towed away. Did you know about that? What is it all about?"

"Well," begins Jonathan, "let's sit down before I fall down, and I will tell you what it is all about."

Jonathan recounts all that had happened with Deputy Chapman and Deputy Wheeler. He shared the encounter with the man in the next room, and he shared the phone call to Ma and Sir.

Jonathan then wrapped it up with the statement, "I think that Louis Herring next door is a member of the Alliance, along with his brother in Denton County.

"Further, I think they are trying to extort something from my parents, but I have no idea what it would be.

"The final thing is that they hauled my van off for my protection. It will be in the police impound lot until tomorrow when you and I are to go pick it up. Last thing is that I have promised the deputies and my parents that I will be going home tomorrow. How does that all sound to you?"

"Well," Michael begins, "since you asked, it all fits perfectly in my opinion. Your immediate mission here in the Quanah area seems finished, and you have not received any instructions to do otherwise. Have you had any conversation with Prairie Flower during this time?"

"No I haven't, and that is strange. She is usually right there and ... Whoa ... Whoa ... wait a minute!"

Jonathan becomes animated as his shows excitement. "I have had strong impressions in my mind. The quiet voice in my mind has told me several things!

"Deputies Wheeler and Chapman are trustworthy, they are my friends. The guy next door and his brother in the Denton County Sheriff's Office are not my friends; they are part of the To-sah-wi Alliance. They are trying to stop my quest!

"Prairie Flower has been the quiet voice of my mind all along. Why didn't I recognize it? Wow, that is really profound and exciting!"

Michael laughs and adds, "And *important*; don't forget that. She, or someone like her, will always speak to you as long as your quest, your journey is honorable.

"Jonathan, you have been taught well by Sir and Ma. Sir has been a conflicted man all of your life, especially since your episodes at The Big Trees began.

"But he is a man of integrity, and a man who will make the correct, although difficult decisions when he is faced with the necessity."

"Yes," responds Jonathan, "I have seen him from the mound. I have watched as he has fought with himself over his connection with the To-sah-wi Alliance, and his devotion to Ma and me.

"Chief Peta Nocona has taught me a lot about Pa's internal struggle. Pa has held two opposing loyalties for many years. He did not fully know the trouble that would cause, until my quest began.

"He and Ma had to come to some understandings. But they have a strong marriage and everything is going to be alright. I am certain of that."

Jonathan sinks into a thoughtful mode.

Should I share this thought with Michael? He is my friend and Chief Peta said he can be trusted. But ... I also know that I am to be in control of my quest.

Michael should be able to assist me, especially if my conclusion is correct ... but what if I am wrong?

"What is it, Jonathan? You are hesitating a bit. Do you have something to say? I can tell that there is something in there trying to come out."

"Yes, Michael," Jonathan begins. "There is something. I have come to a conclusion. I believe that Sir has the other part of the artifact. But ... But if I am correct, I could be putting his life ... and the life of Ma in jeopardy."

Michael looks questioningly at Jonathan, "Okay, lay it on me. You have come to a breakthrough, have you?"

"Well," Jonathan decides to open up, "I learned up on the mound, that Ma has had a box in her possession ever since Gramps died. It was handed down since the days of Peta Nocona. She kept it hidden because it represented bad things to her.

"Sir ... Sir ... He was almost threatening to her ...So much so that she gave him the box. She gave it to him ... That's ... I think that's all I know."

He reaches over to his backpack, then places his hand inside and retrieves the envelope. "Prairie Flower is supposed to let me know when to open this envelope. At least, that is what you said when you delivered it to me. I am wondering about that; she has not talked with me for a long time. Anyway, it seems like a long time since we have spoken."

Michael smiles in an understanding way, "Yes, that is what I said. Prairie Flower will never let you down. The important thing for you, for *us* to do, is to lay plans for what we must do now. She will speak at the right time. Remember what you learned about faith?

"You see, when you have a friend like Prairie Flower, you do not need to worry about her duties. You must focus on your own responsibilities. That way, everything will fall into place."

"Okay! Okay! You are right, of course," Jonathan says as he inwardly laughs at himself. "Tomorrow is a big day for us.

"I need for you to pick me up here at the hotel at about nine-fifteen in the morning. We then go to the county impound lot, and spend an hour or so with Deputy Chapman. Then, I must return home to Ma and Sir. Beyond that, I am totally in the dark!"

Michael grins as he speaks, "So what I am hearing, is that you are firing me as your companion after I get you to your van. Is that it?"

"NO!" exclaims Jonathan. "I was just figuring that your errand would be complete. The next step is for me to get the box and then meet with the tribal council ... but I sure don't have a clue as to how to get the box! Besides, maybe the artifact is not inside; then what?"

"Let's look at the scenario that you just presented," says Michael in a serious mode.

"Your van is a target for the Alliance. They all know it, and will recognize it. Maybe Deputy Chapman will hold it in custody for a few days. While the Alliance may know a little bit about my car, it is not as prominent."

Michael continues, "I can drive us back to your home, and have the Quanah segment of your quest behind us. We will be able to figure out how to get our hands on the box during the drive. I have a feeling that we will know exactly how to do it. How does that plan sound to you?"

"You have a marvelous way of simplifying everything," Jonathan says. "How do you do it?"

"Easy," is the rejoinder. "But isn't it time for you to call Deputy Chapman, and tell him what we would like to do, so he can be prepared?"

"Yep, sure is. Thanks." Jonathan lifts the hotel telephone to his ear, and dials the necessary numbers as he looks at Deputy Chapman's business card.

"Hello, Deputy Chapman, here." Just his voice comforts Jonathan.

"Hello, Deputy, this is Jonathan Parker. I am calling to let you know that Michael and I plan to be at the impound lot around nine-thirty tomorrow morning, will that be alright?"

"Actually, Jonathan, I think it will be better if we meet here in my office. I will explain when we meet tomorrow, and nine-thirty will be just fine."

"Great," says Jonathan, "see you then." He hangs up and nods approval to Michael.

Over at the sheriff's office, Deputy Chapman looks across his desk at Louis Herring and says, "They will be here at nine-thirty in the morning."

Chapman glances past Herring to Deputy Wheeler who quietly rises from his chair and leaves the room.

Putting all of your eggs in one basket
Is rarely a good idea ...
Even if you also own the basket

CHAPTER 22 – THE DEPUTY

Earlier, back in their home in Denton County, Sir has just responded to the ring of their doorbell. With the door ajar, he recognizes Deputy Sheriff Herring.

"Yes, Deputy, what is it now?" Sir's impatience is clearly showing and the officer takes note.

Herring speaks, "Sorry to bother you again, but may I come in for just a few minutes?"

"Yes, of course. Come on in." Sir turns to Ma, "It's Deputy Herring ... again." Sir turns his back to Herring and raises his finger to his lips, an indication for her to be cautious in speaking with the officer.

Ma scowls, shrugs her shoulders, and begins to leave the room.

"Please, Mrs. Parker, would you mind staying with us? I will only take a few minutes of your time." Herring assumptively takes a seat and motions his hosts to do the same.

"I just need to clear up a few facts that I am not certain about, if you don't mind. He went to Quanah a few days ago, correct?"

Ma and Sir nod simultaneously, awaiting the next question.

"Can you tell me what his purpose was in going up there? I mean, why did he choose Quanah in particular?"

Ma defers to Sir, having decided she would not answer any questions unless forced to.

Sir says, "He is preparing to go out on his own, and went to Quanah to be alone and plan his future."

"And he took your only family car, is that correct?"

"Yesss," Sir draws out his one-word response, then adds, "is there a problem with that?"

"No, no problem ... but what if you and Mrs. Parker needed to go someplace, but were unable because of no transportation?"

"I cannot imagine what that would have to do with anything Jonathan might be involved in!" Sir is beyond impatient and fully perturbed.

"Well, they probably don't have anything to do with each other, I'm just curious. What kind of future is he looking for? I mean is he going to go to college, or is he looking for a job? What are his plans? What are his special interests?"

"Mr. Herring," Sir speaks defiantly, "you are here searching for something, and you think we will spill out some information that we know nothing about. In fact, earlier you said that you didn't know what it is either, but that you will know when you see it. That is totally irrational, and I think you should leave now!"

"Mr. Parker, please don't threaten me. I am an officer of the law, and I am on official business. Your son was missing, and I am trying to get to know him so that I can assist getting him home. Anything that I can learn will be important.

"I will leave for now, but rest assured, I will be back and will expect your total and complete cooperation. Goodbye for now!"

Herring lets himself out of the house, and leaves the premises in haste.

Ma, who seems to have held her breath throughout the entire visit speaks first, "What in the world was that all about? What do you do you suppose is in the box? That is what he is after, isn't it"

Sir stands, walks to the door, and looks outside to be certain that Herring's car is really gone. He heaves in a large amount of oxygen, and blows it out in a huge sigh of relief.

"He is trying to get me to say something that he can take to the Alliance. If he can get me riled up enough, and cause me to make some kind of mistake, they will come after me with a vengeance. I must … we must be very careful!"

Ma's cell phone rings. She doesn't recognize the calling number, but decides to take the call anyway. "Hello, hello," she tries to calm her voice, but isn't very successful.

She listens for a moment and tries to understand what is being said. Disbelief and gratitude are intermixed in her mind. She is both mystified and thankful as she exclaims:

"Oh, oh! SIR, PETA! It is Jonathan! It is Jonathan! Here I will put it on speaker phone. Hurry Sir, it is Jonathan!"

Several minutes later, the phone call is completed and the gratified parents are still sitting in silence, their minds and bodies weakened by the flow of energy so recently expended.

Finally, Ma is able to voice her thoughts and feelings, "He's coming home. Our Jonathan is coming home tomorrow. Oh, I need to see him. Can you believe it? He's coming home tomorrow!"

Sir looks at his princess with compassion mingled with concern, "Yes, he is safe and coming home tomorrow. However, we are now being watched every minute of every day. We cannot have him come home, but I don't know how we can stop him.

"That phone call verifies that Herring is part of the Alliance. He is, and has been lying to us right from the start. The To-sah-wi Alliance is baiting us, and trying to stop our son before he goes any further ... Hmm, interesting questions Jonathan asked, I think."

"Yes, he did seem a bit shocked. But ... But what can we do?" Ma asks. "I think we are powerless aren't we?"

"They are hoping we will try to do something that will expose all three of us. I think the best thing for us to do is this: Do nothing other than our normal daily activities.

"We must not indicate that we know Jonathan is alright. We must continue to be concerned for his safety, especially whenever that deputy is around. And I suspect that he will not only be *around* us, but will be all over us until we make the fatal mistake that he is looking for."

Ma makes a somewhat lighthearted observation, "Well, it shouldn't be difficult to show concern for his safety. We are certainly in that category!"

Sir observes, "Yes, but you can expect Herring to lean on your emotions and motherly care for your son. He can be merciless, and I expect him to not hesitate to show his true commitment; not the commitment to upholding the law, but his commitment to the To-sah-wi Alliance."

"Do you think Herring is alone in the sheriff's department, or that there are others involved with him?" Ma's mind suddenly expands to recognize the possible magnitude of the issue.

"I don't know, but my feeling is that he is working alone in this department, but quite possibly has someone in Quanah as a contact. It could be in their department, or just someone who is active in the Alliance."

Ma looks admiringly at her husband, "Sir, Peta, I am so very proud of you for what you have done today. You have placed everything in the proper perspective and prioritization. We will overcome the evil of the Alliance and hopefully never hear of them again.

"You remember what you have always taught Jonathan? The part about the quiet voice of your mind?"

Sir nods and says, "Yes, I remember it very clearly."

"I am hearing it now," says Ma. "I am feeling calm, and at peace. I think the voice is telling me that everything is going to be alright. It is saying that as long as we remain calm and alert, Jonathan's quest will be successful. I am still not certain how it all fits together, but I know he is, and will be safe."

"I agree," confirms Sir. "We must not leave the immediate space around our home. Not only must we not visit The Big Trees, but we must not even acknowledge them.

"Jonathan is being led, or tutored, or something, and through this he will somehow gain access to the box if it is important."

Ma snuggles into Sir's arms and thoughtfully asks, "If over the years you have reported Jonathan's special place, The Big Trees, don't you think they will know about the current place?

"And further, If they know about it won't they be asking you about it? Or maybe even go searching there?"

"Yes," is the reply, "except Herring is acting pretty much on his own, and is hiding his affiliation with the Alliance. Until they are ready to expose themselves, he will not go that direction. In fact he may not know specifically about The Big Trees.

"If my theory is correct, he is dealing with a personal informant from the Quanah area. They are trying to build their personal influence by stopping Jonathan together. They are treading down a dangerous path themselves. Herring cannot afford to report his activities to the To-sah-wi Alliance at this point."

Ma asks, "So you think that neither the sheriff's department or the Alliance know what he is up to right now?"

"Yes," says Sir with confidence. "That is what I am thinking. Also, Herring's partner, what's-his-name, is a minor player. He was clearly the junior officer, and not even aware of what was going on during their visit. I doubt that he has any connection to the Alliance."

Ma is absorbed in the verbal illustration being painted by her husband. She thoughtfully asks, "Do you suppose that neither of those men are really deputy sheriffs? Could they be imposter deputies?"

"Holy cow!" Sir sits up straight and performs a fist pull. "That's it! Elizabeth, you have hit on the truth! They are renegade members of the To-sah-wi Alliance who are independently trying to stop the Fifth-Son Prophecy from happening.

"Somehow, they have learned of Jonathan's quest and are trying to make names for themselves. You have solved the questions in my mind.

"We must let things play out on Jonathan's schedule and not interfere. Herring wants us to slip up on something; therefore we must only play his game up to a point, and not be intimidated by threats or coercions. He and his little buddy are complete frauds!"

Challenges in life are but tests
Obstacles in life are but challenges
Overcoming obstacles means we passed the test

CHAPTER 23 – TEST

Jonathan and Michael are still in Jonathan's hotel room when the telephone rings. Jonathan answers in a voice that displays hesitancy, "Hello?"

"Hello, Jonathan. This is Deputy Wheeler; this message is short and urgent. Deputy Chapman and I want you to meet us at the impound lot tomorrow morning at eight o'clock, instead of the office at nine-thirty. Is that clear?"

"Uhh, yeah, I guess so. What is going on?" Jonathan is trying to be both trusting and careful.

"Chapman just took your call, and signaled me to call you back immediately. Don't ask questions. Just you and your friend meet us at the lot at eight o'clock. See you then. This is important! Goodbye."

Michael looks at Jonathan's stunned face and asks, "What was that all about? What is going on?"

"That was Deputy Wheeler," says Jonathan robotically. "He said that we are to meet him and Deputy Chapman at the impound lot at eight o'clock in the morning. I have no idea what is going on. I'm not sure it is legitimate! What do you think?"

"I think that we need to consider and talk about everything we know," answers Michael in his confident, analytical manner.

"First of all: Do you trust Wheeler completely? You have indicated that you do. Are you still feeling that trust?"

Jonathan responds, "Yes, I believe I do. My mind is clear and not muddled ... Yes, I do trust him."

"Good! Then the plan is set. No need to second guess anything. Now all we need to do is make our plan fit theirs. Right?"

Jonathan laughs and says, "Like I said, you sure know how to simplify things! So, our plan was to arrange for Marc to keep my van impounded for a few days and travel to my home near Ponder in your SUV. I think that is still a good plan; I just hope Deputy Chapman will buy into it."

"I agree," encourages Michael. "I also think that we have friends in those two men that goes beyond mere friendship. They may even be trying to trip up the Herring brothers. Did you notice how quickly they moved on Louis Herring? It was just like nails drawn to a magnet."

Jonathan purses his lips, whistles, then says, "I sure did notice how quickly they acted!

"Sooo, tomorrow our steps are: First, we must sell Chapman on the car idea; second, we must determine our next course of action while we are driving to Ponder. It will take us about two and a half hours to make the trip. We should be able to make plans in that much time. Wouldn't you say?"

"Yes, okay," says Michael, "I will pick you up tomorrow morning at seven-thirty. I will be at the side door again. It is still important that we be very careful.

"Now, let me take everything that you don't need before you leave in the morning. You are traveling light however, aren't you?"

Jonathan thinks momentarily, "Yeah, I only have some dirty clothes, everything else is in my backpack, and I will keep that with me. Here, I will put the clothes in this laundry bag and you can have it. Good thinking.

"By the way, where are you staying? Do you live around here somewhere?"

Michael just smiles as he turns to leave. At that moment they hear the chime of the elevator signaling that someone is either arriving or leaving. He looks through the peephole in the door, "Oh my gosh," he whispers, putting his finger to his lips.

"Herring just got off the elevator. I had totally forgotten about him! Why would they release him?"

"What?" whispers an alarmed Jonathan. "What do they think they are doing? Let's rethink our plan."

Michael returns to his place in the desk chair, and puts his head into his hands. "We must trust the deputies. But ... why ... Why would they ..."

Jonathan, unexpectedly looks up, and over at Michael, "They probably didn't have any legal reason to hold him. Even if they did, and our theory is correct they are giving him some loose rope.

"Michael, the deputies are trusting us as much as we are trusting them! Let's talk a little more."

"Yes, you are correct." Michael quietly agrees, then continues, "The elevator is a dead giveaway. Herring is right next door, and so you must not use the elevator when you leave tomorrow."

"Good thinking. Actually, perhaps you should leave by the stairs this evening. What do you think about that idea?" Jonathan asks.

"You may have a good idea there. Let's consider our alternatives. I leave now, and you stay here is our present plan.

"Another idea is for both of us to leave tonight but that presents two problems: First, where would you stay? And second, what if someone, especially hotel staff or the deputies need to contact you.

"The third alternative that I see is for me to stay here with you tonight, and we both leave quietly, early in the morning.

"Gosh, I'm getting tired of whispering everything I say, but we must do so."

Jonathan, listening thoughtfully, whispers his own observations, "I like the third alternative, but where will you sleep? I have dibs on the bed."

"Stop being funny, I cannot laugh quietly," giggles Michael. "I can sleep on the floor, the easy chair and ottoman ... or in the bathtub."

"Okay, You do whichever you want. There are extra pillows right here and a spare blanket in the closet. I'm going to turn the TV on so that Mr. Herring next door will know that I am in my room."

Jonathan flips the television on and searches for a suitable station. He settles on the Home and Garden channel.

"That should be harmless enough," he mumbles with a snicker.

Jonathan scribbles a note to housekeeping, using the hotel notepad and pen. He thanks them for their efficiency, then lays a five-dollar tip on the note, securing both with the clip on the pen. He ends the note with: "I look forward to returning tonight."

The two young men who have quickly become good friends are both soon asleep; Jonathan in his bed, and Michael in the easy chair with his legs stretched out on the ottoman.

Jonathan, you are smart ... You have a good memory ... You make correct decisions ... Your parents are proud of you ... Continue to listen to the quiet voice of your mind.

Jonathan rolls over and turns the television off; he smiles as he sinks deeper into sleep.

Suddenly, it seems, Jonathan is awake.

"Michael, it is five-fifteen," Jonathan whispers to his friend. "I think we should be on the move as quickly as possible. It is very early, but I just heard Herring's shower start. Let's get the jump on the day."

"Huh? Oh, good. No shower for me. I will be ready in three minutes," says Michael, overcoming sleepiness quickly.

"Me too," Jonathan whispers back. "Let's get out of here now, while the bad guy is showering and cannot hear us."

In five minutes the two fellows are silently closing their room door, and moving toward the stairwell located at the far end of the long hallway. Jonathan is carrying his backpack and Michael has the bag of dirty laundry under his left arm.

They quietly make it to the emergency exit. On their way down the stairway, Jonathan stops and puts up his arm to halt Michael.

He says, "There is an exit door right at the bottom of the stairs, on the main floor. It is rarely used, and goes basically nowhere. Let's go out that door and walk around the back of the hotel.

"It will be dark, and we should make it to your car without being seen. Where are you parked, anyway?"

"At the east end of the hotel in an out of the way spot. I did not want anyone to make any kind of connection to either of us."

"Great move, my friend," responds Jonathan. "We should be able to get out of the immediate territory without being noticed. Okay, let's go."

Reaching the main floor exit door, Jonathan pushes on the panic bar as silently as he can, and opens the emergency exit. There is an audible click, but fortunately the door is in a secluded area of the hotel, and no one is within hearing distance.

The two emerge from the hotel, successfully exiting the building. They make their way around the rear, to the opposite end of the hotel where the car is parked.

"I think we are in good shape, Michael. We are ahead of the plan by a couple of hours, but when I heard his shower start, I decided that Herring is up to no good. He probably plans to keep an eye … ahem, an ear on us … and report to his brother in Denton County."

"Well," comments Michael, "despite the fact that I could have used a few more minutes of sleep, I think you are correct. Herring is a bit of a snake.

"If he follows up on what Deputy Chapman told him, he won't be expecting us to leave the hotel until around nine o'clock. We should have a good hour, maybe two hours jump on the bad guys."

Jonathan says, "Yep, we can be almost home before they even start to watch for us on the road. For now, how about we go to the impound lot and wait for Deputy Chapman? Who knows, he may even be early."

"Okay Christopher Columbus, you have the address of the impound lot. Where are we going?" Michael is his typical self.

Jonathan reads the address aloud as Michael puts the information into the GPS of his Volvo.

"We are on our way," Michael cheers. "It is in the northwest part of town and will only take a few minutes to get there."

It is shortly after six a.m. when they arrive at the designated address.

The sign on the small building at the front of the lot indicates it is a storage lot; the place is surrounded by a tall sheet metal fence. A light is glowing behind the blinds from inside the office. They pull into a vacant lot on the opposite side of the street, and stop.

Jonathan makes a suggestion, "Let's see if there is a more private place, rather than parking in clear view."

Just as Michael is about to turn the headlights back on, a sheriff's department car approaches from the opposite direction, and parks in front of the storage facility.

"Hold on, Michael, let's see if that is Deputy Chapman. It's still kinda dark outside but maybe I can recognize him."

No one gets out of the officer's car for several minutes, until another official vehicle arrives and parks alongside.

Both drivers emerge from their cars, then stand between the cars while engaging in a lengthy conversation.

Jonathan speaks with hesitation, "I think those officers are Chapman and Wheeler, but it is difficult to tell, with them standing between the cars."

At that point a third vehicle, a dark pickup pulls into the parking space marked *reserved*. It is a familiar dark pickup and Jonathan's heart sinks; his stomach suddenly feels sick. They watch as the driver of the pickup walks toward the officers who emerge from between their cars, and begin to talk with the new arrival.

"Oh, Michael," Jonathan chokes as he speaks, "those officers are Chapman and Wheeler. The third guy is Marc, the owner of the tow truck. But ... But ... The pickup is the ... It is the one that has been shadowing me ever since I first arrived in Quanah."

Taking a step into the dark
Is sometimes the only way
To get to the light switch

CHAPTER 24 – THE REVISIT

After another moment of stunned disbelief, Jonathan is able to find some words, "I am afraid that we are in huge trouble! We have been so very cautious … And yet, we are in serious danger. I think … I think that … I don't know what to think … The truth of the matter is that I am totally confused!"

Michael is dumbfounded. He leans back in his seat and moans. "Oh my gosh! Jonathan, how could this possibly have happened? There is something really wrong with this picture; we must figure it out.

"Tell me about the pickup. What are the circumstances, and how has it hampered your activity?"

Thinking back, Jonathan's mind is filled with recollections of the numerous incidents, all the while briefly relating them to Michael.

"There was the initial contact: The near miss on 287 when the pickup screeched near me as I crossed the highway. I thought it was probably just a sloppy and careless driver, until later.

"After that first episode, it seems like the pickup was always parked in front of the hotel whenever I returned. As soon as I got out of my van, it would hurry and be gone. It raced away as though the driver wanted to be seen."

Michael listens carefully to the descriptive portrayal of events leading up to this moment. Jonathan can tell that his friend is processing everything he hears.

"Jonathan," Michael clears his throat as he begins to speak, "do you remember the first encounter that you had with me?"

"I sure do! I thought you were a total nut job!" responds Jonathan.

Michael continues, "Yes, I know, and do you remember that I told you that I needed to get your attention in a dramatic way? I had to do it that way to make an impression ... and also to help raise your awareness to the ever-present dangers that surround you.

"Jonathan, think about the possibilities of this situation, the here and the now."

Jonathan closes his eyes and rests his head against the back of his seat as he processes.

I'm trying to take it all in. Just what is Michael saying to me and how does it apply? What am I missing?

This is so very critical, and I know our plans have been good. My mind is nothing but a huge muddle! ... Wait ... That's it, my mind is muddled which means that I am drawing the wrong conclusions!

"Michael, are you saying that the pickup ... That Marc, the tow truck owner is on our side? Are you saying that he got my attention, and kept showing up just to keep me alert?"

"Well," says Michael, "it seems plausible to me, and it fits the pattern of your learning, doesn't it?"

Jonathan grins and answers, "Yes, I guess it does. Let's join my three friends across the street, and either prove or disprove that theory."

Jonathan and Michael watch from across the street as the three men enter the small office building. Michael speaks, "We have a lot to get done today, and it has to be done without any missteps; especially what we are starting now!"

They look at each other and take deep breaths as Michael turns the ignition of his SUV to the on position. He pulls across the street, taking a parking place beside the dark pickup.

Jonathan states the obvious, "We are very early, almost an hour early. I hope they will be ready to get on with it."

Giving each other a fist-bump, Michael says, "I think our theory is correct, and they will probably be very happy to get a jump on the day."

The office door is unlocked so the two walk in. Marc, hearing the outer door open and close, quickly appears at his personal office doorway. He speaks, "Yes? Wha ... Oh, it's you, Jonathan! Hey you guys," he calls out, "it is Jonathan and his friend.

"You are early, we just got here ourselves a few minutes ago. The deputies are here in my office. Come on in."

The deputies are standing when Jonathan and Michael enter the inner office. Jonathan says, "We know we're early, but we were impressed to leave the hotel early to be ahead of my next door neighbor. I hope that is alright."

"That is perfectly alright," says Deputy Chapman. "Actually, it is better than alright. It is smart that you made that decision. This will give you a big jump ahead of the bad guys."

Jonathan makes the introduction, "Guys, this is my friend Michael. He has also been my ride provider."

"Good to meet you, Michael," all three of the hosts greet him warmly. "We appreciate you for stepping up to the plate and helping Jonathan out."

Chapman begins to ask a question, "How long ..."

Jonathan quickly interrupts and says, "We have a proposed change to previous plans and ..."

Deputy Wheeler interrupts Jonathan with this: "We think it is important that you know something else that we discovered yesterday.

"We checked with the Denton County Sheriff's Office and learned that they have no Deputy Herring. The Herring brothers are only imposters. They are working together, against you."

Michael responds, "We kinda have that figured out. But we think it is important that you hear what we have to say first, because of the time element."

Deputy Chapman holds up both hands, "Wait a minute, sounds like we have plenty of new information to go around. Let's have some order to this.

"Jonathan, please tell us what you two have come up with. Just know that I agree that time is very important, but so is accuracy."

Jonathan clears his throat and says, "We propose that you keep my van impounded for a few days. The Herrings will be looking for it on the road. Michael and I will drive to my home in his SUV. While they may know about it, I doubt they will be on the lookout for it."

Deputy Chapman stares at Jonathan for several seconds, his mouth agape. He then says, "That is genius. There will be a double fake for them: Time and vehicle. Wonderful!

"Marc, can you hold the van inside your workshop for a few days? Long enough for these fellows to do what they need to do?"

He turns to Jonathan and asks, "How long will Marc be required to hold your van?"

Jonathan is somewhat shocked by the favorable response he received from Chapman, "Uh, ... Probably only a couple of days, three at the most is my guess; that is if we have no problems. Otherwise, I don't know."

Marc, having enjoyed the rapidity of the change of plans, jumps right into the conversation, "Yes! I can do that ... Except, not here. I rent indoor storage space down the street; that'll do much better."

Deputy Chapman extends his hand to Jonathan and says as they shake hands, "It is quite clear that you are on a very important mission, otherwise no one would be trying to stop you. Hopefully, you will be able to be successful.

"I would be very happy to hear from you when all is done. Do you think you could do that?"

Jonathan's mind is swirling; he is happy, surprised and gratified. "Absolutely, I will do that! Thank you so very, very much."

He turns to Marc and declares, "You have certainly kept me on the alert these past few days, Thank you, also. Thank all of you for your help."

Marc, being surprised simply states, "So you figured it out? My actions, I mean. You are really on top of it!"

Deputy Wheeler speaks, "Jonathan ... Michael, remember this, there are more good guys out there than there are bad guys. Sometimes it is hard to tell the difference. We must learn to listen to the quiet voice of our mind."

"Well," declares Chapman, "this is a nice party but you must get on the road. Drive carefully, and good luck on your quest. Again, drive safely."

Being settled in Michael's car, and back on Highway 287 driving eastward to Wichita Falls then turning mostly south, the two friends have time to think about what just happened.

Jonathan says, "Interesting two references by Deputy Chapman, 'voice' and 'quest,' I think."

Michael agrees, "Yes, that is what I thought. I wonder if ..."

They drive in silence for several minutes then Michael picks up the conversation again, "We need to discuss what we are going to do after we get to your home."

"Yes, we do," responds, Jonathan. "This may sound a little strange to you, but I have been having strong feelings that we should not go straight to my home."

He pauses while he processes more thoughts, "I would really like to go to my special place. I call it The Big Trees. That is where I first met Prairie Flower, and is where I have been tutored for the past thirteen years."

Michael's interest is piqued. "So, are you saying that there might be some new insight gained by going there first?"

"I don't know what to expect," answers Jonathan. "It's just that it is a place of peace and comfort for me. But ... we do need to see my parents on this trip. There are a number of things that must be done before this whole thing is finished."

"Okay," says Michael, "Let's list those things. That will help us put together a plan."

"There you go, simplifying things again!" Jonathan laughs at his own propensity to overburden his mind with random issues; issues that just seem to pile up, creating a mental backlog. *Ugh, I hate it when that happens.*

"Alright," says Jonathan in an admiring tone, "I will start, and you fill in the gaps.

"First, we must locate the treasure box and see if the other part of the artifact is in it.

"Second, we need to see Ma an …"

Michael stops Jonathan in mid-sentence, "Just list the items that *must* be done in order to complete your quest. Seeing your parents is not vital to your quest…"

"It will be, if the artifact piece is not in the box," says Jonathan in an argumentative tone.

"Okay … Okay, I'll concede the possibility. Put the visit in the list as a dotted line event. But, I have a serious safety concern about that, just for the record."

Jonathan thinks for a moment about the relatively short time he has known his friend: *Michael not only simplifies, he analyzes. The more I am around him, the more I like the guy.*

"Got it, I agree." Jonathan starts again, "First, find the box!

"Second, verify we have the piece.

"Third, return to Medicine Mound and get the original piece.

"Fourth, meet with the tribal counc … Oma' gosh. I haven't even given that a thought. When and where do they meet? I hope we don't have to go far away for a meeting!"

Michael makes a more urgent observation, "Possibly the most critical thing we need to be doing right now, is being alert for any one following us. We are probably way ahead of them right now, but we still need to be on the watch."

Michael continues, "As for the tribal council, I imagine that either Prairie Flower or Chief Peta Parker will advise you how to find the meeting.

"Your quest is partially putting the pieces together for the good of the Comanche Nation, but it is partly to teach you faith and trust in your errand. In other words, as long as you are pursuing and fulfilling your errands, you will be led in the right direction to properly complete your quest."

Jonathan sighs, "You are right ... of course. Everything in its own due time. Correct?"

"You got it, my friend. Now why don't you lean back, and think about all of this; I will alert you when we are close to Krum. We are probably only about an hour away."

"Ahhh, This is what I love, a comfy reclining passenger seat." Jonathan reclines the seatback to the maximum, lays his head against the headrest and closes his eyes. Shortly he appears to be sleeping, but in reality his mind has gone into recall mode.

Remember, always listen to the quiet voice of the mind ... Truth Honesty and Integrity ... Faith ... Always remember this, I will never say it to you again: Quanah Bananah is the key ... go for the good, the bad will always try to intercede ...

... Good luck on your quest... Always ... The Big Trees ... You are Smart ... The box ... You ... That's me ... That's Jonathan ... Chief Peta ... Medicine Mound ...Cactus ... People are good ... People are bad ... How to tell which is which ...

Jonathan, this is Prairie Flower. Please listen carefully. Stay the course and you will find the artifact. Stay the course ... Stay the course. Continue to listen to the quiet voice. Stay the course ... The quest ... Soon finished ... Quiet voice ...

Jonathan opens his eyes but remains in reverie. *My mind is clear, I recognize the feeling of warmth throughout my body, and I know we are on the right path.*

He ponders the route they are taking for a few moments, then he turns to Michael and speaks. "I feel we should not drive close to my parents' house until after we have been to The Big Trees.

"I will direct us past our turnoff, we can then circle around and approach The Big Trees from the south. Are you good with that?"

Without hesitation, Michael answers, "I am totally good with that. It sounds like you have been directed, or at least have been listening to the quiet voice."

"Actually," says Jonathan, "I think it was a combination of the two. After we go to The Big Trees, it will probably be alright to visit Ma and Sir for a few minutes. Then we must return quickly to Medicine Mound.

"It might be possible to be on the road before the Herring brothers even realize we have been around."

"We've just passed the town of Henrietta, how would you like us to proceed?" asks Michael.

Jonathan answers, "Let's continue on to Rhome, then take 114 due east over to 156. We can turn north, and come into our place that way."

"Okay, Bud, you are a great navigator. Let's do it."

Within the hour, they are on Highway 156, headed north toward Ponder. After driving a few short miles, Jonathan directs Michael to turn on a graveled county road. Soon they are winding slowly through the countryside.

Jonathan says softly, "Pull over and stop in that grassy area ahead. I know this seems very surreal, and I don't know why I am talking so quietly, but you stay with the car.

"I want to be alone in that small grove right over there. It is hard to see, but our home is just a short walking distance beyond that group of trees." Jonathan points ahead and to his right.

"Those are The Big Trees. I don't think that I will be very long, but if you see anything suspicious, give me a toot of the horn."

Michael, wanting some clarification asks, "So, to get to your home, is there an intersection ahead of us that takes us there?"

"Yes," says Jonathan, "and if someone, such as 'Deputy' Herring comes to our house from Krum, he would probably approach from the other direction."

"Sounds like a plan," observes Michael. "Actually, it sounds like a good plan, and I will be right here waiting when you return. Do you have any idea why you are going there, to The Big Trees?"

"Nope, I just have the incredibly strong impression ... No ... Not exactly true. I heard from Prairie Flower ... I think ... while you thought I was sleeping on our drive. What I heard was 'stay the course.'"

Jonathan thoughtfully continues, "The 'course' would be what we have already discussed. The decision for me to be alone in the trees came to me later. Okay, I'm on my way, see ya' later. I don't think I will be gone long."

He hops over the fence and proceeds across the pasture.

I wonder what reason there is for me to come here first, before going home. Maybe Prairie Flower wants to give me additional instructions. Perhaps ... I wonder ...

He approaches the trees.

Gosh, since I'm on the opposite side of the trees, I am not certain where to enter. I think my place is over to my right ... Yes!! ...

Jonathan steps into his personal sanctuary.

DENNIS BOYD CALL

The visual is what one sees
The obvious is how one perceives the visual

CHAPTER 25 – THE OBVIOUS

Earlier that morning back at the Best Western in Quanah, Louis Herring rises early.

Jonathan will probably be on the move soon, and I must listen carefully for his departure.

It is important that I keep my brother informed of Jonathan's movements so he can watch for him back in Ponder. At some point, the treasure box will appear, and we must get possession of it!

Herring relaxes on the couch in his room and listens. The couch backs against the wall separating his room and the one Jonathan occupies.

I will not turn on the television but will sit here, silently working on my laptop. That way I will be able to hear when he awakens.

Eight o'clock arrives, and Herring becomes concerned that he has not heard any movement from next door.

Jonathan is supposed to meet the deputies at nine-thirty so maybe this would be normal. After all he is young and probably likes to sleep in ... On the other hand he needs to gather his things, and be prepared to leave town.

I've got to find out if he is still in his room! How can I do that without raising suspicion? What in the world is going on?

Let's see, he is to be at Chapman's office at nine-thirty which means leaving the hotel shortly after nine. It will soon be eight-thirty. He should be up by now and moving about. What ... How ...

Herring leans back and tries to concentrate on the room next door; he is listening for any sound that will indicate activity.

It is almost nine. I suppose I could drive to Chapman's office and hang out, just watching. Actually, I see no other way.

This is not good, Herring thinks to himself as he leaves the hotel.

There is something really wrong here; what is it? Could he have left early? If so, why? His friend was to pick him up, and I would have heard them ... Panic starts to take over Herring's mind.

After driving to the sheriff's office, he finds an inconspicuous spot to park his car. It is a place where he can see everyone who enters and leaves the building.

Unless Jonathan came really early, I should be able to see when he and his friend arrive. They will then arrange to get his van out of the impound lot and be on their way to Ponder.

It's nine-thirty ... Something is very, very wrong ... or ... or ... NO! It can't be. I have been tricked! Marc ... Did you? ... I'm going to your place right now!

Immediately, Herring starts his car and is on his way to Marc's office, arriving in short order.

Well, at least the dark pickup is parked in its regular place ... which is a good sign. I cannot see over the fence to know if the van is still here, but I sure hope it is!

He enters the towing and storage facility's small office building, then moves stridently to Marc's personal office.

He is met at the door by Marc. "Hey Louis, what can I do for you?"

Louis Herring glares at Marc as he speaks in a demanding voice, "What is going on? Do you still have Jonathan's van? He was supposed to be at Chapman's office this morning, and he didn't show up! What are you trying to pull?"

Marc looks blankly at Herring and calmly responds, "I am not in charge of Jonathan, or his van. I do as I am instructed by the sheriff's department. If you need information, talk to them."

Herring is infuriated, "You watched him as he traveled; you were at the hotel every time that he arrived there. You reported to me when those things happened. You should have told me about the van, and what was going on! YOU BETRAYED ME!"

Marc, maintaining his composure responds, "Yes, Mr. Herring, I did the things you just mentioned. I did them because you asked me to ... but I also did them because Deputy Chapman approved it.

"You see, I have not bought into your attempt to put Jonathan in jeopardy. The things I did were very harmless to him. Actually, it helped raise his awareness to the various dangers that surround him.

"You are assuming that just because I agreed to do a couple of things for you, that I have no character or self-respect."

"Why you traitor, you have misled me and the entire ..."

Herring's face is red with rage as he speaks. "I trusted you. You said you would report everything Jonathan did."

"No, Mr. Herring, You asked me to do two specific things. One, you asked me to harass Jonathan on the highway, and let him be aware that I was doing so.

"And two, you asked me to be at the hotel every night when he returned, then let you know that he knew, that I was there. I did both of those things."

Herring, his anger increasing says, "You knew what I wanted all along and you lied to me. You are in serious trouble with me and … and …"

"And what Mr. Louis Herring?" Deputy Chapman and Deputy Wheeler emerge from the hallway. "Just who besides yourself and your brother, is he in trouble with?"

Herring, surprised and totally incensed turns around and looks toward the office door. "Who … Why … What are you two doing here?'

"Mr. Herring," replies Deputy Chapman, "we will ask the questions. You said that Marc had mislead you and the entire … something. Just who are you speaking of?

"You also said the he is in trouble with you and someone else. Just who are you referring to in your threats?"

"I'm not talking! I'm not talking to you or anyone else!" says Louis Herring adamantly.

"Okay, if that is what you wish," concedes Chapman. "But tell me this: Just why are you trying to stop Jonathan from whatever it is that he is doing?"

Herring fixes his glare first at Chapman, then Wheeler, then Marc before turning his gaze back to the senior deputy, saying nothing.

Deputy Wheeler enters the questioning, "Have you spoken to your brother in Denton County this morning? I believe you said he is a deputy with that sheriff's department, didn't you?"

"I talk to my brother every day, so what?" comes the surly retort from Herring. "He and I are very close; Our momma taught us real good, she did!"

"Alright, Mr. Louis Herring," says Deputy Chapman. "You come with us down to the station.

"Marc will you please put Mr. Herring's car in your lot? We will have it on hold for a while."

"Wait a minute!" says Herring. "I guess I have no choice but to come with you; but I need some things from my car. And, I want to see where you park it."

Marc speaks up, "You can either let me have your key, or I can tow it into the yard. Which would you prefer?"

"I don't want no tow truck pulling my car anywhere. I will drive it around back for you." Herring's disdain for Marc shows clearly.

Chapman takes charge and speaks, "Sorry Mr. Herring, we cannot allow you to do that. Marc, you go ahead and make the tow. It will only take a few minutes; we have plenty of time don't we, Louis?"

"I wanna see the lot, and how he parks my car. I want to know it is safe."

"That's fine. Marc you go ahead and take care of his car; we will go out into the yard, and wait for you to bring it around." Deputy Chapman resolves the issue with his verbal directive.

As the two deputies and Louis Herring stand at the rear of the towing service office, Herring looks all around the lot.

"Hmm," he says to whichever deputy will answer him, "I see Jonathan's van is not here. I guess that means he came over here early, and is well on his way to Ponder. Is that correct?"

Deputy Wheeler remains motionless, but Chapman looking at Herring says, "Well, you are correct. The van is not here, is it?"

The discussion ends with that brief answer, and a sneer from Louis Herring.

Marc adeptly backs Herring's car into an appropriate space in the partially filled storage yard. He exits his tow truck, dismantles the towing mechanism, then turns and walks toward the three who are watching him.

"Does Mr. Herring need to get anything from his car?" Marc looks at Deputy Chapman for a response.

However, Herring is the one who immediately responds. "Yes, of course. My wallet and cell phone are in there. I need them," he says as he practically bolts from the two deputies.

"Hold it, Louis," says Deputy Chapman, "Deputy Wheeler and I will go with you. We need to look at your phone."

"Yeah, sure you do," Herring mumbles beneath his breath before saying, "okay, then let's go. I have the key right here."

Deputy Wheeler joins the other two as they walk to Herring's car and watches as he unlocks the driver's side door.

Chapman is the first to speak after the door is open, "Mr. Herring, please unlock all of the doors, hand your keys to me, and keep your hands in sight. Do not get inside until tell you to do so.

"Deputy Wheeler will walk to the other side of your car. After I give you the word, you may get inside … Then slowly get your wallet and hand it to me."

Louis Herring does as he is instructed. "Here it is, your honor," he says derisively. "Now what would you like me to do?"

"Now, slowly get your phone in the same manner, and hand it to me," says Chapman.

Herring reaches across the car to the passenger seat, and picks up the phone; he touches the home button, then attempts to navigate to another screen.

Wheeler immediately opens the passenger door and commands, "Stop! Hand the phone to me, and do not touch anything!"

Sometimes the truth is bitter
But the truth is always the truth
And some people see it as the enemy

CHAPTER 26 – CONFRONTATION

Louis Herring's brother sits in his home on the outskirts of Krum, and drums his fingers on the table.

I wonder just what does all of this mean: Louis reported yesterday that Jonathan was to be at the deputy's office at nine-thirty this morning ... So far: Nothing! Louis reports that there is absolutely no indication of any activity in the young fellow's room.

Either he has overslept, left early or died; I think we can rule out the third possibility ... Louis was up very early so he could monitor Jonathan's room, and has heard nothing ... He said he was going to watch for activity at the sheriff's office and get back to me.

He looks at his watch then picks up his cell phone. Dialing Louis's number, his mind returns to their arrangement of this morning.

It is nine o'clock, and Louis should have called me by now. Why isn't he picking it up? There must be something wrong! Now it's going to voice mail ... What should I ... I probably shouldn't ...

He abruptly ends the call.

I think it would be best to go to Highway 287 and park somewhere within sight ... That way I can intercept Jonathan before he gets to his home ... Yeah, that'll be the plan.

No ... I don't know just where he will turn off 287 ... I think I ought to go to the Parker home ... No ... I think I will go to a place near their home. That way, I can see when he arrives ... I don't know which is the better ... The most sure place is their home ... So ... Why isn't Louis ...

Finding a wide spot at the roadside about a quarter mile from the Parker home, Herring parks his car and leans back in his seat.

I can see Jonathan if he comes from the north, or from the south. I think that when he pulls into the driveway, I will follow and park right behind him ... That way he won't be able to move his van.

I could go to the house after he arrives, and conduct another interview ... That way, I will see what I can get someone to admit to ... Probably, it will be good to put a little pressure on Jonathan ... His parents will undoubtedly tell me anything I want to know if it appears that their son is in trouble.

Becoming very restless and concerned about the passing of time, and nothing to show for it, Herring is faced with a decision.

There is something not right here ... Could it be that Jonathan wasn't planning to come home ... Maybe he has had an accident ...

Perhaps he is still in Quanah, and with the sheriff or the deputy right now ... Maybe ... Maybe ... Maybe ... This is getting me nowhere ... I will go over there and force something out of them!

In just a few minutes Herring pulls his car into Ma and Sir's driveway. Getting out of the car, he surveys the place, looking beyond the small area immediately surrounding the Parker home.

Within his sight are grasslands where he sees Texas Longhorn cattle grazing. He observes a couple of new homes under construction and a few patches of trees close by.

He stops all action as his memory kicks into gear.

Hold on, he mentally exclaims. *There has been a rumor about the Parkers' son spending time at some trees.*

Looking at the several groups of nearby trees, he senses some movement in one of the groves. Herring moves swiftly to the house.

I think I just saw movement in those trees ... There is someone in there ... The kid? ... Jonathan ... Can it be? ...

****

Meanwhile, Jonathan has stepped into his private sanctuary in The Big Trees.

This is so very comfortable; I love this place. I think I am going to sit, and just contemplate for a few minutes. Maybe Prairie Flower will be here ... I sure hope so ...

He leans against a tree and closes his eyes.

"Jonathan, this is Prairie Flower, you do not have time right now to relax. There are things you must accomplish today and tomorrow. The tribal council will be meeting the day after tomorrow, and you need to get the other part of the artifact."

Jonathan opens his eyes and slaps his forehead with his right hand.

I hoped she would be here; but that is not the message I hoped to hear from her.

He repositions himself, preparing to stand; then he blinks at a startling glimmer on the ground in the underbrush.

The sun is high in the sky, and something just glistened at me. Must be a piece of glass, but that is strange.

His curiosity causes Jonathan to visually search the ground near the reflection

It was over here to my left ... looks like there is something partially covered by some leav ... It looks like a jewel ... It is a jewelry box! Oh, my gosh! Could it be?

Jonathan rolls onto his knees, and picks up the box. His hands are shaking as he holds it.

Box? ... Treasure box? Ma ... You must leave ... Now ... Chief Peta gave treasure box to ... Other piece ... Could it really be?

His mind races through everything he has heard and learned while on Medicine Mound with Chief Peta Nocona. His hands tremble as he prepares to flip the latch.

****

Back at the Parker home, Herring knocks on the door.

I'm just going to be tough with these people ...

Ma excitedly opens the door wide, "You know you don't ... Oh my, I was ... Uuh ..." Her voice trails off disappointedly.

"Peta ... Peta ... It's Deputy Herring," she calls out.

Sir is already on his way, thinking that his son has arrived, "Oh ... Hello Herring," he says coldly, "what is it that you want now?"

Herring speaks, "I'm just letting you know that I am going to be looking in the groves of trees in the area. Is it true that your son spends a lot of time there?"

Trying to thwart Herring's assumptive question, Sir gives his answer, "We haven't seen Jonathan for a week. What do you expect to find in a bunch of trees, anyway?"

Herring turns, and begins to walk away from the house. Sir grabs the interloper's arm and shouts, "Just who do you think you are, coming into our home making demands of us? You claim to be a deputy sheriff, but I think you are a fraud! You are an imposter!"

In a responsive loud tone, Herring responds, "I could arrest you right now and lock you up! I am going to those trees, and you are not going to stop me!"

"Then I am going with you. You will go nowhere on this property without me!" The shouting has escalated to an uproar of mammoth proportions.

Together, the two angry men push each other out of the way, and begin trekking toward The Big Trees. Their shouts continue to break the silence of an otherwise beautiful and peaceful day.

"You have no authority …" shouts Sir.

"And you are interfering with an officer of the law!" responds Herring.

In his semi-secluded sanctuary in The Big Trees, Jonathan begins to lift the lid of the newly discovered box. Suddenly he hears a din coming from the direction of his home.

He looks toward the noise and momentarily freezes. *Oh my gosh!! Sir and someone else are on their way here. They are coming to The Big Trees. I've got to get out of here.*

Jonathan jumps to his feet. With the box in his hands, he quickly leaves his beloved place, running to where he left Michael and the Volvo.

"What's going on? What's happening?" Michael jumps to attention and is clearly unsettled as he sees Jonathan running toward him.

"Don't ask questions now! Get in the car and turn around. We need to get out of here. Quick, let's go!" Jonathan is inside the SUV and ready to leave.

Michael immediately gets into the driver's seat and has the engine running.

In haste, the car is turned around and leaves the area.

"Now what?" he asks his breathless passenger. "What has happened?"

"I'm not sure," says Jonathan, "Sir and someone else were shouting, and heading toward The Big Trees. We need to get back to Quanah right away. Prairie Flower told me that the tribal council will be meeting in two days."

Michael eyes the box and asks, "Is the missing piece in the box?"

"I don't know," answers Jonathan, "there's not been time to look. I had to leave The Big Trees too suddenly."

"Let's open it now; if it is not here, we will have no choice but to go see Ma." Jonathan slowly raises the lid; he peers inside the box.

****

Herring shouts to Sir, "See, there is someone in those trees! Is it your son?"

Sir is adamant in his response, "I don't see anybody. What are you talking about?"

"See there, he is running away from the trees! Who is it? Where is he going?"

Herring is on a dead run now, moving as quickly as he can toward the grove of trees.

By the time he reaches the trees, and reaches the other side of the grove there is no one to be seen.

I saw a vehicle of some sort disappearing from my sight! It had to be the kid; I know it had to be Jonathan.

Sir is just now entering the confines of the trees, having slowed his own pace in order to hinder Herring in his objective.

Leaning over, and resting his hands on his knees, Sir asks between breaths, "What … What did you … What did you see, Herring? I don't think you saw anything!"

Herring looks in contempt at Sir and says, "You know what I saw! I saw your son running out of these trees, and I saw a vehicle rounding that turn in the road. It was probably your van!"

Herring is accusatory in all he says, "What have you been hiding here in the trees? You have been lying to me all of this time! Haven't you?"

As they argue and shout at each other, Sir is furtively trying to study the area.

Is the box gone? … I tossed it right over there … It appears to be gone … Jonathan must now have possession of it … The special box … With its special contents … Please, Jonathan be safe … Do not try to visit us now … I will assure Ma that you are alright.

The two antagonists begin their angry tromp back to the home of Ma and Sir. Because of their moods, it is a relatively fast walk that is done in silent, mutual scorn.

DENNIS BOYD CALL

Puha does not reside in one's self-importance
It lies within the heart and soul of the
One who chooses to do right

CHAPTER 27 – NEW PUHA

The two young men are returning to Quanah, reversing their direction from an hour previous. Jonathan raises his eyes from the box as they drive.

He says, "I am nervous, Michael. Let's pull over at the first wide spot. I don't want to see everything that is in here by myself. You need to be a part of this!"

Soon they are in the parking lot of one of the many warehouses in the area.

Jonathan, with a lump in his throat asks, "Are we ready?"

Michael nods his head, and Jonathan begins his emotional task. One by one he removes the four items.

"First is this ring," Jonathan states. "It looks like a wedding ring, maybe. Next are these two pictures of a very pretty lady; on the back side of one is written the name 'Priscilla' which I believe is my Grandmother Finley."

He holds his breath as he extracts the fourth and final article from the box. It is wrapped in some sort of covering that is thin, but protective. The wrapping is yellowed and appears very old.

Jonathan whispers both to himself, and to Michael, "Ready?"

Then he unfolds the wrap. It is double wrapped, and as the content is revealed Jonathan becomes faint; his eyes begin to shed tears.

"This is it … Michael, this is it," he says very softly. "This is the piece that completes the Quanah Bananah."

It is a very reverent and sacred moment as two friends stare at the artifact, then at each other. They are starting to grasp the impact of the quest; the quest that has been so many years in the making.

"Michael," Jonathan says with great humility, "I have always considered this journey as *my* quest. That is not true. It is the quest of five generations; five generations of people who have been waiting for this moment, and for the moment that will come in two days."

They sit in silent contemplation for several minutes.

Daring to break the silence, Michael finally asks, "So, Boss-man, where do we go from here?"

Jonathan considers his response for several seconds, then answers, "Well, I am sure that Sir knows by now that I have been to The Big Trees; he will certainly tell Ma that I am alright.

"We must get back to Quanah tonight because I have to return to Medicine Mound tomorrow.

"I will retrieve the buried box and the artifact. Then, I need to get myself ready for my meeting with the tribal council in two days; the day after tomorrow.

"So the answer to your question is this: Let's return to Quanah now. Does that make sense to you?"

"It does," says Michael, "but what does the quiet voice of your mind say?"

"It says, 'go to Quanah,' at least that is what I am hearing." Jonathan is learning to listen to, and rely on that voice; he has been a good student.

"Ya' know, Michael, I am feeling really, really good. This quest is making more and more sense to me all of the time. But … at the same time, I am feeling very weak."

"Yes," says Michael. "I am weak, too. We will do our very best!"

****

Sir and Herring return to Ma who is waiting at the house. She has been outside watching the two as they hurried to The Big Trees and then return.

Sir stops before they reach Ma; he reaches out, and stops his unwanted companion.

He turns, faces his nemesis, and pokes his finger into Herring's chest, "You have made a lot of bad comments to us, and have been very demanding. I don't know exactly who you are, but I do know that you are not a member of law enforcement."

Herring sneers as he answers, "You are not only in big trouble, you are a traitor to the cause of the To-sah-wi Alliance. A huge price is going to be paid by you and your family."

He is surprised by Sir's response, "You may be right, and if so we are willing to pay the price. However, I think you have a larger problem; I think you do not represent the Alliance, nor do I think you represent the Denton County Sheriff's Department."

Sir concludes with a forceful statement, "You are trying to make a name for yourself so you can claim leadership of the Alliance. The To-sah-wi Alliance will soon implode under its own weight. Mr. Herring, you are a doomed man."

Herring looks at Sir with a venomous look in his eyes, "We will stop your son. We will crush the Fifth-Son Prophecy, and we will rule all.

"My brother is waiting for your son right now. He will stop Jonathan before he has opportunity to go further with his unwise pursuit!"

Ma has moved closer to the two men as they have been talking.

She intervenes, "Mr. Herring, I think it is time for you to leave our home, and never return. Our son will be able to take care of himself, and none of your threats will change that."

Her powerful statement is not to be demeaned, "Now leave before I call the real sheriff's department, and report you for trespassing on our property. We are not afraid of you or your precious ambitions. Now get out of here!"

Herring, not being used to having a woman speak to him with such force, or puha recoils. He opens his mouth to respond, "Don't … Who do you … I never …"

Unable to bring a sentence to fruition, he turns and walks defeatedly to his car. Looking back, he glares at Ma. Then he climbs into his vehicle and drives away.

Amazing things can be done by ordinary people
Ordinary people do amazing things
By rising to the occasion

CHAPTER 28 – REMARKABILITY

Continuing their return drive to Quanah, Jonathan and Michael turn onto Highway 287, traveling in a northwesterly direction. A lot of silence exists as they each have many issues to consider.

The discovery of the other piece of the Quanah Bananah has had an enormous impact on their introspection. Jonathan holds the piece reverently in his two hands as he looks down at it.

This is so very exciting, but beyond that it is historical, and beyond that it is the very honor of Chief Peta Nocona's family. I am actually holding the completion, and success of what was prophesied about one-hundred and sixty years ago.

He shivers and tears form again in his eyes.

I am just Jonathan, the son of Elizabeth Finley and Peta Parker. How could I be chosen for this?

Michael looks over at his friend, and traveling companion, "Hey, Bud, are you alright? You seem a bit preoccupied. Wanna share?"

"Oh, I don't know," says Jonathan appreciatively, "I guess I am just thinking of the improbability of it all. I'm just a home-schooled Native American boy who has lived a rather remarkable, unusual life."

Michael adds an observation, "Kinda makes you wonder what is yet to come, doesn't it? I mean following the quest; what will be coming your way? I imagine you will be worshipped by many, and there might be those few who will hold you in great contempt."

"Ya' think? I don't want worship, and I cannot comprehend the reason of contempt. Can you explain what you mean?" Jonathan is finally beginning to view his future in a new, enlightened fashion.

"Well," begins Michael, "There will be a few dedicated to the To-sah-wi Alliance who will never give it up. They will be dissidents because it is the cool thing to do. They will never give up the past.

"On the other hand, there will be those who are extremely grateful for you, and your actions. They will see your contribution to the remaining Native American culture, in particular to the Comanche, as so magnificent that you will be memorialized by them.

"The two opposing opinions can be equally dangerous. The first is more temporal, or physical. The second is more subtle and elusive; it goes to who you really are, on the inside."

Jonathan sits quietly on the passenger side of the Volvo SUV.

He looks over at Michael and asks, "Michael, you have become a good friend, but I really don't know who you are. Can you answer that question for me? Who are you, really?"

Michael looks at the control center of his car, and exclaims, "We need fuel. How about we pull off at the next off-ramp and get gas? It is the Henrietta exit; the Pecan Shed is a delightful place, and they have gas pumps there as well," Michael chuckles.

Jonathan remains silent so Michael continues, "The Pecan Shed is right next door to the Best Western Hotel, that should impress you."

Jonathan laughs, "Okay, let's do that but don't think that I will forget my question. I will still want to know who you really are, and how you came to be my friend ... and now my tutor."

They take the off-ramp, cross over the freeway, and negotiate to a Pecan Shed gas pump.

Michael observes, "There is a nice looking older couple sitting on the wooden rocking chairs in the shade of the store awning. I said that this is a delightful place, didn't I?"

"You sure did," acknowledges Jonathan, "I think I will go inside and get a cold Dr Pepper. Do you want anything?"

"I will follow you in, and see what appeals to me. You will probably like some of their pecan candy ... or they have a terrific little bakery ... and the staff are all very friendly, especially the nice lady named Suki." Clearly, Michael is very familiar with this place.

Jonathan walks briskly to the entrance of the store, and passes close by the couple whom they had seen from the car. They watch him as he approaches; their friendly smiles are infectious and Jonathan responds in kind.

"Howdy," the gentleman speaks first, "do you come here often?"

Jonathan stops and responds, "No, this is my first visit, but my friend has been here several times."

The man reaches out, offering a handshake and says, "My name is Brian, and this is my wife, Gay. We stop at this place every time we travel to Oklahoma to visit family. We really like it here."

"Jonathan ... my name is Jonathan. My friend and I are just traveling through. I have been past here a number of times but this is my first time to stop."

"Well," Brian waves, and says, "enjoy your visit to the Pecan Shed, Jonathan ... Oh, by the way, try to get acquainted with Suki in the bakery department. She is a neat, neat lady."

Jonathan enters the store.

What a friendly couple. Quite typical of most Texans, I think ... But I must remember caution.

Michael completes his task of pumping gasoline, and joins Jonathan inside the store.

"Friendly folks outside, aren't they?" Michael comments. "I also spent a few minutes chatting with them. They are from the town of Bedford, Texas. Do you know where that is?"

"Sure do! Ma, Sir and I have been there several times. It is a very nice place, in my opinion," Jonathan answers. "I sure hope that I didn't say anything that I shouldn't have said."

Michael thoughtfully says, "I doubt that you did. They are neat people who seem genuinely friendly and interested.

"In fact, they said that if we need to spend the night in the area, that the Best Western next door is an excellent hotel. They told me that they have a friend who stays often, and really loves that place.

"The folks gave a high thumbs up when they spoke of individuals who work at the hotel. Let's see ..." He begins to recall what he had been told.

With a grin, Michael rattles off the hotel staff names as best he can recall, "There are Josie, Pennie and Debbie; the rhyming trio! ... Hmm, wonder if they sing, too." Jonathan gives a dull groan.

Cheerfully, he continues, "Let's get our stuff, and get on the road. We have a pretty good drive ahead of us."

They leave the Pecan Shed, say goodbye to Brian and Gay, and are soon back on the road toward Quanah.

They drive in silence for a short while until Jonathan cannot hold his questions any longer. He speaks, "Alright, Michael, I'm going to ask this question again. Just who are you and what is your connection to Prairie Flower?"

Michael ponders for several seconds then looks over at his friend; Jonathan has a sincere look on his face.

He says, "Jonathan, I wish I could give you the answer you are looking for. I cannot do that.

"But, I can tell you this universal fact: At different times in our lives, there are people who come to us for no apparent reason. We often do not know them, or how we are brought together, but they help us in unpredictable ways."

Jonathan is listening intently, but is unclear as to what is being said. He raises his eyebrows questioningly.

Michael continues, "There will be a time in your future when you will have the opportunity to become someone's teacher or mentor. You may not know them, but you will understand the situation because of your experience, and you will be able to help.

"When, and if it becomes important for you to know anything about me personally, you will be told. I will say this to you: Never give up your Big Trees experiences.

"You have learned that those experiences can occur any place. All you need to do is listen to the quiet voice of your mind. The trick is to always be ready."

Jonathan is in serious consideration of what he just heard.

So, Michael has just put into a few words, many of the things I have been learning from Prairie Flower. I can do more than just bring Chief Peta's family together; actually it is my family that is being brought together. Chief Peta is the father of all five generations.

I can help others ... The quiet voice of the mind ... When one goes for the good, the bad will try to intercede ... Truth, Honesty, Integrity ... The envelope ... Precaution, Protection, Proceed ... What's in the envelope ... Prairie Flower will tell me when ... The tribal council ... Ma ... Sir ... The box ...

"Jonathan ... Jonathan, it's time to wake up." Michael is speaking, "We are almost to the Best Western. You have had a good snooze, now it's time to wake up and get on with life."

Jonathan shakes himself awake, runs his hands through his hair, then says, "Wow, guess I fell asleep. I was thinking about what you told me. I thought how it matches much of what Prairie Flower has taught me. It makes a lot of sense ... Hmm, very interesting ... and very revealing, isn't it?"

Michael acknowledges the question, "Yes, it is revealing ... and important."

He continues, "Okay, Jonathan. I will let you out here, and will return in the morning at eight o'clock. We will go to Medicine Mound where you will get the buried artifact. Is that the plan?"

"Ahhh, yeah, I guess so. Where will you be staying?" questions Jonathan.

Michael smiles, "Oh, I will be around. You need to have solitude and peace now. It has been a very exhausting couple of days for you, and I am sure that Prairie Flower has much more to share.

"Grab your backpack and anything else of yours. I will see you bright and early in the morning. Be cautious, Jonathan."

Jonathan opens his door then hesitates, "Is there anything in particular you are referring to? ... Where do you think Louis Herring is right now? ... Will he be in the hotel?"

"I have no idea about any of your questions," answers Michael. "I only know that you are very near the end of the quest, and *they* know it too.

"Regarding Herring: I doubt that he is anywhere but in the pokey right now; but caution is the word of the day, for you."

"Got it!" responds Jonathan as he grabs his backpack, and exits the black Volvo SUV that he has come to know so well.

He walks through the sliding door into the lobby of the Best Western. Anita looks up from behind the reception desk and delivers a cheery greeting.

"Hi there, young man. Good to see you. I have a message for you. There was some sheriff's activity this morning in the room next to yours. I don't know much about it except that I am to offer you a different room if you would like. Would you prefer to change?"

"Uhhh, I don't know. Is there a really good reason to do so?" asks Jonathan.

"I think I would move, if it were me," says Anita in a protective fashion. She looks at Jonathan, offering a slight smile and nod.

"Okay, I will do it. Where do you want me to go? I mean, which room will I be in?" He smiles at his own misspoken question.

"I have a room ready for you. It is on this floor right down there. The room next to the exit door. It is all ready for you."

Anita places a keycard in his hand, along with a handwritten note extending out of the protective envelope that holds the key.

Jonathan looks at Anita with a questioning look on his face.

She, in response, smiles and nods toward the location of his newly assigned room.

What one says is just that
But what one means
May be different from what you heard

CHAPTER 29 – LAYING A PLAN

Early the morning of that same day, Louis Herring is in the custody of Deputies Chapman and Wheeler of the Hardeman County Sheriff's Department.

"What were you trying to delete from your phone, Louis?" asks Deputy Chapman. "You were trying to do something."

"I ain't talkin' to you or anybody else!" Herring's belligerence is clear evidence to the deputies that he is hiding something of importance.

"That's fine. Just come with us, and you will wait at the office while we get search warrants. We'll need to search your car, your phone and your hotel room." Chapman is being professional in his demeanor, while keeping Herring occupied for as long as possible.

On their way to the local jail Chapman says, "We will keep you behind bars on obstruction charges while we get the search warrants ... unless you want to give us access to everything. It will save a bunch of time for all of us if you will do that."

The deputy looks at his passenger in the rear view mirror as Herring sneers and shakes his head.

Deputy Chapman pulls his patrol car into the facility parking space and Wheeler parks his car beside. Then together they escort Louis Herring into the building where he is processed.

Wheeler takes the necessary steps to procure the warrant. Within the hour, the two deputies approach Louis Herring.

Wheeler speaks, "Mr. Herring, would you like to come with us, or wait right here while we conduct our searches? Actually, we can examine your phone right now."

Chapman says, "That's a good idea. Let's go for it."

Together the two men sit at a desk in full view of Louis Herring who is showing increasing uneasiness.

Wheeler switches the phone to the on position, then asks, "Louis, what is the password?"

He looks at Herring who is ignoring him. "You can either tell me now, or we will have a tech guy here in about five minutes who will get it faster than you can say AT&T."

Chapman enters the verbal standoff and says, "Mr. Herring, you know we will get everything we need; there is absolutely no reason for you to delay us. If you do, you will only be hurting yourself."

"So if I cooperate, will I get out of this zoo cage today?" Louis asks.

"It's very likely that you can. Depends on what we find, and how valuable your cooperation is to us." Chapman is sensing some progress and welcomes it.

"Alright, alright ... Here it is: MONK4309." Louis states it twice then waits for Wheeler's success.

Wheeler chuckles and asks, "Any reason for the monk part?"

Herring looks at the two deputies and answers, "Yeah! That's the nickname Ricky gave me. Ricky is my brother. What of it?"

"Nothing at all, just being curious," Deputy Wheeler responds.

"So this morning you sent a text to Ricky, the message says, 'The kid must have left already.' It looks like you sent it at 8:43." Wheeler is looking at Herring for verification.

"If that's what it says, I guess that's what it was," Louis knows that to deny, or argue will only make matters worse for him.

"Is this what you were trying to delete? This message to your brother, is this what you were trying to get rid of?" Chapman is pushing for an answer.

"You're just assuming that I was trying to delete anything," Herring challenges the two deputies. "Maybe I was just trying to keep my phone from getting away from me."

"Fair enough," says Chapman. "Tell us this: What business is it of yours, or your brother's what *the kid* is doing?"

"I dunno. You are the cops; you figure it out!" Herring is determined to not give up any information.

Chapman turns to Wheeler and speaks, "Have the jailer come in and take custody of this man. He can continue to cool his heels inside the zoo cage, as he calls it, while we are checking out his car and hotel room."

He looks back at Herring and asks, "By the way Mr. Herring, what do you do for a living?"

"What's that got to do with anything?" retorts Herring.

"Well, maybe a lot and maybe nothing. That's what I'm trying to find out. Are you here just to harass and follow the young man, or are you here on business?" Deputy Chapman continues to press Herring for any information he can gather.

"I'm just here because I want to be here. Why don't you guys go search whatever you want to search? I will be here, just waiting for your return," Herring mocks.

Wheeler returns with the jailer who makes certain that Herring's cell is secured.

"Okay Deputy Wheeler, let's do as he says. With a little luck we may be back in a couple of days," Chapman smugly mocks the mocker.

With great disdain, Herring retorts, "Whatever you're looking for, it ain't there!"

Outside, Chapman says to his partner, "Let's go to the hotel first. I suspect that if there is anything, it will be in his room."

Taking their separate cars the officers arrive at the Best Western in a matter of minutes. They enter the lobby, approach the desk clerk, and present the search warrant; soon they are escorted into Louis Herring's room on the second floor.

Sifting through Herring's personal belongs, they begin to share thoughts on the best way to handle the situation.

Wheeler observes, "You know, Jonathan will probably be back here tonight. They were going to the Krum area for something, but they did not expect to be gone long.

"He asked us to hold his van for a couple of days; it seems to me though, that he has other things to do here."

"Yeah," says Chapman, "I've been thinking along the same lines. His room is next door to this one, Herring's room. For his protection, let's have the hotel move Jonathan to the bottom floor … and … I think right next to the exit door on the east end."

"Sounds good to me. That way he will have separation from Herring, and a quick exit if necessary." Wheeler is in full agreement.

"We will have the hotel move Jonathan, and have them notify us when Jonathan checks in. We will release Herring, and take him to his car at that point; he will probably return directly to his room in this hotel." Chapman lays out a preliminary plan.

Wheeler expands on the plan a bit, "We should somehow make certain that Jonathan does not leave his room after he checks in, just in case Herring is wandering about."

"Yes," says Chapman, "and with a little bit of luck, Herring will slip-up somewhere, and we will have something solid to bring him in on."

The two men go to the lobby and begin putting the plan into action. Speaking with the Manager on Duty, Chapman states their case.

"We have been conducting a search of Mr. Louis Herring's room on the second floor."

"Yes, I know," says the manager. "I was notified immediately after your arrival. Is everything alright?"

"We would ask you to relocate Jonathan Parker to a room on the main floor, particularly in the room closest to the east end exit. Can you accommodate that?" Wheeler speaks for both deputies.

Checking the room availability on the hotel computer system, the manager says, "Yes, we can do that. Do you know when Mr. Parker will be returning?"

"Not for sure," says Wheeler. "But we think it will be late afternoon or early evening. There is a possibility that he may not be back until tomorrow, but probably today."

Deputy Chapman interjects, "What time will you have a shift change, and who will be at the desk this evening?"

The manager responds, "The change will occur at three o'clock and Anita will be here, at the front desk. I will notify her of the change."

"Wonderful!" is Chapman's response. "We may come by periodically in the meantime, if that's alright."

"Anytime, Deputy Chapman. You and Deputy Wheeler are welcome whenever you want to stop by. You know that."

As they exit the hotel and start the short walk to their cars, Chapman says, "Let's go to the impound lot and go through Herring's car. I want to come back to the hotel in an hour or so, after Anita comes on duty. Okay?"

"Sure," answers Wheeler. "Want to give some special instructions to Anita?"

"Not exactly, I just want to be sure things are being carried out correctly."

Chapman leads the way out of the hotel on their way to the auto storage yard and Marc's office.

Marc hears the front door of his auto storage lot chime, indicating the entrance of someone into his building. He stands and walks from his desk to the hall doorway.

"Well, deputies, you are here a little earlier than I expected. How are thing going?" Marc is being inquisitive.

Chapman answers, "We are here on official business; we have a warrant to search Louis Herring's vehicle. I guess that is where we will begin, if we may."

Marc smiles, "Absolutely! You can pretty much have the run of the place. Do you have the key?"

"Sure do," Wheeler dangles the keyring on his left hand's little finger.

Marc escorts the two police officers to the lot behind the building and says, "Knock yourselves out, gentlemen. I will be in my office when you return."

It is about thirty minutes later when Chapman and Wheeler re-enter Marc's office and take a seat.

Marc inquires, "Did you find what you were looking for?"

"Not really," says Chapman. "We found no evidence of any wrong-doing or anything unexpected. We want to hang out here for a little while if that's alright with you. There are a couple of things you might clear up for us."

The response from Chapman startles Marc just a bit. "What are you talking about? Did I do something wrong?"

"No, not that we are aware of, anyway." Chapman smiles, and continues, "It was very evident this morning that Herring was not happy with you at all. Did he say anything about his purpose in being here, in Quanah?"

"I don't think he said anything new," says Marc very thoughtfully. "Nothing other than his displeasure with me for not doing all that he expected me to do.

"I explained that I did exactly as he and I had agreed. I also informed him that everything I did was with your blessing; that you were aware of all my activities in this matter." Marc smiles as he recalls the tense interchange with Louis Herring.

"Of course, in his eyes, I am a traitor to him, his brother, and their cause! That concerns me a bit, from a personal standpoint." Marc's expression shows some concern.

"Yes, that could certainly be a bit unsettling," Wheeler says.

"Well," comments Deputy Chapman, "we will do our best to keep an eye on you, and your safety. You know that. And we will expect you to let us know of any dissonance in your life. Okay?"

"Uh-huh … And just what is dissonance, other than a big word?" The tow truck operator grins and pushes back at the deputy.

"Guess the college education didn't teach you much, did it? Dissonance means discord, or out of order. In other words let us know if anything appears wrong." Chapman laughs and reaches his arm out to shake hands with Marc.

Wheeler also shakes hands with Marc, then says, "I think the vocabulary lesson won't cost you more than a late lunch at the Old Bank Saloon. Actually, their Mesquite Grilled Steak dinner might be a better idea."

They all have a good laugh and the deputies are on their way to the Best Western.

Anita is at the registration desk when both men walk through the front door of the hotel. She looks up and welcomes them in.

"I understand we have a slight change in room assignments," she says as they draw close to the counter. "Is there anything special that I should know?"

"Yes there is," answers Chapman. "Will you please call me as soon as Jonathan Parker returns, and is directed to his new room?"

"Certainly will. Is that all?" Anita asks.

"Just one more thing," says Chapman as he reaches for a notepad. "I want to leave a note for Jonathan."

He quickly scribbles a short note, folds it and says, "Please put this in the cardkey envelope for the young man, Jonathan Parker."

DENNIS BOYD CALL

You must first know
Where the buffalo live
Before you go for buffalo steak

CHAPTER 30 – FOLLOWING THE PLAN

Earlier at their home near Ponder, Sir and Ma are walking into their house after the deputy imposter, Herring has driven away. Jonathan and Michael have left the area.

Sir says, "Elizabeth, I think we will not see Jonathan today. I am certain that he was in The Big Trees and retrieved the treasure box.

"I believe it was our son that Herring saw when he got a good look in that direction. By the time we got there, Jonathan was gone."

Ma, looking tired and resigned, speaks, "Are you telling me that you feel he is alright? Do you really think that is true?"

"Yes, My Love. That is exactly what I am saying." Sir takes Ma into his arms as he speaks. "I just feel strongly that everything is as it should be. The quiet voice of my mind strongly says that to me."

****

Later in the day in the town of Quanah, Jonathan walks to his newly assigned room at the Best Western hotel.

How can I feel so very good ... and at the same time be scared to death? ... I really need a good night's rest tonight ... I will meet Michael tomorrow morning at eight o'clock ... Sure hope Sir tells Ma that I'm safe ... at least that I have been there and have the box ... Use the hotel phone ... Safety issues ... Leave it alone ...

Oh how I have come to love Medicine Mound ... It is probably my second favorite place to spend time ... The Big Trees is clearly my most favorite.

I wonder just what went on in the hotel this morning that caused them to have me change rooms ... Something to do with Louis Herring, surely ... but I wonder what it was.

He pulls the cardkey from its holder, and sees the note.

Okay, I will read the note as soon as I get settled ...

Jonathan sets his backpack on the desk and pulls the note from the cardkey protective sleeve, unfolds it and reads, "Jonathan, I hope you enjoy the room – Stay in it! - Meet me tomorrow morning - outside east hotel exit - 6:45 – Deputy Chapman"

Well, that's interesting. I wonder if he knows I am meeting Michael at eight. Hmm ...

The young man is physically worn out and plops onto his bed.

Does this note from the deputy have anything to do with Herring? ... Room change ... Hmm ... It does get me away from him ... Wait a minute ... I thought he would be in jail ... Sooo ... Stay in room ... Why? ... Meet Chapman early ... What about Michael ... Stay in room ...

Maybe Herring is upstairs ... Getting me out at six-forty-five is for my own good ... Wow, very interesting ... It's been a very long day ... I should take a shower ... Tomorrow is going to be a good day ... I'm tired ... Sleep ... Quanah Bananah ... Tribal council ...

Back at the front desk, Anita is busying herself with hotel records and maintenance schedules when Louis Herring enters. He strides through the lobby then stops, and returns to the registration counter.

"Good evening." He is speaking to Anita, "Has my neighbor in the room next to me returned yet today? His name, I believe is Jonathan. Nice young man."

Anita looks up from her sitting position and replies, "I am sorry, but we do not give out information about our residents. What is your connection with the person? ... Jonathan, I think you said is his name. How do you know him?"

"Oh," says Herring, "he and I have become elevator buddies, that's all. He seems like a fine young man."

She reaffirms her earlier statement, "Well, like I said, we do not give out information regarding our residents. If you are friends, I am sure it he wouldn't mind if you were to knock on his door when you get up there."

"Mmm, maybe I'll do that," is his response.

Anita smiles politely as he walks away; she returns to her desk duties.

****

Jonathan awakens early.

Well, morning has arrived right on schedule again. I need to be outside to meet Deputy Chapman in about thirty minutes. Good thing I woke up at ten last night so that I could shower, and kinda' make myself feel human again.

From the sound of his note last night, I should not go for breakfast this morning; just silently go through the exit to my right when I leave the room.

Jonathan knows that this is going to be a very special day, and he feels the need to properly present himself. After shaving and brushing his teeth, he looks through the minimal number of clean shirts remaining is his bag.

I think I will wear this royal blue pull-over shirt, and these khaki slacks; after all I will be hiking to the top of Medicine Mound, and comfort is important to me ... I feel good about wearing these.

No matter what I wear, it will be dirty by the time I return ... But I do want to be respectful of the artifact ... and who knows, I may see Chief Peta Nocona again ... or maybe even Prairie Flower.

I wonder why the deputy wants me to meet him this morning. Does he know anything about my quest? I am sure he is trustworthy because of the good feelings I have, and his work against Louis Herring.

Michael will be here an hour and a half later. I don't know how to contact him ... And what about Michael ... I sure would like to know more about him.

Jonathan leaves his room, turns right and exits quietly through the east door into the darkness.

Suddenly his eyes are blinded by red and blue flashing lights; he is frozen between automobile headlights from his right, and from his left.

"Just stay where you are, put your arms in the air." Jonathan thinks he recognizes the voice, but cannot see the face.

Two men emerge, one from each of the two automobiles. They approach the stunned young man. "Jonathan Parker, you will come with us right now!" commands the voice.

The men are at his side in a matter of moments; Jonathan stutters, "D ... D ... Depu ... Deputy Chapman? ... Whe ...Wheeler? What is going on? Why ... Why are you doing this?"

"Just be quiet and get into Wheeler's car ... Now," is Chapman's hard and uncaring response.

Feeling faint, totally confused and disbelieving, Jonathan does as he is told. He gets into the rear seat of Deputy Wheeler's official vehicle and slumps, overcome with emotional fatigue.

In moments they are on their way to the detention center; Chapman is following close behind.

Back in his second floor room, Louis Herring smiles as he watches the scene below.

I will send a text to Ricky to let him know that the situation is under control; that my offer of information about Jonathan's holding some stolen articles has paid off.

Also, I need to show up at the sheriff's office around nine o'clock this morning.

Herring sits back in his hotel room chair, puts his feet on the ottoman, and begins his text to his brother.

DENNIS BOYD CALL

One makes a plan
To have a route to follow,
To follow the route shows confidence in the plan

CHAPTER 31 – PLAYING THE PLAN

The sun is now bringing light into the north Texas community of Quanah; Deputy Wheeler watches Jonathan through his rear-view mirror for several minutes as they drive to the sheriff's office. He sees a glum, silent, and clearly befuddled Jonathan staring out of the tinted window.

This young man is not defiant or belligerent; how remarkable that Jonathan controls his passion so well! It is very clear that anger and disobedience are not a part of his behavior, but it is equally clear that he is struggling internally. He needs some reassurance.

"Jonathan, please try to relax just a little. Things are going to be alright. I do not know a whole lot about what is going on, but I do know that what we are doing is for your protection." Deputy Wheeler's is a pleasant voice of reassurance.

The young passenger turns his gaze to the front of the vehicle, and thinks momentarily of what he just heard the deputy say. He struggles with his words and finally asks a question.

"What about Deputy Chapman? Is he my friend or is he working against me?"

Wheeler answers quickly, "Chapman is the lead officer in this entire matter. He is doing what he feels is best. Here we are at the station, and Chapman is right behind us."

Inside Deputy Chapman's office, the three of them sit around the small conference table. Chapman speaks first, "Jonathan, I am sorry that we had to do things this way; it was important for you to be surprised and shocked by this morning's events. Otherwise, it would not be believable by those who were observing."

Jonathan looks squarely at Chapman in a questioning manner. He says, "Believable? Observing? What are you talking about? I am not sure I am comfortable here."

"You are under surveillance by those who would have you fail in whatever errand you are pursuing. Louis Herring was probably watching from his hotel room window." Chapman is successful in helping Jonathan to feel at ease once more.

Jonathan, being his responsible self takes up the conversation. "I am supposed to be picked up this morning at eight o'clock, at the hotel. Michael will be expecting me; that is about forty-five minutes or so from now. What do you suggest that I do. I do not know how to get in touch with him."

"Oh, yes," Chapman chuckles, "that too. Michael will be here any minute now. For your information, here is the plan:

"We believe that your arrest this morning was observed by at least one other person. There could be more than just Herring. As far as anyone knows, you are now being held here in the detention center. In actuality, you and Michael will be wherever you are supposed to be in plenty of time."

Wheeler picks it up, "You will not return to your hotel until your mission is complete. The bad guys will be under the belief that you are being housed here, compliments of Hardeman County.

"Louis Herring is meeting us here, in this office at nine o'clock this morning. At that point we will take him into custody. The

Denton County Sheriff's Office will arrest his brother Ricky, at the same time. There are plenty of things to charge them with."

The room door opens, and the front desk clerk enters. "A fellow by the name of Michael is here to see you. Shall I bring him in now?"

Deputy Wheeler gives an affirmative nod of his head and the clerk steps aside, allowing Michael to walk inside.

"Hey, guys," Michael has a way of brightening everyone's day. "How are all of you? How'd you like the sudden change of plans this morning, Jonathan? Pretty slick, wouldn't you say?"

Jonathan looks at Michael and asks, "So how did you manage to pull it off? I'd say you all did a darn good job; I'm still shaking!"

"Deputies Chapman, Wheeler and I have been in touch with each other over these last few days. We had to keep you out of that loop for your own safety, and for the protection of your quest." Michael is clearly pleased with the success of the execution of their plan, so far.

"Okay, you two," says Chapman, "you better get out of here. Now, go do what you need to get done today. I am not certain what it is, but I do know it is important.

"Herring and group, whomever that may include, do not know for sure how you get around since your van has not been seen for several days. They do not know about the warehouse where it is being kept."

Deputy Wheeler adds, "They might be getting a little suspicious of your SUV because it has been around the hotel a bit, Michael … But we doubt it because their pattern of harassment has not changed. We want you to continue with the plan as we now have it. Alright, now go!"

Jonathan and Michael leave the sheriff's office through the back door where Michael has parked his SUV. They carefully leave the secured parking lot, and are soon on their way to Medicine Mound.

The twenty minute drive is filled with excitement and chatter about how the deputies outsmarted Louis Herring and any other members of the To-sah-wi Alliance that may be involved.

Jonathan speaks, "Louis and Ricky Herring will both soon be in custody ... I will also have the original piece of artifact in my hot little hands ... Wow, what an adventure this has been ... But I still don't know about the tribal council meeting, except that it is held tomorrow ... Somewhere around here, I suppose."

Then teasingly, Jonathan adds, "What do you know about it, the council meeting, that is?"

Michael looks blankly at his friend and answers, "Sorry, Bud, but you are on your own in that regard."

"Well, it was worth a try, as they say," grins Jonathan.

They arrive at Medicine Mound, and park near the spring at the north end of the mound.

Jonathan says somewhat quizzingly, "In the absence of direct communication and instruction, I guess I will just trek to the top and retrieve the box. I know where it is kept."

Michael comments, "Makes sense to me. You have been in training all of your life to listen to the quiet voice, and to take action on your own." Michael is simply reinforcing what Jonathan already knows, but is still a bit unsure of.

With his backpack strapped on, Jonathan goes to the spring, takes a cool drink, and begins his climb through the juniper bushes to the top of Medicine Mound.

The time alone as he trudges through the heavy low brush, is good thinking time for Jonathan.

Am I going be told more today about the council meeting? Is Prairie Flower's assignment to me finished, or will I hear from her one more time?

I would love to spend a lot more time with Chief Peta. Just imagine, he is my third great-grandfather. Wow, that's really exciting ... I am proud of my Native American heritage ...

Sir is such a good man ... I love Ma very much ... I hope they are alright ... I will soon be able to see them ...

"Jonathan, please take time for a break. Find some shade beside a juniper bush, and sit for a few minutes. Let me review a few things with you." It is his first mentor, Prairie Flower speaking.

Jonathan reacts, "Oh Prairie Flower, I am very happy to hear from you again. Thank you, thank you! Thank you for visiting me today."

"You are welcome, Jonathan. There have been many lessons brought to you over the years, and you have learned them well.

"The reunification of my father's family has been long awaited. I have some messages for you now. Sit, relax and listen carefully to me."

Jonathan rustles around in the Redberry Junipers and settles on a gentle sloping portion of the hillside in the meager shade provided by the juniper.

Prairie Flower proceeds, "Today the entire plan comes together, and will be presented at the tribal council tomorrow. Your quest will be completed at that time; I will give you some direction now.

"When you arrive at the top of the mound today, do not go directly to the box. Spend time in meditation, walk around the open area, and contemplate further the plant and animal life. In this way you will grow closer to the Comanche.

"Chief Peta will be close and I will be close. You will be prompted as to when to retrieve the box. When you have the box, open it and become more familiar with the piece inside.

"Spend the night here at the mound; stay at the base with Michael. When you return to the base and are with Michael, you are to open the envelope. He will be your witness as to the content. Keep the content; it will be needed at the tribal council.

"The tribal council will meet tomorrow at the top of the mound, when the sun is high in the sky. You will present your case and be heard by them at that time."

Prairie Flower pauses in her instruction, then asks, "Do you have all of the notes that Chief Peta Nocona instructed that you write?"

"Yes, I do," answers Jonathan. "I keep everything here in my backpack." He pats the pack that he has set by his side.

"That is good. Now continue your trek to the top and listen to the quiet voice of your mind." Prairie Flower sounds wistful in her concluding comment.

It is early afternoon when Jonathan arrives at the top of Medicine Mound. He feels a closeness to his Comanche heritage, a closeness that he has never before felt. It is as though he is living among his ancestors of more than a hundred years ago.

After a brief rest, he starts his walk around the perimeter of the open area at the top of the mound. Again, he walks a counter-clockwise pattern.

I wonder why I am going this direction. Just for no reason, I guess; but it feels like the thing to do.

Jonathan views closely for the third time, the bounteous plant life and creatures that are all around him, from the tiniest insect to evidences of larger animals. He thinks about how things might have been in Chief Peta Nocona's time. He sees some hoof tracks.

Probably deer; I wonder if they are mule deer or whitetail. I remember when Sir talked about both species. I think he said that the Mule deer is larger ... Oh, there is a snake of some sort ... and some bees around the few blossoms that still exist on the plants ... This is so good for me ... to change my focus for a little while ...

Having made the full circle, Jonathan is now back at the north end of Medicine Mound. He knows it is time to remove the stone lid from the container and view the contents of the box inside.

He kneels at the side of the stone container that was fashioned by Chief Peta Nocona, more than one-hundred-fifty years ago. His hands begin quiver, and his body seems overcome with a strange sense of weakness.

For some reason, I am very nervous right now. I wonder why ... This is what I have been directed to do ... I have been diligent in everything concerning this quest.

A soft light gradually begins to surround the area. The protruding boulder that serves as the lid to the unusual stone container is especially highlighted.

A deep voice intones, "Jonathan, this is Chief Peta Nocona. You are right on schedule, and I am here to give you some last words. The trail has been long, weary and treacherous. You have learned to fly high; you fly as does the eagle."

Jonathan's transfixed mind sees the image of Chief Peta standing above the box. He is dressed in full Indian regalia; elegant and majestic, as befitting a Comanche of such prominence.

Peta continues, "Remove the lid from the container and take the secret box from inside and open it. Then remove the piece that lies within."

No wonder I am nervous and my hands are shaking. Chief Peta is my idol and my example. He is here with me; I must listen and observe.

Jonathan removes the secret box, then with care and reverence he removes its content.

"Jonathan," the Chief begins, "what is it that you hold in your hands?"

At first the answer to the question seems very simple and straightforward. Jonathan starts to offer his answer, "It is a part ... No, it is the reunification of your family. It is not *part* of anything ... Yes, it is the reunification of the family of Chief Peta Nocona!"

"Very good, my son. Now, what is the key to reunification?" The chief is pushing Jonathan for accuracy in detail.

Jonathan responds after a slight hesitation, "... Quanah Bananah is the key."

Chief Nocona nods his head slowly, almost in ceremonious fashion and says, "You have learned well; you are prepared for the tribal council meeting at this spot tomorrow.

"Now give me the piece," concludes the great chief holding out his two hands.

Jonathan makes an observation.

Chief Peta has tears in his eyes as he raises the piece to his lips. I must, and I will perform perfectly during the council meeting.

Chief Peta places the piece back into the secret box, and sets it in the stone container, then steps back. Jonathan begins to restore the site as it was. He feels the sacredness as he replaces the flat-bottomed cover. He brushes some leaves and dolomite soil over the protruding stone.

It is time to walk back to the base, and to Michael ... I wonder what I will find inside the envelope ... Actually, I have been so caught up in so many other things ... I have almost forgotten the envelope ... or at least I had forgotten about the importance of it.

Jonathan begins his trek down to the base of Medicine Mound.

It is late in the afternoon, and the shadows are long by the time Jonathan reaches the base. He calls out to Michael, "Hey, partner, I'm back. Are you still here?"

Hearing no response, he looks around the area for signs that Michael is near. There is no evidence of his presence, but the black SUV is right where they had parked earlier in the day.

Oh my gosh! What in the world is going on? This is supposed to be a safe place. This is Medicine Mound ... a sacred place ... a place of peace. Michael must be around here ...

Think, Jonathan, think ... I don't need any more drama ... The key ring is laying on the console; typical of Michael ... sooo ... he must be around here ... somewhere close-by ...

He walks to the driver's side of the car, opens the door and sits sideways in the driver's seat; his legs are hanging out of the open door. Jonathan bows his head into his hands with his elbows resting on his knees.

DENNIS BOYD CALL

Taking responsibility means to care
The trick is to care about the right things

CHAPTER 32 – THE PROTECTOR

"Jonathan, Michael needs your help." It sounds like Prairie Flower but it is a distant voice, not what he is used to hearing.

"Jonathan, go to Michael now!" The voice is clear and distinct, but Jonathan is still not sure he really heard it.

"Michael is around the hill, go now and follow the road. Take the car." This time the voice is firm and clear.

Immediately, Jonathan plants himself in the driver's position and starts the engine. *Wow! This is really different for me. All I have ever driven is our large van. I like it!*

He drives back to the dirt road that travels along the west side of all four mounds.

Michael must be in danger or perhaps hurt. He probably went for a walk to take up time while I was up on the mound.

Jonathan slowly heads south following the narrow dirt road, looking for any sign of Michael.

I'll roll down all of the windows just in case Michael is calling for help ... Other than just look for the man ... I don't know if I should look up the side of the mound or down toward the valley ... or what!

Approaching Cedar Mound, the second largest of the four mounds, Jonathan sees Michael to his left, on one knee by the side of the road.

Oh no! There is someone lying on the ground. What in the world is happening? ... It looks like someone is hurt ... Did Michael do something bad?

He accelerates the car for a short moment, until he is alongside Michael and ... *and ... Sir? ... Sir? What is he doing here ... Why?*

Jonathan hits the brakes and slides to a dusty stop; he is quickly out of the car, and rushing to Sir's side.

"Sir ... Sir ... What happened? What is going on?" He is out of breath, worried and confused.

In near panic he looks at Michael and screams, "This is my father! What? ... How? ... Is he alright? Michael, what is this all about?"

"Jonathan, I will explain later, but right now we need to get him to the spring where we can get him a drink; and a wet cloth for his head." Michael is springing into action as he speaks.

With the help of the two young men; one on each side of him, Sir is able to stand and slowly hobble to the SUV.

Michael says, "Jonathan, you get in the rear seat beside him. I will do the driving ... How did you know ... I am confused ... but I am also very grateful."

Sitting in the seat next to Sir, Jonathan is looking curiously at his father, "What ... How ... When ... Tell me ... Is Ma alright?"

Michael remains silent as he drives to the spot near the spring where he parks the car.

He has been listening to the mostly incoherent conversation taking place in the rear of the SUV. Grabbing his flask, he rushes to the spring, fills the container and hurries back to the vehicle.

Jonathan takes the flask of water and holds it to Sir's lips, "Here, Sir, just take a little at a time. You are going to be alright."

He looks at Michael, and asks, "What is going on? How did you find him?"

Michael is still somewhat confused as he tries to tell his story. "I decided to take a walk while you were on the mound.

"As I came around to this side of the large mound, I saw this man stumbling and wandering on and off the road. He tried to speak but was totally unable to say anything. I had no idea of who he is!"

"This is my father, but how did he get here?" Jonathan's voice has calmed a bit, but is still loud and distraught.

Turning his attention to Sir, Jonathan asks in a guarded tone of voice, "How did you get here? Is Ma alright?"

Sir tries to speak but the words all come out haltingly and nearly impossible to understand; but in Sir's mind he is telling the story.

The fake deputy Herring came around, and was threatening Ma and me. He is with the To-sah-wi Alliance, and is a bad man. Herring was looking for the box, and he said you would be in serious trouble if we didn't cooperate.

When he couldn't find the box in the house, he wanted to go to your private place. He saw someone running away from The Big Trees. Was that you, Jonathan? I think it was you.

Holding the thermos to Sir's lips, his son speaks, "I think you asked if I was at The Big Trees. Is that what you said?"

Sir nods his head and whispers a faint, "Yes."

Jonathan answers the question, "Yes, we went to The Big Trees instead of stopping at the house. I saw you and a man coming to the trees. I hurried and ran away with the box."

Sir continues, his strength returning slowly, but his voice remains almost as though he is trying to recall a very faint dream.

Ma and I became very concerned for your safety. I know that the fraud deputy will try to stop your quest. He will do anything for the Alliance.

I got a ride with a trucker. The voice told me to get out of the truck at Dam Site Road. He stopped because I said I could walk to my destination. I remembered this special place, your special place.

Michael and Jonathan look at each other in amazement. Their shared expressions were followed by concurrent thoughts and statements, "He walked several miles. He was led here! But why?"

Sir's voice is becoming stronger, "I am aware of the tribal council meeting, and so are some members of the Alliance. I … I … I just want …"

Sir reclaims his composure, although his voice is still weak and scratchy. He says, "I just needed to know that you are alright. My life has been filled with deceit and I want to make it up to you.

"Oh, Jonathan I have been trying to travel two paths. It worked until the distance between the paths became too wide to straddle. Please forgive me, my son. Can you ever forgive me?"

Jonathan cannot contain his feelings. He throws his arms around the large man who has suddenly become like a small child, a papoose as it were.

"Sir, I understand your life. It has already been revealed to me, and I forgive you entirely. You taught me right; you taught me how to be honest and to have integrity. I am proud of you, and I am proud to be Native American. I am proud to be Comanche!"

Michael, observing the humbling of the older gentleman, and the strengthening of the young man, has a strong moment of reflection.

This is really a role reversal. The youngster takes the character of leader while the leader has taken the persona of the child.

"Sir," says Michael drawing attention to himself, "my name is Michael, and I am Jonathan's friend and companion. He speaks of you often and holds you in high respect."

Sir acknowledges Michael by smiling and reaching forward a feeble arm to shake his hand, "I'm very happy to meet you, Michael. Jonathan is a good boy ... a good son."

"There is one question burning in my mind, Sir." Michael looks at Sir intently.

"Where did you stay the night, last night? Did you sleep here, near the mound? If so, how did you manage? You have no blanket or covering other than what's on your back."

Sir considers the questions carefully before answering, "I grew up Comanche. I know how to sleep in the wild ... I am Comanche!"

Jonathan, after several moments of silence, and quiet expressions of appreciation for his father says, "Sir, there is something that I must do in preparation for the council meeting tomorrow. I must do it with only Michael as witness.

"You please wait here in the car while we walk a few paces away for a brief discussion. We will be back shortly." Jonathan picks up his backpack and motions for Michael to follow him.

They walk a few yards away, and stand behind a juniper bush. Michael says, "What's up? Is there a problem?"

"Oh no," comes Jonathan's response. "You are to be my witness as I open the envelope that you delivered to me back in Denton. Do you remember that?"

"Of course I remember. But I did not know that I was to witness the opening." Michael's interest is piqued.

Jonathan sets his backpack on the ground, reaches inside and brings out the familiar envelope.

He looks at the article in his hand as he turns it over, exposing the flap. Anxiously, he places his forefinger under the flap on the corner of the envelope. He tears it open carefully, and reaches inside.

A new day to live
Is a new opportunity to serve
To serve is to recognize another's need

CHAPTER 33 – THE MORNING BREAKS

Jonathan reaches into the envelope with his right hand and extracts a second smaller envelope. On the outside are written the words:

"You know the key.
Inside, find the lock."

"Now that's a headscratcher," declares Jonathan as he looks blankly at Michael.

Michael looks at the message on the smaller envelope and comments, "I don't have a clue what any of it means. Do you?"

"I know the first part, and I think it will be revealed tomorrow, but the second part is a mystery to me," mumbles Jonathan. He is speaking half to himself and half to Michael.

"Unless I hear otherwise, I am not going to open this envelope until tomorrow. Right now, it is my impression that I should not open it here." Jonathan shows confidence in his decision.

"Well," concludes Michael, "at least it will give you something to think about as you go to sleep tonight! You don't have anything else on your mind do you?" He grins at Jonathan, who gives a scowl in return.

The two young friends walk back to Michael's car where Sir is waiting. The older gentleman is sitting upright with a smile on his face. He appears to have recovered significantly from his experience last night, and earlier today.

He speaks, "I am sure glad that you came along today, Michael. The heat, along with lack of food and water, was overcoming me quickly.

"But mostly, I am grateful to know that you Jonathan, are alright. Ma needs to know that you are safe, but I have no way of contacting her. I learned some time ago that all modern communication means are forbidden at tribal council meetings … so …"

Jonathan finishes Sir's thought, "So you left your cell phone at home. Correct?"

Sir nods affirmatively.

Michael says, "I have an idea. Listen to this: Jonathan you must stay here at the mound tonight, so you have no option.

"How is this for a plan? I will take Sir to Quanah; he can stay at the hotel tonight. Then, he and I go to the impound lot tomorrow and get your van. After that we return here in the late afternoon. How does that sound?"

Michael and Sir look to Jonathan for approval; he responds, "No, that will not be safe for either or you. The Alliance is out in full force right now. They are probably aware of your Volvo, too."

Jonathan steps out of the car, and walks a short distance away; he appears to be listening to someone. After a slight nod of his head, Sir's son returns to the Volvo and shares his thoughts with his two companions. Says he, "Slight change of plans, Michael.

"You should take a back-road to Chillicothe, and spend the night at a hotel there. Sir, phone Ma as soon as possible from your hotel.

You should leave now, then travel to Quanah tomorrow. Meet with Deputy Chapman, and have him help you retrieve the van.

"Sir can drive the van back here to Medicine Mound tomorrow, late in the afternoon. Deputy Chapman will be of great assistance to both of you. I will get my sleeping bag out of the back now.

"Thank you Sir, for being so concerned for me. Give Ma my love when you speak with her. I will see you tomorrow."

The father and son give each other a warm meaningful hug as Michael starts the car. He then gets out of the SUV, walks around the vehicle to Jonathan, and says, "Goodbye, my friend. We must never forget ..." There are tears in the eyes of both young men.

Jonathan begins to pull the sleeping bag from the rear of the car when he stops and says, "Wait a minute, please. There is something else. Wait right here."

He takes his backpack, and again with Sir and Michael watching, Jonathan walks a few paces away. He stops, and with his back turned toward the two, Jonathan appears to retrieve something from his pack. In a few minutes he returns to the SUV.

He says while holding something out to Sir, "Please keep these in your care for Ma. They are very precious to her."

Sir reaches out, taking the two pictures and the wedding ring from Jonathan's extended hand. The older gentleman shows emotion as the black SUV begins to pull away, leaving his son alone.

Pensively, Jonathan then begins to find his spot for the night; he knows of a nice spot toward on the east side of Medicine Mound.

There he has some protection from any wind that might blow; plus, he will be out of the way of anyone who might follow the typical entrance into the area. He settles in for the night.

****

The morning sun rises from the east and its beams awaken Jonathan. The air is chilled, and he hunkers down in the warmth of his sleeping bag.

It feels so good inside this double filled bag. I have quite a lot of time before I need to be up on top of the mound.

I want to hurry and meet with the council ... But I am so very scared of the things they may expect of me ... And Sir, did he make it to a hotel and contact Ma? ...

Will Michael be back? ... Oh, how I hope so ... His companionship is so normal that I cannot imagine giving it up ... But I don't know who he really is ...

Sir will drive the van back here ... Will we just go home? ... Is that the end of my quest? ... Come on thoughts ... focus ... focus ...

I hear voices? ... It sounds like people walking through the brush ... I hear a sort of chant ... It's them ... The council members are arriving ... It's really happening ...

I think they shouldn't see me yet ... The best thing is for me to stay here ... in my sleeping bag ... until time to hike to the top ... Wait two more hours ...

****

Michael knocks on the door to Sir's hotel room, and is quickly greeted by his young friend's father who says, "I am ready to go. I feel the urgency to get back to Medicine Mound."

Michael responds, "Yes, I am sure you do; however Jonathan must not be distracted by your presence, either before or during the tribal council meeting.

"We should not be in a rush ... The wise old chief said, 'The brave who hurries to battle, puts his companions at the greatest risk.' Your son will be just fine."

Sir looks at the young man who has just expressed much wisdom and says, "Yes, of course you are right. I must not get in the way of the quest."

"And," offers up Michael, "you must not put yourself in jeopardy by being impulsive. Remember, you have just infuriated the To-sah-wi Alliance. They will stop at nothing to get even with you. Also Jonathan's mother is still at risk."

"Okay, yes, you are absolutely correct! Just tell me when and where throughout the day, and I will do as I am told!" Sir makes the all-important commitment.

"Good," says Michael. "We will drive to Deputy Chapman's office and hopefully he will be available to help us. He is a good man and can be trusted."

****

At the Hardeman County Sheriff's Department, Deputy Chapman looks at Deputy Wheeler and comments, "Well, I guess we can only assume the best. Everything seems to have gone well; the Herring brothers are in custody, we have not heard anything about Jonathan, and it is quiet around here."

"Yep," agrees Wheeler. "Looks to be a great day, but I cannot stop thinking about young Jonathan. I don't know what he is all about, but I sense a great work being done by him."

Chapman looks carefully at his partner.

What is safe to tell him? ... I know he is trustworthy ... It has been really difficult to keep things to myself these last several days ... A lot of people have heard about the Fifth-Son Prophecy ... I think it will be alright ... Maybe just a little ...

The entrance door to the reception office opens; in a moment a familiar voice is heard. "Are deputies Chapman and Wheeler here?"

Chapman gets up and walks to see who is looking for him, "Michael! What are you doing here? Is everything okay?"

Deputy Chapman eyes Sir in a questioning manner, and puts his hand up to Michael as a signal to not talk until he identifies the unknown visitor.

Michael begins the introduction, "Deputy Chapman, this is ... this is ... Sir?" He suddenly realizes that he does not know Sir's real name.

"Sorry, this is Jonathan's father," Michael finally gets it out.

Sir speaks as he extends his hand, "Hi, Deputy, my name is Peta Parker, Jonathan's father, as Michael said."

Acquaintances are made all the way around as they laughingly make their way into the deputies' office.

In a few succinct statements, Michael outlines their reason for being at the sheriff's department. During this time, Chapman has been watching Wheeler very closely for signs of doubt or inquisitiveness.

Wheeler's facial expressions are indicators that he is pulling the many events of the past week into place. He shows he is about to speak when he is cut off by Chapman.

"Fellas," interjects Chapman, "I need to explain a few facts to Deputy Wheeler before you go any further in your explanation."

He turns to face Wheeler eye-to-eye, "Etsel, have you ever heard of the Fifth-Son Prophecy ... or the To-sah-wi Alliance?"

Wheeler answers in a tentative tone, "I have heard the words during this past week, but ..."

Chapman then launches into a brief description of the situation. Then concluding he says, "This fellow Louis Herring and his brother Ricky Herring are prime examples of the objectives and goals of the Alliance."

Startled, Sir jumps in his seat, "Herring? ... Herring? You know about Herring? He should be in jail ... he is a fraud ... He posed as a deputy down in Denton County. He is trying to destroy my son, my Jonathan!"

Chapman quickly moves his hand to Sir's arm and squeezes it as he tries to calm the man. "Peta ... Sir, both of the Herring brothers; your Ricky Herring, and our Louis Herring are in custody, and have been so this entire day."

Thoughtfully, Sir says, "Let me get this straight. The fake deputy Herring that came to my house has a brother here who is also a member of the Alliance? And they have been working together to destroy my son?"

"Yes, that is the way we see it. Louis, the brother here, has been feeding information to your man Richard or Ricky Herring. That is the way we see it." Deputy Chapman sees this as the conclusion of their meeting.

Sir says, "I have one more question: With the two brothers in custody, is Jonathan now safe from the To-sah-wi Alliance?"

"Probably not entirely," responds Chapman. "We believe that the brothers are only a part the danger ..."

Sir interrupts, "I think that the Herrings are not working under direction of the Alliance. It is my opinion that they are independently trying to stop Jonathan.

"The purpose would be to get respect and glory from the Alliance, after they have destroyed the Fifth-Son Prophecy."

"Well," says Chapman, "certainly makes sense and it might help fill in some gaps for us.

"Okay, let's go to the impound lot, and get your van. After doing so, where will you be going, Peta?"

"I want to return to Medicine Mound, and be there when Jonathan is finished with his mission. I am so very proud of him! Besides, he will need a ride home," Sir grins.

Deputy Chapman laughs and replies, "Let's go get your van."

Something worth having
Is something worth working for

CHAPTER 34 – REUNIFICATION

Near the northeast portion of the base of Medicine Mound, Jonathan pulls himself out of his sleeping bag.

The sun is at about a forty-five degree angle. It will take quite some time for me to make it to the top, so I better be on my way.

My stomach is in a bit of a turmoil, and the feelings in my mind are mixed. But I know that I am in the right place, doing the right thing ... Sure would like for Prairie Flower to hold my hand the rest of the day!

Jonathan walks to the western side of Medicine Mound; to the area he has found to be the least difficult route to the top. He hikes for about thirty minutes when he pauses at the side of a breach, or a wash in the hillside.

This wash is about a dozen feet across at the top. I wonder if it was here a hundred-fifty years ago, or if it is a recent development ... Funny that I would stop now and think this. Just a diversion, I suppose.

"It is fine that you take a short rest, Jonathan. But you must remain focused," Prairie Flower is speaking. "Now is not the time to cause a delay by diverting your attention. Keep your mind trained on your quest, and what you will say to the council."

She continues reassuringly, "I have said that I will be with you during your quest. All will be well, and you should arrive quickly. The council will be ready for you."

"Thank you Prairie Flower, for your support," Jonathan whispers. "I will not let you down."

Walking into the flat, football-sized open area at the top of Medicine Mound, Jonathan is suddenly the focus of attention. Thirteen men are sitting in a small semi-circle around a tiny stack of smoldering branches.

They are seated about thirty feet from the stone container housing Chief Peta Nocona's secret box.

Simultaneously, Jonathan is both overcome and curious.

So this is the tribal council ... Combined, they must surely represent several hundred years of experience ... Their dress is ceremonial, and I suppose there is a ranking of some sort among them.

The old gentleman who sits at the center of the semi-circle says, "Come in, young man. Please join us in our meeting. We have made a place for you to sit in sight of all of us. I am White Eagle."

Jonathan, being uncomfortable, takes his place on a three legged stool fashioned from small mesquite sticks and a triangular piece of leather. He looks around at the thirteen men who appear to be sitting in judgment of him.

I know they are wondering about me. These are the wise men of the Comanche ... Prairie Flower ... Are you here? ...

Jonathan notes the magnificent headdress of the man who welcomed him. *He is obviously the man in charge, and the one to his right is probably the Medicine Man.*

White Eagle speaks, "Young Man, please tell us who you are. What brings you to this council?"

Jonathan answers, "My name is Jonathan Parker. I am the son of Peta Parker, who is the son of Daniel Parker, the son of Bodaway Parker, who is the son of Quanah Parker and his wife, Ta-ha-yea, a Mescalero Apache.

"I am the third great-grandson of Chief Peta Nocona. This makes me the fifth-son. The one that was prophesied by Chief Peta Nocona."

Jonathan pauses for any questions; there are none so he continues. "The second question asked by you is to explain why I am here at this meeting.

"I have been selected and assigned by the fathers before me to bring the two sides of the Peta Nocona family together."

Wow! This is not the normal Jonathan speaking. The words are being placed in my mouth for me. I am amazed!

White Eagle instructs, "Please explain the division that you claim to be bringing together."

Jonathan sits erect, and begins the story, "Quanah Parker's wife, Ta-ha-yea, was an Apache who was driven away from the Comanche and from her husband Quanah Parker.

"She returned to her own people. Unknown by Quanah at the time, she was carrying their child. She gave birth to him, and named him Bodaway. She held great hatred toward Quanah because of the circumstance."

The members of the council lean forward, not wanting to miss any of the story Jonathan is reciting to them.

He continues, "Quanah's younger brother Pecos, did not die of smallpox, or any other childhood illness as reported at the time ..."

Jonathan then reveals all that he had been taught by Chief Peta Nocona during the previous week.

There are gasps and chatter among the council members. White Eagle raises his hand and says, "And young Mr. Parker, what do you offer up as proof of the words you speak?"

Reaching into his backpack Jonathan says, "I have the notes that Chief Peta Nocona instructed me to write following our meetings.

"He revealed these truths to me during my several sessions with him during this past week. Chief Peta tutored me in meetings we held right here, at this spot on Medicine Mound."

"Please give your notes to me," White Eagle instructs.

White Eagle takes the notes, and hands them over to the man to his right. He then turns his attention to Jonathan, "Your notes are very important, but what other proof do you bring to this council?"

Jonathan inhales heavily as he hears Prairie Flower, "Have them open the box."

The nervous young man says, "Chief Peta buried an artifact on this mound at the time he received the Fifth-Son Prophecy. Although some of you, and your fathers have frequented this place, the artifact has been hidden from your view.

"White Eagle, please have someone walk with me, and do as I say." Jonathan rises from his position while White Eagle nods to the man on his far left; the one seated at the end of the semi-circle.

After turning, and walking to the stone ahead of him, which is slightly protruding, Jonathan stops.

He opens his left hand in the direction of the stone, drawing his follower's attention to the spot.

Jonathan says to the man who has been behind him, "Brush away the leaves, dust and dirt. Then trace your fingers around the edge of the stone until you feel a wide notch."

The man kneels and does as instructed. The protrusion is cleared, and he feels around the stone. Suddenly he stops. With a look of surprise, tempered with satisfaction, he looks up at Jonathan.

Jonathan takes one small step aside, looking at the group of men. They are all moving closer in anticipation; they clearly want to see everything, and be involved.

When all are gathered around, Jonathan says to the kneeling man, "With your fingers under the notch, raise the stone."

This, the council member does. The side of the stone lifts; it becomes obvious that it is flat on the bottom, revealing a container beneath.

The silence is dominate, and is broken only by the audible intake of air by all of those present. Each member of the council is intent on hearing and seeing everything that transpires.

Jonathan further instructs, "Remove the box from inside and give it to White Eagle."

This is done; White Eagle takes possession of the box. He says, "We will all return to our council seats. It is then that we will open the box."

Everyone, including Jonathan are reseated in their prior position, and White Eagle turns the latch. Dead silence fills the air as he raises the lid and peers inside. With a sort of puzzled look, he reaches into the box and carefully removes the artifact.

White Eagle looks down at the item as he holds it with two hands. His gaze turns to his right, and he raises the piece into a perpendicular position making it easier for the medicine man to observe.

It has become rather evident to Jonathan that the medicine man is the senior member of the council, and is held in high regard by all members. Therefore it makes sense that he would be the one to whom White Eagle might defer.

The medicine man reaches for the object; with a broad smile on his face, he holds the piece as high as his arms will reach. The group of men are mystified by what they are seeing.

Finally one man speaks, "I see only something that is crescent shaped with puzzle-like bubbles on the inside portion." The group applauds in agreement.

The medicine man raises his left hand to indicate silence. He then speaks, "My brothers, in the process of establishing honor and respect to the entire Peta Nocona line, several steps must be taken.

"But there are some here within this council, who belong to another side.

"That is the side of Chief Peta Nocona's family who desire that the two sides not come together. They work to stop the Fifth-Son Prophecy from being fulfilled.

"If this young man meets all requirements, the sides will be joined together; your Alliance will dissolve. You can either accept that fact, or be driven from the council. You will know what to do."

He pauses to visually survey the enamored and intense body of tribal leadership. He is looking for any sign of discomfort or disbelief.

There is none and he continues, "We have had verbal testimony, we have had written testimony, and we now have seen some physical testimony. There is more yet to follow, and our young friend here may be able to provide it; but only if he is truly the fifth-son, as he proclaims.

"I will further explain. There are characters engraved on this piece. They are unknown to all except to the one appointed to read them.

"I will read them ... but I cannot ... until the missing part is given to us." He turns and looks at Jonathan, then White Eagle.

White Eagle takes charge and asks, "Jonathan, are you prepared to provide the missing piece?"

"Yes, I am." He reaches deep into his backpack, then pulls out the treasure box.

This is what I coincidently found in The Big Trees ... But it is really proof to me that there are no such things as coincidences. It is also proof to me that I must always listen to the quiet voice of my mind!

He extends his arms to White Eagle who takes the box from him. White Eagle repeats his previous action and moves the latch. All eyes are upon him as he carefully lifts the piece from its container.

Speaking to Jonathan, White Eagle asks, "Young man, how did this piece happen to come into your possession?"

Jonathan answers, "My mother, Elizabeth Finley, is fifty percent Comanche. The box was passed to her by her mother, Priscilla; she received it from her mother, Chenoa. Chenoa's mother received it from Chief Peta Nocona when she was a young girl.

Removing the double wrap, White Eagle again raises the piece to the view of the medicine man. This time, the puzzled look on the face of White Eagle is replaced by a large smile.

The medicine man holds the new piece up for all to see, then says, "Jonathan, can you explain the significance of the two pieces?"

Again, Jonathan silently asks, "Prairie Flower are you here?" He does a quick look at the council of tribal leaders who are watching his every move. Their anticipation is unmistakable.

He stands, and in a clear and distinct tone of voice responds, "The outer edge of each of the two pieces is smooth and easy to hold. This represents the family. It is how a family should be, except Chief Peta's family is broken just like these two pieces. There are rough and fractured places on the inside.

"The inner part of each piece has both rough edges and smooth parts; this is how Peta Nocona's family is right now. Each side of the family stands by itself. But like a jigsaw puzzle, both pieces can fit together and be secure."

The medicine man slips the balloon-like portions of each piece into the reciprocating opening in the other piece. It fits perfectly into an oval, almost football shape.

The other twelve men making up the council, show astounded looks with expressions of delight. One-by-one, every man stands and applauds.

There is not one who indicates anything other than belief and support. The medicine man takes his seat just before one of the council members speaks.

"What do the characters say? You said you would be able to read them."

The medicine man holds the combined pieces carefully as he looks at the engravings. His countenance changes as he seems to be in a hypnotic trance.

After about two minutes he looks up and says, "Jonathan, you are to go to the far end of this open space; wait for a signal from me before returning."

A surprised Jonathan rises; he begins to do as instructed, thinking: *Who am I to question the authority of this man? This is good!*

Once Jonathan is many yards away from the group, the medicine man speaks softly to the other twelve men.

He says, "After we know that Jonathan is well out of earshot, I will read the engravings aloud to you. When he returns, White Eagle will ask him one question. His answer must be exactly as I have read the words on this object to you.

"After that, there will be one other piece of proof that he must provide."

Turning to look at Jonathan's progress, White Eagle says, "He is at the end of the opening. What do the engravings say?"

The medicine man answers, "The words, as written on the combined pieces, simply say 'Quanah Bananah is the key.' Those are the words he is to say to you, White Eagle. His answer will come after you ask one question.

"When he returns, and we are in our places, you are to begin the discussion then ask this question: 'What is the key?' He must then answer exactly. Following your exchange, turn to me so I can complete the verification process."

The medicine man steps apart from the others. He waves to Jonathan, signaling him to return to the council. Jonathan comes on the run, and is in their midst within a minute or so.

All members of the council are resettled in their original semi-circular places.

White Eagle looks squarely into the eyes of Jonathan. He comments, "Young man, you have been very impressive in your presentations to us. There are a couple of other things that we must take care of.

"First, I have a question to ask you ... What is the key?" The entire council is sitting erect, and listening intently.

Jonathan takes a deep breath, and remembering his practice run with Chief Peta says, "Quanah Bananah is the key."

It takes a split second for everyone to assimilate what was said. They then erupt into wild cheers while spontaneously offering a sort of ceremonial dance and chant.

White Eagle tries to calm the group's celebration which he, himself has been participating in. "Attention, everyone. Please ... We have one more piece of business to conduct before the process is complete."

The men quiet themselves, and turn their interest to their leader, White Eagle. He looks at the medicine man and gives him a nod to conduct the final act of verification.

The medicine man looks at Jonathan, and with great compassion comments, "Young man, this has undoubtedly been a long quest for you. Can you share much of your journey with us?"

Jonathan replies, "It has been years in the making, and it is all very personal. But let me say this, the tutoring and education have been more valuable than I could ever express.

"Additionally, I have learned that there are evil forces among all people. This has been proven to me, time after time. We must never forget who we are or where we come from.

"But, I think there is one more thing we must do. I ..."

White Eagle interrupts, and turns to the medicine man, "It is up to you now."

The medicine man states, "Yes, Jonathan there is one more step. I believe you have something else to share with us. This will be the final step, bringing the quest to completion."

Jonathan again reaches into his backpack, and pulls out another item. This time it is an envelope; he hands it to White Eagle who respectfully hands it to the medicine man.

The Medicine Man takes the envelope, but before opening it he says, "The artifact that Jonathan has provided to us is still just two pieces, and can easily come apart. It is called the 'Quanah Bananah' because of the unique shape of each piece; and because of the location from where it came.

"The fact that it can easily come apart is also symbolic of the family. It has been five generations since our family, the family of Chief Peta Nocona came apart. This must never happen again.

"The missing part; the part that we must have is given to us in this envelope."

He holds the envelope up for all to see before tearing off one end.

After looking inside he says, "Jonathan, will you please take the paper out of the envelope and tell us what is written on it?"

The surprised Jonathan walks to the front, takes the envelope into his hands, and pulls out a faded, yellowed sheet of paper. He looks at it and chokes a bit as he says, "On the top are numbers apparently written by a shaky hand; written, as if by an old chief. The numbers '1855' are given as a date.

"The message written below the date reads, 'The final part of the Quanah Bananah is found at the end of this trail.'"

In a shocked sort of way, he stops reading. Becoming emotional, Jonathan hands the note back to the Medicine Man.

He in turn, reverses the paper to face the group, he then turns it so he can read aloud the final brief statement, "Remove the bottom piece of the stone container."

Oh, golly! thinks Jonathan. *Is Chief Peta playing with us? It does sound like something he might do!*

The group moves to the opened stone container from which the first piece of the Quanah Bananah was taken.

One of the younger members of the council volunteers, "I will go to work on it."

He drops to his knees and begins to loosen the various pieces of the container with his bare hands. Soon another is on the opposite side of the container; the two of them working in concert.

To the amazement of all, they discover another, very shallow space. "Oh my gosh," says Jonathan, "there is a false bottom to the stone container. What is that lying between the two bottoms?"

The first man to have begun working on the box reaches toward the object, then stops. He looks at White Eagle who peers into the hole.

White Eagle exclaims, "It looks like a thin piece of leather, or perhaps a slice of buffalo stomach. It has been lying there between two slabs of stone for scores of years, since about eighteen-fifty-five. Chief Peta was a very wise man ... But why this?"

White Eagle reaches down, lifts the leather piece out of its place, and unfolds it. It is an oval shaped piece with nothing unique about it. He looks at the medicine man who takes it from their leader and offers a wisdom-laden smile.

The medicine man lays the Quanah Bananah face down, on one of the flat stones. He proceeds to lay the thin leather piece over the symbolic family representation. It matches in size perfectly.

He speaks, "Chief Peta Nocona is telling us that we are to affix this to the back of the full artifact. We should use a permanent adhesive that will not allow any separation to take place. In that way, the Peta Nocona family will forever remain intact!"

White Eagle puts his arm around Jonathan's shoulder and draws him close. He says with tears in his eyes, "Jonathan, your quest is now complete.

"The To-sah-wi Alliance no longer exists. They had only a few dedicated followers. Most of their followers have been in name only, and have done what they did out of fear."

All of a sudden there is the sound of rushing wind, but no one feels as much as a breeze. As they look southward from where the sound comes, their eyes are filled with cloudy imagery.

The cloudiness lifts, and the imagery becomes focused. Jonathan is delighted to recognize many of them; those he has come to know are standing at the front of the multitude of Native Americans.

He declares enthusiastically, "I know some of these people!"

Aloud, he begins to identify those standing in the front, "There is Chief Peta Nocona ... and his wife, Cynthia Ann Parker. I recognize Quanah Parker from pictures I have seen; his wife Ta-ho-yea is next to him. There is Prairie Flower, her real name is Topsannah. And next to her is Pecos ... Pecos? ... Mic ... Michael, is that you? ... Is that really you?"

At his side Jonathan feels a warmth; he turns ... and falls into a warm embrace by the outstretched arms of his father, Sir.

ABOUT THE AUTHOR

Dennis Call was born and raised in Rigby, Idaho. He and Connie Wheeler married shortly after high school graduation, and enjoyed 63 years of glorious marriage; Connie passed away in 2016. Their marriage produced three daughters, three sons, and 25 grandchildren. As of this writing they also have 34 great-grandchildren, with many more to come.

Having lived in north Texas for the past 24 years, Dennis became enamored by the history of the area, particularly the history of the Native Americans. He holds great respect for those people who helped shape the Texas country he has now come to appreciate.

As a result of this respect, and his penchant for writing, it is a normal consequence that a novel such as Skullduggery at Quanah be on his list of accomplishments.

Dennis Boyd Call has written many "Quick-Read" books that can all be viewed on his website.

dennisbcall.com

Made in the USA
Columbia, SC
18 January 2020